Conducting Terror

Julian Hopkins

RED LEAD PRESS
PITTSBURGH, PENNSYLVANIA 15222

The contents of this work including, but not limited to, the accuracy of events, people, and places depicted; opinions expressed; permission to use previously published materials included; and any advice given or actions advocated are solely the responsibility of the author, who assumes all liability for said work and indemnifies the publisher against any claims stemming from publication of the work.

All Rights Reserved
Copyright © 2007 by Julian Hopkins
No part of this book may be reproduced or transmitted in any form or by any means, electronic or mechanical, including photocopying, recording, or by any information storage and retrieval system without permission in writing from the publisher.

ISBN: 978-0-8059-8524-5
Library of Congress Control Number: 2007927911
Printed in the United States of America

First Printing

For more information or to order additional books, please contact:
Red Lead Press
701 Smithfield Street
Third Floor
Pittsburgh, Pennsylvania 15222
U.S.A.
1-800-834-1803
www.redleadbooks.com

Acknowledgments

I wrote Conducting Terror at home in Germantown, MD after convalescing from multi-bypass heart surgery, and it is dedicated to the team at the Heart Centre in Washington DC where I was looked after so compassionately.

Thanks are due to those who helped me while I was polishing the manuscript, especially my son Justin, daughter-in-law Grainne, daughter Julia, sister-in-law RoseMarie Snarski, mother-in-law Minnie Marino, cousin Michael Wells, and family friend Susie Jones. Their contributions have all been deeply appreciated.

Much of the action in the novel takes place in and around the Royal Opera House, Covent Garden, London, and the Metropolitan Opera House, New York City. I know both theaters well, and love them, having spent many nights enjoying performances of operas there. I have an enduring admiration for all those in the opera world who bring us so much pleasure, especially the conductors, singers and orchestral players. As much as anyone, they inspired me with the idea to set key scenes in the book in the two theaters.

Conducting Terror would not have been written without encouragement and assistance from my beloved wife, Stella. I would like to pay a heartfelt tribute to her for her wonderful support, love and friendship.

JH
St Albans, UK
2007

Prologue

Growing numbers of voters in Great Britain believe their Government is off course. The Prime Minister and his Cabinet are allowing a crucial foreign affairs policy difference with the United States to get wider and wider. Disagreements on how to deal with international terrorist threats are erupting. Tensions between London and Washington are escalating, and the special relationship between Great Britain and America is becoming more and more fragile.

The accumulation of intelligence concerning the build-up of terrorist cells, and the fear of the deployment of weapons of mass destruction against America, provide the basis for an increasingly proactive and aggressive approach by the Administration in Washington.

The Opposition benches in Westminster include many who want to fall in line with those they regard as their natural allies in the United States.

Part I

Chapter 1

Alexandra did not know where she was. The room was dark and there were blindfolds over her eyes. She only knew that she was near other people. She could hear their voices outside, but she was confused because some of them seemed to be Russian. Her hands were bound behind her back, and her legs were tied together at the ankles. She was lying on a mattress on a concrete floor. She thought she could hear children playing in the sea. She cried out for Quentin.

Quentin had agonized over her torture a thousand times. These terrible images had become imprinted in his mind. How could it have been different? What else could he have done? The events of just two weeks had totally changed his life …..

THURSDAY

It was a damp, humid evening in late June. The traffic along the Thames Embankment was heavy, and Quentin realized he was going to be late. Alex had said to be at her place by six, and they could have cocktails, change, and get a cab over to Covent Garden. They had to be in their seats by seven thirty.

He wanted to get to her apartment in time to change, as the performance was a charity gala, black tie. He was still wearing what Alex called his scruffy suit. The drive from Wapping to Chelsea was about forty-five minutes, at the best of times. He wished he had left earlier.

Jack Barker, his managing editor, had called him into a meeting at very short notice that afternoon, and had asked him to cover the Lincoln Center Festival in New York. He was thrilled to have this opportunity, and he planned to surprise Alex with the news and invite her to go with him. It would be a three week trip.

Alexandra had previously lived and worked in Manhattan for about ten years. She remained very fond of the Big Apple, and he suspected she missed it more than she said, at least to him. They would have a lot of fun, and all at The Times' expense. Bitter sweet, in a way, he thought, for he could not forget that while she was there she had worked and lived with Gubin. Petya Mikhailov Gubin was such an over-achiever. Quentin could never compete. But New York would be good, and they might be able to bury a few of her skeletons.

Leo Connell and the agency still represented Gubin, and Alex was always slightly coy about the agency's star client, when talking to Quentin, at least. Quentin assumed that she had some professional dealings with Gubin's people in New York from time to time, but they very rarely discussed it, and in any case Gubin had not been to Europe for the whole of the two year period she had been in England.

It started to pour down. The traffic going west almost stopped altogether. He decided to turn round and go straight to the opera house. He pulled out his mobile phone from the glove box and plugged the earpiece into his left ear. He dialled and she picked up straight away.

"Hi. I'm not going to make it, I'm afraid. The traffic is impossible."

"OK," she said immediately, "I'll see you there, my darling. I'll bring your clothes. Meet you in the lobby. Love you."

That was a relief, but now he had to get back from the Embankment to Covent Garden. He did an illegal U-turn and pulled the car into the Vauxhall Bridge Road, heading for Victoria, surprised that he had left behind most of the traffic, at least for the time being. He turned on the radio, and pushed button 1, which was automatically tuned to Classic FM. "The Pathetique," he said out loud, "Might be Gubin's version they're playing." He had to admit it was good. Full of vivacity, life and color. Authentic Russian flavor. He started to sing along. He loved Tchaikovsky. It appealed to his romantic nature.

He glanced at himself in the rear view mirror. Not bad, he thought. But he needed to shave. He was not good looking in a conventional way, and in fact he thought he had a weak face. He was sometimes mistaken for Tony Blair. His hair was not receding, however, and was not showing any signs of grey. There were no apparent lines or wrinkles. He needed a trim, perhaps, but so many men in the arts world wore their hair long, and Alex said she liked it that way. In fact he loved the fact that she would comb his hair with her fingers, and caress his brow at the same time, often in public. She was demonstrative and loving. He liked that, especially when they were with their friends. He told himself he was luckier than he deserved to be. A hot-blooded Ukrainian girl, and so beautiful. He loved everything about her.

Quentin Dart and Alexandra Matviyko had been engaged for nearly eighteen months. She was born in Nezhin, near Kiev. Her given name, Aleksandra, meant "Defender of man", she had told him, and her family name meant "God's gift". Her father had deserted her mother when she was a young girl, and she had been raised by her grandparents.

Quentin was the third son of Sir James Dart, the MP and Financier, and had been raised in Washington, West Sussex. They had met at a reception given for the new Head of BBC Music, at Broadcasting House, and immediately got on well.

She told him she worked as Executive Vice President for Connell Artists, representing several leading conductors, instrumentalists and singers in Europe. She was fluent in Russian and French, and knew a little Italian. Her English was faultless, albeit with a Russian accent.

They had arranged to meet for dinner the night after the reception, and they talked ceaselessly. Alex showed a genuine interest in the fact that Quentin was one of the UK's leading music writers, and she deeply respected his knowledge. He was a little bit of a nerdish highbrow, she thought, and she pulled his leg about it sometimes, when she was feeling mischievous. But he took it well, usually, and they quickly became inseparable. "Q and A," as he liked to refer to themselves when joking with her.

After a month they slept together and he was soon living with her in her Chelsea apartment, at least during the weekends. He kept his apartment in Wapping. It was near The Times office, and very convenient, but he was spending more and more time in Chelsea.

Following a Christmas party at The Times that year, they went out for a celebratory dinner, and he popped the question over the salad course, much to his own surprise, for he had not planned it that way. "Q wants an A," he told her suddenly. She did not hesitate to accept.

The radio disturbed his thoughts. "You are listening to Classic FM. It is six o'clock and here are the news headlines." There were the usual items about growing tensions between Washington and Westminster over terrorism, the prospects for peace in the Middle East, and insurgencies in Iraq. He was only half listening. There was a high security alert in New York. Nothing new there, he thought, but he hoped it would not make the trip difficult. And then suddenly, "Do not forget to catch Classic FM's live relay from Covent Garden tonight. The world-renowned Maestro, Petya Gubin, will lead an international cast in a new production of Tchaikovsky's "Eugene Onegin," in a special gala performance, starting at eight o'clock. The performance is in aid of UNHCR. Only on Classic FM."

Quentin wondered whether he and Alex would be obliged to visit Gubin backstage after the performance. He hoped that Leo would cover it for the agency, and that they would not be placed in an awkward situation.

He was now pushing through Mayfair. He knew all the back streets. He would park off Long Acre. Plenty of time.

He suddenly remembered that he had not mentioned the tickets to Alex. They were on the table in the living room, in her apartment. He pulled out his mobile phone again. No answer this time. Still, not to panic. He could always see Douglas in the box office and get duplicates. They were comps in any case, fourth row orchestra stalls, right aisle, if he recalled correctly. He often had those seats. He was working, after all, and would also see the second performance in the series on Saturday. He would then write his piece, for publication the following Monday.

He moved the car into heavy traffic in Holborn, wondering what Alex would say to Gubin if they did meet after the performance. How long had it been? Two years. She had not said much about him since she heard he was scheduled to do "Onegin" at The Garden, and that was over a year ago. Surely it would be difficult for her. After all, Gubin had broken it off, or so he had gathered from the little Alex had said to him, and she was quite clearly hurt by it. He wondered whether Gubin knew Alex was now engaged to be married. The music world was notoriously gossip-ridden, so he had probably been told. Would Gubin bring his wife with him, he wondered?

Quentin drove into Long Acre and found the multi-story car park half empty. It was only six forty-five. Pretty good, he thought. Lots of time to change. He put his mobile phone in his jacket pocket and locked the car.

He hurried past Café des Amis, into Floral Street, and just as he was walking into the entrance lobby, there was Alex. She was wearing a long, dark blue, sequined gown, with a deep, plunging neckline, adorned with her favorite quadruple string of pearls. Her shoulder length dark hair was pulled back. She was wearing a full-length fur coat, thrown over her broad shoulders. She was a tall woman, but the outfit made her seem even taller than her five feet ten. She looked like a million dollars, he thought.

She caught Quentin's eye and stopped. He kissed her and gave her a hug, being careful not to disturb the fur coat. "You look fantastic! But why the coat? It's too warm. Everything OK?"

"Fine, scruffy pants," she said, and pulling a small bag from under the coat said, "Here are your things. I found the tickets as well."

"You're so good. I'll have to find a place to change. Maybe I'll go into the gents in the lobby. Can you amuse yourself for fifteen minutes?"

Alex looked momentarily unsure of herself, but then she said, "Sure. I'll just go and say good luck to Petya. Is that OK with you, Quentin?"

Quentin felt as though he had been punched in the stomach. He could not believe how blatant this was. "Now? Do you have to? Where is Leo?"

Brushing off her sense of his insecurity, Alex responded quickly, "I don't know. But it will get it over. And it will save you any embarrassment, my angel. See you in the lobby in fifteen?"

With that she turned on her heels and went back out of the lobby, and walked left into Floral Street, down by the side of the theater, making for the stage door.

Quentin quickly thought he would let it be. This was probably the best way of dealing with it. Alex was smart, and she had a no-nonsense, practical, instinctive way of coping with tricky situations. But questions started to cascade in his mind. What would they say to each other? How warm would Petya be towards her? Would they kiss? Would she tell him she was going to marry him?

He made his way into the largest cubicle, reserved for the handicapped. He took his dress suit and shirt out of his bag and hung them on the hook on the back of the door, and started to undress. He realized he had no shaver, and wondered whether there would be one in the restroom.

There were hushed voices outside the cubicle. They sounded strained. Two men talking, arguing, it seemed. There was the sound of running water. The voices became louder. "You have no choice," one man said. Then another, "Maybe, maybe not, but I'm not doing this for you." And then they were whispering. Then gone.

How odd, Quentin thought. But his mind quickly went back to Alex. "Please, let's get tonight over and done with," he said to himself out loud.

He strolled back into the lobby, carrying the bag, now containing his daytime clothes. He had not shaved, and he hoped Alex would not mind.

He stood by the bottom of the stairs leading up to the Dress Circle lobby, and waited.

*

As he was waiting, his thoughts went back to the first time Alex had told him about Gubin. They were at The Royal Festival Hall for a concert the previous summer, and had gone backstage during the interval to meet Dominique Lieberman, the young French violinist. Leo had badly wanted to sign Dominique. Since Alex knew her, and they were on quite familiar terms with each other, it was decided that Alex would make the first pitch. As they entered her dressing room, Alex introduced her to Quentin, and she said how much they had both enjoyed her performance of the Sibelius Violin Concerto.

Dominique was a tiny woman, probably no bigger than Edith Piaf. She reminded Quentin of Leslie Caron.

"Thank you," said Dominique in her best English, as she put her violin back in its case, "I am glad you liked it."

"Leo wants to meet with you, if that's OK," said Alex. "He feels he can help. Also he is planning a few engagements for Gubin here in London next June, and he wants to explore the possibility of recording the Tchaikovsky with you, I think at Maida Vale. The combination would be just fantastic."

"That would be very interesting to me," said Dominique. "Please let me know and I will surely try to make myself available."

Alex and Quentin both gave her their business cards as they left the dressing room, and Alex said she would call her. "Delighted to meet you, Ms Lieberman," said Quentin, gently taking her hand.

As they returned for the second half of the concert and moved into their seats, Alex tugged on Quentin's arm, and quietly said, "I must tell you something. It's about Petya."

"He's just great," said Quentin jovially, "I would love to see him at The Garden."

"He's coming to do "Onegin" next June", she said.

"Wow! That's great. I hope they mount a decent production for him."

"Yes, I'm sure they will. But it's not that." She hesitated. "I've been meaning to say this for a while." She hesitated again. "I know him, Quentin. I knew him, I mean," she said, correcting herself. "You know, er … oh my God, this is so awful! How can I say this? I was ….I knew him quite well, actually. When I was in New York. You know, we ……" Her voice tailed off.

Quentin immediately understood what she was trying to tell him. She and Petya Gubin had been an item. He felt sick, and yet he wanted to say it was OK.

But the words didn't come out as he wanted. He said, "Gubin is one of best conductors around," he added weakly. "He is an amazing musician. How long did you …I mean how did it happen? He's married, isn't he?"

Alex chose her words carefully. "We became very good friends. The whole family. He and his wife, Maria. The children. Well, mainly him, actually." And then, after a long pause, "We had an apartment just off Columbus Avenue, for a while."

"You mean you lived together?" Quentin couldn't quite believe what she was telling him. "Did people know?"

"I suppose so. Anyway, Maria and the children knew, and eventually I wanted out of the relationship. Well, I thought I did, but it was difficult. We worked together. I had known him since going over to the States from Kiev. He kept insisting we should go on professionally, and that it would be OK. He was going to get a divorce, he said. But he never did, and eventually it ended."

"What ended?"

"He told me I would have to leave. He said it was for the best. He got me the job with Leo. Here."

The enormity of what she said then began to sink in. This girl, the girl he adored, loved, hoped to spend the rest of his life with, had a past. But a past that he never remotely suspected. And with one of the major musical figures of the time. A world figure. Someone he regarded very highly, if he was honest. An inspiring musician, a genius, or so many thought. Petya Gubin! He was fifty-five years old, maybe more. Old enough to be her father. OK, she must have been around the block a few times. But the two of them living together. Oh shit! Why hadn't she mentioned it before? What should he do, or say? His heart pounded.

"What was the job you were doing, exactly? I thought you were with the agency."

"I was his Personal Assistant," said Alex weakly.

*

Quentin still sometimes felt the pain from that discovery almost a year before, as he stood waiting for Alex, in his best dress suit.

"You managed, then," said Alex, as she walked up to him.

"Uh?" Quentin noticed that she was now carrying the fur coat, and that she looked flushed. "How did it go? Did you see him?"

"Yes. It was fine."

"What do you mean? Tell me!"

"Well," said Alex evasively, "he's just about to conduct. What would you expect?"

As they walked into the auditorium, and took their programs from the attendant, Quentin couldn't think of anything else to say. She would tell him more later, he thought.

The house was almost full already, and there was a buzz in the air. They knew many of the people around them. Quentin nodded to Sir David Wright, Lady Porter, the Wellingtons and the Spencers. He talked courteously with the music critics from The Telegraph and The Guardian. Alex chatted with the Russian delegation and another large group from the record company that Leo had invited. They found their seats, and Quentin placed the bag with his clothes in it under his. He took the aisle seat, Alex to his left.

The orchestra was tuning up. Quentin did his usual scan of the house while the lights were still up, and he noticed that the front row in the Dress Circle behind him was empty. He assumed there was a VIP group coming in at the last moment, probably with Lord Jaeger, the Chairman of the opera house board. Not unusual for a gala performance.

Quentin absent-mindedly started to thumb through his program. Alex was doing the same. He noticed that she was already looking at Petya's biography and photograph.

The house lights went down, and the audience was hushed. There was a long pause, and then isolated clapping started to break out in the amphitheater above, gradually spreading throughout the theater, as Petya Gubin bounced on to the conductor's rostrum, baton in his left hand, caught in the white of the spotlight directed from the top of the auditorium. The intensity of the applause had increased by now, and there was cheering. Even a few bravos. This was quite a welcome. Audiences at Covent Garden were notoriously guarded with visiting conductors, and were not usually generous in their applause, especially at the beginning of an opera.

Gubin beckoned the orchestra to its feet, and acknowledged the ovation, his hands above his head, the bright spotlight trained on his head and shoulders.

He was a very distinguished looking man. Quentin thought he seemed even more imposing and charismatic than he had remembered. He had a presence about him. Gubin was at least six feet five, and had grey hair and a goatee to match.

Even four rows back from the orchestra Quentin caught a whiff of Gubin's after-shave lotion. It seemed very strong, sickly sweet.

Quentin looked to his left to see what Alex was doing, as Gubin indicated to the orchestra to resume their seats. She was still clapping politely, smiling, and she seemed radiant, he thought, almost serene.

Gubin waited for the audience to quiet down, baton raised in his right hand. There was movement and hushed voices in the Dress Circle, and Quentin turned round just in time to see Leo Connell taking his seat next to Lord Jaeger, with the Russian Ambassador on the other side, he thought. He assumed the elegant woman wearing the purple dress, sitting next to Leo, was Maria Gubin. It would make sense. The wife of the conductor would be given VIP treatment. The group was at least ten in number. He wondered if it was Maria, and whether she had been in the dressing room before the performance when Alex had been there.

The prelude started. Tatiana's theme sounded particularly poignant, Quentin thought. Then his mind turned to rehearsals. He suddenly realized that Petya must have been in London for at least a week to prepare the performances, and to direct final rehearsals. Alex hadn't mentioned it. But then he hadn't said anything either.

Quentin was now back into the music. It sounded wonderful. The strings had a strong, vibrant yet sweet, lyrical quality that few other conductors could achieve with Tchaikovsky, especially those without Russian blood in their veins. This was the real thing, Quentin thought. The opera was one of his favorites. It had a melancholy, not to say tragic, feel to it, reflected in some of Tchaikovsky's best music. The libretto was based on a story in verse by Pushkin, perhaps the most notable of all Russian writers. Quentin felt it was one of opera's true masterpieces.

The curtain opened to the first scene of Act I of "Eugene Onegin". The widowed Madame Larina sits in the garden of her country estate with her devoted servant Filippyevna. Her daughters, Olga and Tatiana, sing a love song that reminds the older women of days gone by. It is a pretty scene.

Quentin noticed that Alex was concentrating, and carefully checking the surtitles above the proscenium arch, to monitor the line-by-line translation from Russian into English.

By now, through the second scene, Tatiana has fallen in love with Onegin, and she has written the famous love letter. In the last scene of the Act, Onegin tells Tatiana he admits he was touched by her letter but adds he would tire quickly of marriage. Though she has all the virtues he might wish for in a wife, the most he can offer is a brother's love. He advises more emotional control, lest another man fail to respect her innocence. Crushed, Tatiana rushes away.

Quentin thought he must have seen the opera at least ten times, and on each previous occasion he had thought Onegin totally blind and stupid for rejecting Tatiana. But this performance seemed different. He understood, and his sympathies were with Onegin.

The first Act had gone well and the audience greeted the curtain with loud bravos.

During an interval of over thirty minutes, too long Quentin thought, he fought to find words to open up discussion with Alex again concerning her visit to Gubin's dressing room before the performance, but he could not.

Instead, over gin and tonics at the bar, and rather limply, he asked, "What did you think?"

"Wonderful," Alex responded. "It's going really well, isn't it?"

"Is Maria here? His wife?" Quentin was not looking Alex in the eye.

"Yes, I think so," she replied.

"She wasn't backstage, then?" he asked.

"I would like to see Leo during the next interval, if I can," she quickly interjected, ignoring his question. "Maybe I could come up to the Dress Circle and find him. He's with the Ambassador."

"But he will also be with Jaeger and the VIP party," Quentin said, "and I'm not sure we'll be able get to him."

"I know," Alex replied quickly, "so I'll come up on my own. You needn't bother. It will be a bore for you anyway. Why don't you stay down in the stalls?"

They were now back in their seats, the house lights were dimmed, and Gubin was returning to the conductor's rostrum, this time accompanied by even more bravos and prolonged applause. Quentin thought it very strange that Gubin did not acknowledge the audience at all this time, and that he had abruptly turned to the orchestra and raised his baton, without waiting for the clapping to die down.

"That was a bit out of order," he whispered in Alex's ear. She did not respond, just shrugged.

Act II takes place some months later, in Madame Larina's house. A party is under way in honour of Tatiana's name day. It is a showpiece for the full company, and Quentin was overwhelmed by the excitement and beauty of the performance. He watched Alex, as she too seemed enchanted by the colorful scene.

Onegin dances with Tatiana but clearly is bored with the country people and their provincial sensibilities. To get back at the poet Lenski for dragging him there, he dances with Olga, who is attracted to him momentarily and she responds to his advances. Lenski jealously confronts Onegin. The merrymaking stops. Madame Larina implores them not to quarrel in her house. Lenski is remorseful but cannot contain his rage at Onegin, who accepts his challenge to a duel.

Quentin thought that Gubin had caught the drama of this scene particularly well, as the performance went into the Act's final scene.

At dawn on the banks of a stream near an old mill, Lenski and his second, Zaretski, await Onegin. Reflecting on the folly of his brief life, and saddened by its now unalterable course, the young poet imagines his beloved Olga visiting his grave. Onegin arrives with his second. The two men, standing apart and without looking at one another, sing a cannon in which each admits privately that they have acted rashly — that they would rather laugh together than fight — but pride and impulsiveness prevail. The duel is fought and Lenski is fatally shot.

It is always a stunning theatrical moment.

The curtain quickly fell, and the audience was silent, just for a few seconds. Then there were sudden outbreaks of cheering, and shouts of "bravo" and "bravi."

Quentin immediately turned to Alex, and without thinking, whispered, "I love you." "Me too," Alex said, as she smiled and stroked his hair. "I think I'll go and find Leo now, if you don't mind. I've got thirty minutes, I assume."

Without hesitation or saying anything further, she swept past Quentin to the rear of the stalls. Quentin noticed she had left her fur coat on the back of her seat. He then looked up to the Dress Circle, and he saw that Leo, Lord Jaeger and the entire group had already left their seats.

During the interval, with Alex's coat under his arm, Quentin strolled around the front of the house, stopping here and there to talk with some of those in the audience he recognized and knew on speaking terms. With ten minutes left before the Act III curtain, he decided to walk down to the pit, and look at the placements Gubin had for the orchestra. He went right down to the very front of the stalls, leaning over the pit, and as he did so, he felt something hard in Alex's coat pocket under his arm. He put in his hand, and pulled out a CD, without its case. There was nothing else. The CD was unmarked. He put it in his own jacket pocket, next to his wallet, to remind himself to ask Alex about it later. It crossed his mind that Petya might have given it to her.

"How nice to see you," a voice beside him suddenly said, as he was looking into the pit. He turned to his left and there was diminutive Dominique Lieberman. He momentarily did not recognize her. She was wearing glasses, and her hair was different, very short.

"Well, how delightful," said Quentin, holding out his hand. She took it and held on to it. It surprised him, since the last time he had seen her was the previous year, when they had first met.

"Are you working, or is this just pleasure?" Dominique smiled into his eyes. She was obviously flirting with him, and he was flattered.

"Oh, I'm working. I'm here again on Saturday night," said Quentin. "Are you doing anything with Gubin while he's here?" he asked.

Dominique turned away. "No, unfortunately. Not at all. Maybe in New York."

As he stood there, now with his back to the orchestra pit, he spotted Alexandra in the back of the Dress Circle, in animated conversation with Leo. She was gesticulating. She seemed upset. Leo was shrugging and not saying much in response, it seemed. She then walked away from Leo, pointing her finger in the direction of the stage, and disappeared through the back exit.

"I will let you go to her," Dominique said, not commenting on what they had both just witnessed. "Au revoir, mon ami." And with that she moved swiftly away.

Quentin returned to his seat. He was pleased to have bumped into Dominique. Alex didn't talk about Dominique very much, although he knew they met from time to time. He would suggest the three of them got together for dinner, he thought.

He placed Alex's coat over her seat, next to his. He was suddenly very hungry, and he wished they had eaten something in the first interval. He soon felt Alex's hand on his shoulder. He stood up, and let her slide into her seat beside him. She had been crying, and her face was flushed.

Quentin asked, "What's the matter? Are you OK, darling?"

Alex nodded her head, but said nothing. She was staring ahead vacantly at the safety curtain which was now rising. "I can't talk about it. Not now."

Quentin decided to change the subject. "How would you like to come with me to New York? Next week." Quentin took her right hand in his, and looking into her eyes, said, "I have to cover the Lincoln Center Festival for the paper. It's three weeks. All expenses paid. You could come. I would have to confirm that with Jack Barker, of course, at the office."

"Really? Wow, that's wonderful," she said, without smiling. "Let's see how things work out. I have a lot on at the moment, and it would take some arranging."

Quentin persisted. "But it would be great. We've always said we would like to be in Manhattan in early summer when the weather is half decent, before the real humidity sets in. And I would love you to come with me, I really would."

"Maybe. Let's see."

Quentin went on, "The thing is, I have to get the air tickets and make the hotel reservation this week, by the weekend, at the latest. And I should talk with Jack tomorrow."

"Don't push me Quentin. Let's talk about it later. OK?"

After an awkward pause, Quentin said, "I just saw Dominique Lieberman, by the way. I thought we could get together with her, for dinner or something."

"She lives in New York now. Maybe whenever we're there," Alex said coldly.

The audience was now fully settled and ready for Act III. The lights went down, and Quentin waited to see what sort of a reception Gubin would get as he made his last act entrance, when traditionally the audience gives the conductor and orchestra a special ovation. He was also looking forward to the spectacular St. Petersburg Ball scene, always a favorite of his.

The wait seemed endless. Surely there had been ample time to set the last act scenery. After all, the interval had been at least thirty-five minutes. Still they waited. No sign of activity in the orchestra pit. Still more waiting.

The audience now started to get restless, and began to chatter.

Quentin whispered in Alex's ear "What do you think the delay is?"

"I have no idea," she said, "but I hope everything is OK back there."

"Back where?" he asked.

Then Quentin noticed the orchestra leader stand up and answer the house phone on the conductor's rostrum. He said nothing, but nodded several times, and then sat down.

The audience at the rear of the amphitheater had now started a slow hand-clap, and then suddenly a spotlight was turned on, not on the conductor's rostrum, but this time on the stage curtain. A public announcement was imminent, it seemed. The audience went quieter, and there was an almost imperceptible groan from the back of the amphitheater. Perhaps one of the singers was suddenly indisposed, thought Quentin.

Geoffrey Wright, the Opera Company General Director, walked on stage from the wings, and into the spotlight, holding a wireless microphone.

He cleared his throat, and then said, "Ladies and gentlemen. Please bear with us. We are dealing with an emergency right now and the performance of "Eugene Onegin" must be abandoned. We are truly sorry."

The audience reaction was immediate. "Oh no!" Then there were isolated cries of "Why? What's going on?" And "This is a disgrace!"

Geoffrey Wright continued, "I appreciate how you must feel. But it is unavoidable. We have no choice but to terminate the performance now. Please be assured that we will try to accommodate patrons by offering tickets for future performances of "Eugene Onegin," by way of compensation, if we can. This is an unforeseen emergency."

There was now total silence in the theater, except for Geoffrey Wright's voice. "I would only add that there is no cause for alarm, and that this is not a security related incident. I must make that clear. Ladies and gentlemen, please leave the auditorium quietly. Once again, may I say on behalf of the Royal Opera House how sorry I am that your enjoyment of this evening has been spoiled. Good night."

He then left the stage, and the spotlight was turned off.

Quentin noticed that members of the orchestra had already started to pack up their instruments and leave the pit.

The house lights then came up, and he took Alex's arm and they stood up. Alex was silent.

He asked her, "What do you think is happening?"

Alex did not respond, but indicated with a gesture to Quentin that they should walk to the back of the auditorium, to the exits.

As he turned, Quentin's eye was drawn to the Dress Circle. Lord Jaeger was on his mobile phone, and the Ambassador was talking to an aide. Leo was nowhere to be seen. Neither was Maria Gubin, if that was who it was.

As he and Alex reached the lobby, Quentin saw Leo Connell rushing in from the street outside, and he was making directly for Alex. He pushed aside several people who were leaving in order to make his way through. He was not wearing his suit jacket, and his hair was ruffled. He was breathing heavily, and sweating profusely.

He grabbed Alex roughly by the shoulders with both hands, and looking at her straight in the face, said, "It's terrible. Petya's dead!"

Chapter 2

Leo was a large man. He had shaken Alex physically. But she was oblivious to this and the news had struck her like a lightning bolt. She collapsed into Quentin's arms, moaning loudly.

Quentin guided her to the nearest seat in the lobby, and Leo sat down beside them. She closed her eyes, and rested her head on Quentin's shoulders, breathing heavily.

Leo spoke. "I don't know what happened. But he was found in his dressing room when he didn't respond to his Act III call. There was a bullet wound in his neck. It's nasty. Unbelievable." There was a pause. "Alex dear", he said, "this is horrible for you, but we have to go backstage. They want to see you."

Quentin snapped, "That's ridiculous. What can she possibly know?"

"I agree," said Leo, "but there it is. They have a Detective Superintendent on the scene already. From Scotland Yard."

Alex was now sobbing uncontrollably. "Let's wait a while," suggested Quentin. "She really can't see anyone just yet."

"Alex, you have no choice," said Leo. "But here's what I suggest. I'll go back there now, and say you're on your way. That should be fine. OK with you?" Leo did not wait for a response, and he got up and left the lobby, the way he had come in.

Quentin looked around. He saw that there was a commotion building. Some people near them must have heard Leo's first outburst, and word was spreading quickly. A voice was heard asking patrons to leave the theater as quietly as possible.

After a pause of a few minutes, Alex was now quieter. "Let's do it, Quentin. I think we should go back there," she said.

"I'm not sure that's wise," said Quentin.

"We must." She hesitated, then added, "I knew something was wrong earlier. Badly wrong. I spoke to Leo about it during the interval…" She started to cry again. "But I can't say much to the police. Not now."

Alex got up. Quentin stood beside her, and draped her coat around her shoulders. He felt strongly protective towards her. She seemed very vulnerable.

Quentin suddenly remembered his daytime clothes that he had left under his seat. "My bag is still in there," he said. "I'll go and fetch it. No, wait a moment, I'll get it later, perhaps at the stage door. We can't go into the theater now, anyway. They won't let us back in."

Quentin then walked Alex out into Bow Street, and down Floral Street, as far as the stage door. What he saw there took him by surprise. There were throngs of people, and many were shouting and gesticulating. There were four marked police cars, and two ambulances, all with their lights flashing. Quentin noticed some reporters, and there was a BBC news journalist and cameraman interviewing some bystanders. They were brightly lit by temporary television lights that cast long shadows across the scene, giving it a surreal atmosphere. The police had put up a temporary barrier just by the entrance to the stage door area, and there were several uniformed officers barring entry to the public.

They worked their way through the crowd. Quentin spoke to one of the police officers at the barrier. "My friend and I are expected backstage. Quentin Dart and Alexandra Matviyko. We need to get through."

The policeman called someone on a radio. He was mentioning their names, although he mispronounced Alex's last name.

"No, Alexandra Matviyko, Matviyko" said Alex.

"Come with me please, Madam. And you, Sir."

Quentin and Alex followed the policeman. They went through the stage door, and down a corridor to the left. They were heading for the principals' dressing rooms. Quentin was familiar with the theater layout. He had been backstage several times, and knew his way around.

Outside the conductor's dressing room, near the stage, there were two more policemen. The door was slightly ajar. "Wait here," the policeman said.

Alex had started to cry again. Quentin tried to comfort her. He felt in his pockets for his handkerchief, and he pulled it out of the same pocket into which he had put the CD that he had taken from Alex's coat earlier. As he did so, the CD fell on the stone floor, with a loud clatter.

"How on earth did you get that?" Alex was looking aghast at the CD on the floor.

"I was going to ask you about it," Quentin explained. "Sorry."

"Put it away, immediately," she whispered. "Now! Now! For God's sake! Quentin, please!" He placed it back in his pocket.

He could now hear voices inside. He thought he heard Leo Connell saying, "Ask her. I don't know."

He moved slightly to his left and peered into the dressing room. There were several people standing together in the center of the room. There was a short, bald man, and he could see Leo, and also Lord Jaeger and Geoffrey Wright. The woman in the Dress Circle was also there. Probably Maria, he thought. There were several men who looked like plainclothes policemen.

The uniformed policeman emerged and he asked Alex to go inside. He said Detective Superintendent Roberts wanted to ask her a few questions.

"Stay here if you would, Sir," he said to Quentin.

"But Miss Matviyko is my fiancée. I am with her."

"Please remain here. Thank you, Sir."

"But I would like Mr. Dart to come in with me," Alex said, her voice breaking with strain. "It's important."

The policeman returned into the dressing room. There were more voices, and Quentin thought he heard a woman's voice saying, "Not that woman. No!"

The policeman then emerged again. "You may both come in. You must do as you are asked at all times. Do not speak unless you are spoken to. There can be no exceptions. This is being treated as a crime scene. Please cooperate."

They entered the room. Alex let out a terrible scream. "Oh my God!"

It was a dramatic and shocking sight. The room was almost blindingly bright. Quentin's eye was immediately drawn to the other side of the room, which was cordoned off. By a white sofa there was a floor lamp, giving out an intense light directed at the body that was slumped over one arm of the sofa. Behind the sofa was a decorative screen, where some of Petya's clothes were hanging. There was blood on the seat cushions, which looked surreal, especially in the harsh light. Petya's torso was twisted with his back against the sofa cushions, his long legs partially on the floor, and his head was face down. He was not wearing his jacket. There was a lot of blood, especially on the front of his dress shirt and on his neck. He was still wearing his white bow tie. The score of "Eugene Onegin" was on the sofa, near his body. There were flowers everywhere in the room, and there were forty to fifty greetings cards on the dressing table.

"I am Detective Superintendent Roberts," said the short, balding man facing them. I am making some initial inquiries here. You are Miss Alexandra Matviyko, are you not?" he asked, looking up at Alex's distorted face.

"Yes."

"And you are Mr. Quentin Dart?"

"Yes."

"I am sorry to have to burden you at this time, but I need to establish some preliminary facts. I regret to tell you that Mr. Gubin has suffered a fatal gunshot wound in his chest. I would like you ask you both a few questions. Firstly you, if I may, Miss Matviyko."

He did not wait for her response. "Am I correct in stating that you worked with Mr. Gubin in New York, in the United States?" She nodded. "And did you meet Mr. Gubin again this evening?"

Alex was sobbing. "Yes, I did."

The other woman in the room then pushed her way past two plainclothes men standing between her and Alexandra, and shook her fist at her. She shouted, "You bitch! You rotten, heartless bitch! You are the reason for this. You...."

Roberts quickly intervened. "Please, Mrs. Gubin. Please!" He then indicated to the policeman who had accompanied Alexandra and Quentin into the room, and who was restraining Maria Gubin. "Assist Mrs. Gubin at once. I suggest you take her to Lord Jaeger's office. Er, will that be all right, My Lord?"

Lord Jaeger, who was behind Maria and also trying to restrain her, said, "Certainly. Of course, I will take her myself. Please allow me to make you more comfortable, Mrs. Gubin."

Maria was sobbing as she left the room with Lord Jaeger. Alex was trying desperately to control her emotions at the same time.

Roberts did not delay with his next question. "Exactly when did you last see Mr. Gubin alive, Miss Matviyko?"

Alex struggled to answer. "Before the performance. This evening."

"And where was that?"

"Er …… here, in this room."

"At about what time would that have been?"

"Maybe seven, or seven fifteen," she said.

"Please tell me what the purpose of that meeting was?"

"We worked together. I mean, before. When I lived in the States. Er ….. Leo asked me to see Petya, and give him our best wishes for the performance. That's all."

"And would these flowers have been from you, Miss Matviyko?" asked Roberts, picking up a large bouquet of red roses from the dressing table.

"I don't know. Er, yes, I think so. Well, they're from the agency really," responded Alex.

"I see. Please read the handwritten greeting that is attached to the flowers, if you would, Miss Matviyko. It is written in Russian, I believe. If you are able to, please tell me exactly what it says, in English."

Alex looked stunned. Quentin noticed that she had gone exceedingly pale. She was clearly struggling to retain her composure.

"As precisely as you can. Thank you." He handed the greeting tag to Alex.

Her hand was trembling as she held it in front of her. Roberts persisted, his voice raised slightly. "Am I right that it is written in Russian? Translate, please, Miss Matviyko."

Alex was now shaking visibly and she fought to speak clearly. "We, I sent it. It's a good luck message. It says, Dear Pet. Er ……Petya, I miss you … have missed you, I mean. I wish I could share this evening with you. My …. Superintendent, I can't. I can't do this."

"Please do, Miss Matviyko. Thank you." He was now making notes in a small black book.

"I'm sorry. Oh Quentin, I'm so sorry." She was sobbing.

"Read on, please," urged Roberts.

"Well, it says…. it says that I wish I could share this evening with you. My thoughts are with you, as always. I will try to see you before curtain up, if I can. My fondest love, … er, Your own Alex."

"Thank you, Miss Matviyko," said Roberts, taking the tag from her.

"One other question, if I may. Who was here with Mr. Gubin when you met with him before the performance?"

"No one. There was no one."

"Are you certain of that?"

Alex did not speak.

After a seemingly long pause, Roberts said, "Perhaps I could elaborate, Miss Matviyko. I believe a gentleman met with Mr. Gubin before the performance, at about seven o'clock. The stage doorman confirms the time, according to his security log. He gave his name as Bryce. I am not certain when he left. It is not logged. Are you sure he was not in the dressing room at the time you met with Mr. Gubin?"

Alex seemed unsure as to what to say next. She finally said, "He was not here, no."

"Do you know anyone named Bryce, Miss Matviyko?"

"No. No, I do not."

"I see. Now, Mr. Dart, may I ask you when you last saw Mr. Gubin?"

Quentin was stunned. He was not expecting any questions.

"Oh. Well at least two years ago, I think. Probably when he, I mean Mr. Gubin, was here for concerts at The Royal Festival Hall."

Leo interjected, "It was March, two years ago. That's right. Er, Superintendent, may I ask if this is really necessary. I mean this is a terrible shock to us all, and Alex is extremely upset, as you can see."

Roberts was picking up Quentin's bag from the table beside the sofa. "Is this your bag, Sir?"

Quentin was amazed to see it. "Yes it is. How did it get here?"

"Would these be your clothes?" Roberts pulled the clothes out of the bag, and held them in front of Quentin.

"Yes, they are."

"And is this your phone, Sir?' Roberts was holding the mobile phone that Quentin had placed in his pocket when he had left his car in the car park.

Quentin was flabbergasted. He quickly realized that he had never turned the phone off. It had been in the bag all evening, in his jacket, turned on. It might have rung in the opera. Thank God it didn't, he thought.

"Yes, I believe it is," he said.

"Would you please check the phone, for any recent voicemail messages? Thank you, and Sir, would you please oblige me by putting the speaker on while you play them back."

Quentin pressed "1" and waited. "You have two unheard messages. First message. Hi Quentin. Jack here. It's around seven pm. Please let me know tomorrow about New York. Enjoy the opera. Love to Alex. Talk to you tomorrow. Bye." "To repeat, press 1, to save, press 2 and to delete, press 3."

"Please go on," said Roberts.

"Second message. Hello Quentin, This is Dominique. I have just left the theater. It was nice to talk with you this evening, Quentin. Please call me back on this number as soon as you can. I have something I want to tell you. Don't tell Alex about this. It's important. Please, I look forward to your call." "To repeat, press 1, to save, press 2 and to delete, press 3."

"No more unheard messages."

"Thank you, Sir," said Roberts. "Tell me, who is Dominique?"

"She is just a friend," said Quentin. "Dominique Lieberman. A violinist."

"I see. How long have you known her, Mr. Dart?"

"I don't really know her. Er …about a year, I think."

"And you, Miss Matviyko, how long have you known Miss Lieberman?"

Alex stirred. "I'm not sure. Maybe three or four years. I really cannot remember."

"And where did you meet her, please?"

"I don't know."

"Was it in New York, Miss Matviyko?"

"Yes, I suppose it might have been," stuttered Alex.

"Very well. I would now like to see Lord Jaeger and Mrs. Gubin again, and I will want to interview each of the staff or anyone else that has access to this room, Mr. Wright, if I may. You have not released anyone yet, have you?"

Geoffrey Wright, who had been standing next to Leo, said, "No, Superintendent. You may conduct interviews in my office. It is two floors up, I'm afraid. But we can arrange whatever you want."

"Thank you, Mr. Wright," said Roberts, putting his book in his pocket. "Mr. Dart and Miss Matviyko, you may both leave the opera house, but please give my assistant your contact details before you leave. I will want to see you again, probably tomorrow morning. Thank you for your cooperation."

"Mr. Wright, has any official press release been sent out by the Opera House?"

"No Superintendent, but I should mention that there are several reporters outside, and the BBC is already filming. It will be in the newspapers tomorrow morning, of that I can be certain."

"Then please draft a formal press statement and check it with me before it is released, as soon as possible. Thank you."

"Mr. Dart, here is your bag with your clothes, and your phone. Goodnight Mr. Dart, and thank you again, Miss Matviyko."

Quentin took the bag, put the phone in his pocket. He and Alex then left the dressing room. Alex stole a look at Petya's body as they turned to go through the door.

They left their cards with the policeman on the door.

*

"We need to talk," said Quentin, as they walked out into the late evening air. "Why don't we go and get something to eat. Somewhere quiet. OK?"

"I'm not hungry. Can't we just go home? You could eat a snack there, if you want."

Quentin looked at Alex. "You do look like you've been through the wringer. OK, let's go. Your place or mine?"

"Mine, please. But Quentin, I have to ask you something. Please don't press me too much. Please. I am so tired."

"I understand," said Quentin, mentally listing some of the puzzling questions that had been worrying him. Why had she kept so much from him? And that message with the flowers. And what was the mystery with the CD? She's obviously not over him, he thought. But he's gone now, said Quentin to himself, feeling guilty for even having had the thought.

As they walked to the car park in Long Acre, Quentin's phone rang. He pulled it out of his pocket. "Mr. Dart, this is Detective Superintendent Roberts. I would like you and Miss Matviyko to meet me in the morning, at eleven o'clock. At Scotland Yard. Ask at the desk and you will be taken to an interview room. Thank you. Goodnight."

"That was Roberts. He wants to see us in the morning. At eleven."

"I'm not sure I can take all this, Quentin," Alex said to him, as they entered the car park entrance. "And I don't want you involved. Not at all."

"But I am involved. With you. I love you."

"You may not want to have anything more to do with me now," Alex said flatly, without a trace of a threat. "I wouldn't blame you."

"But, please do one thing for me." She had stopped and was facing him. "Please cancel New York."

"Cancel?" That's ridiculous. Why?"

"I can't go. I can't leave here, Quentin. It's not possible. Not after this."

Chapter 3

Akbar Sattar sat in the driver's seat of a black Mercedes parked in St John Street, about a mile away from the opera house, alone. He waited as noisy crowds emerged from the several pubs in the vicinity.

He was a large, dark-skinned, burly man. At least three hundred pounds. He wore tinted glasses, with thick lenses that distorted his eyes, making them seem tiny. His hair was black, short and neat. He was wearing an evening dress suit.

His phone rang. "We have a change of plan. Wait for further instructions tomorrow, at noon."

Chapter 4

It had been a bright, sunny, warm afternoon in New York City. But clouds were gathering to the east, over Queens.

Martin H. Schaeffer sat in his office going through some paperwork.

It had been a busy season, but the theater was quiet. He had used the downtime to catch up with paperwork. He was now working on final details for the Lincoln Center Festival that would open the following week.

Martin was a rotund, jovial man, with a ruddy complexion. There was something Pickwickian about his appearance. He had a full head of curly, grey hair. Almost Afro style. He tended to wear tweedy, country style clothes, which accentuated his barrel-shaped physique, and which most would have thought would be far too uncomfortable in the mid-summer, when New York could be notoriously humid and sticky. He had an apartment near Lincoln Center, and a weekend home in Great Neck, Long Island. He was a cultured man, with a wide ranging set of interests, not only in the arts. A man of the world, as Marcie, his assistant, would say. He had emigrated from his native Hamburg, Germany, about twenty years previously, and had settled into the American way of life without any difficulty.

Martin Schaeffer was General Director of The Metropolitan Opera, America's foremost opera company. Petya Gubin had been the Met's Chief Guest Conductor for five years, and he was the star of the Met roster. Martin and Petya were friends.

It was six o'clock. Martin picked up the remote and switched on the TV. He wanted to catch the news before he went home.

He sorted some papers as he half watched the weather forecast. He noticed that there was a storm advisory from nine until midnight.

Then, "Here is the six o'clock news, on seven. First, we have some dramatic breaking news." And suddenly there was Petya's face on the screen, a clip of him at a rehearsal at the Met, filmed earlier in the year. "We are getting reports that American conductor Petya Gubin is dead, shot in his dressing room at the Covent Garden Opera House in London this evening. He was in London to conduct performances of "Eugene Onegin". We understand the police are on the scene making inquiries, and that a statement will be made soon. Mr. Gubin has been Guest Conductor at the Metropolitan Opera House in New York City for several years. He was born in Moscow, Russia, and became an American citizen in the eighties. His wife Maria, who was with him in London when he died, is Italian. They have two children, Antonio and Chloe. We will try to go to London later in this newscast to bring you further news, as soon as we have more details. Once again, Petya Gubin has been shot today, in London. Now to local news ….."

Martin was horror struck, devastated. This was huge. A major calamity. This can't be true, he thought to himself, as he pressed Marcie's intercom button. He said, "Marcie dear, get me Geoffrey Wright on the phone, as quickly as you possibly can. At his office at Covent Garden."

He wondered who else he could call while he waited. Then Marcie buzzed him immediately. "It's Leo Connell, Martin, on line two."

"Leo, hi. What on earth is going on?"

The line was clear. Leo's voice was breathless. "I'm still at the Garden, Martin. I wanted to let you know there's been a terrible disaster. Petya is dead. Shot, right here, in his dressing room."

"I know. I just saw the news on TV," said Martin. "They're not saying much yet. For God's sake, what's happening there?"

"The Scotland Yard people are on the scene. They're not saying he was murdered. But I don't see what else it could have been. He was lying there, in his room. Shot in the chest. It happened in the interval, just before the last act. They shut the performance down immediately."

Martin gasped. "Who discovered it?" he asked.

"I'm not sure exactly who it was. But it was after he didn't respond to his Act III call. They went into the dressing room and found him. There was nothing they could do."

"Is Maria there, Leo?"

Leo was still struggling for breath. "Yes, she is. She's with Jaeger. Martin there was a situation, if you know what I mean. Alexandra was here, and they met each other, she and Maria, when Alex was being interviewed by the police. Maria tried to go for her, physically."

"For heaven's sake," said Martin. "Why on earth didn't they keep them apart. How bloody stupid. Where's Alexandra now?"

"I'm not sure. She left with Quentin Dart a while ago. You know, the Times guy she's engaged to."

"Leo, I have a call in to Geoff. Please let him know if you see him. I must speak to him. I assume Covent Garden is putting out a statement. Please tell them to email it to Marcie immediately. We'll have to do something, and I want to be sure we're on the same page."

"OK Martin, no problem."

"Oh, one other thing," asked Martin, "where are Petya and Maria staying?"

"Martin, they aren't. At least not together. When Maria got to London on Tuesday she made her own arrangements. She's at The Park Lane Hotel. He is staying at The Savoy. He was, I mean."

"Leo, keep me in the loop. Please give my condolences to Maria. Tell her I'll be in touch. Thanks for calling." He rang off.

Almost immediately the phone rang again. It was Marcie. "Martin, I have a guy who says he must speak with you. He says he's with the FBI. Assistant Director."

"Put him through," said Martin.

"Hello Mr. Schaeffer. My name is Mark Novelli. I am Assistant to The Director of the Federal Bureau of Investigation. I'm calling you from Washington. Do you have a moment, on a matter of some delicacy?"

"Yes, I do, although I'm expecting an important connection to London any time now."

"I'll be as brief as I can," said Novelli. "You may or may not know that Petya

Gubin was discovered shot this evening, in London. Were you aware of this, Mr. Schaeffer?"

"Yes, I have just heard," said Martin.

"Mr. Schaeffer, the FBI would like to interview you, as quickly as possible. We have some sensitive matters we are investigating, and I would like to meet with you tomorrow morning, at your office, to ask you some questions. In total confidence, of course. Would nine be convenient?"

Martin quickly looked at his calendar. "Yes, I could be here at nine," he said.

"Thank you. Please do not say anything to anyone about our meeting. Especially to the press. In fact I would suggest you do not yourself say anything to the media at all for the time being. I will see you tomorrow. Good bye."

Martin replaced the receiver. He was shocked that the call had been so soon after the report of Petya's death. He knew that there had been some inquiries into Petya's Foundation, by the police and the IRS, in the fall of last year. But he had been told by Petya's Foundation President, Arnold Fischer, that nothing had resulted from any of it. He started to remember other events that might be relevant. He had suspected that Petya and Maria had been discussing a separation and that there were financial issues to be resolved. And then there had also been the new arrangements for payment of Petya's Met fees, into a bank account in Switzerland. As his mind wandered over what might have given rise to the tragedy in London, Marcie was speaking again, "Mr. Wright on line one, Martin."

"Geoff, mein freund. This is all terrible. What can you tell me?"

"Hello, Martin. I just saw Leo Connell, briefly. He said you were up to date with the ghastly news. I have a moment, but this will have to be quick. The police have started to interview our staff here and are taking statements from everybody. I have to be on call."

"Geoff, what on earth happened? Were you around in the interval? Backstage?"

"Yes, I was, in my office. I was called down by the senior dressing room attendant, just as last calls for the final act were being made. I wasn't aware of anything unusual, except that Petya was obviously in a foul mood throughout the middle act. The reason I say that is that Graham Wood, the concertmaster, told me he noticed a difference in him. Graham said Petya was apparently muttering obscenities under his breath to some of the orchestra players. Very unusual. Also he totally failed to acknowledge the audience ovation at the beginning of Act II."

"Yes, but that's hardly an overture to a shooting, is it?"

"No, Martin, but there are a lot of unanswered questions. The police are concerned with a possible visit to Petya's room by some guy called Bryce, before the performance. They seem to think Alexandra Matviyko might know him, but she's denying it. She was here this evening, you know. In fact, she and Maria crossed swords in the dressing room. Very unpleasant. The police are also very interested in Alexandra's involvement with Petya."

"Yes, Leo told me about Alexandra," said Martin. "By the way, have you issued a statement to the media yet?"

"Yes we have. I've asked the press office to email it to you, to Marcie in fact."

"Thanks. What a dreadful thing to have happened. You must be at your wit's end."

"Yes. My Chairman, but of course you know him, Lord Jaeger, is personally taking care of Maria, and the police, I must say, are totally organized. Very efficient. One question, if I may, Martin. Just curiosity."

"Shoot," said Martin.

"Unfortunate choice of words there, my friend. Sorry, bad joke. Er …when Petya got Alexandra that apartment near the Lincoln Center, was he living there too?"

"I believe he was, for most of the time when he was in New York. Why?"

"Wasn't he also seeing Dominique Lieberman, as well?" asked Geoff.

"That's very likely. Dominique's father, Hermann, is a good friend of Petya's, and he used to spend a lot of time with him when he was in town. But what the relationship was between Petya and Dominique, I'm not sure. There were several women he had in tow. You could ask Alexandra about Dominique, she would know."

"She's not in a fit state to tell anyone anything at the moment," said Geoff. "Anyway, I have to go. Sorry old man, but the police want me downstairs. Bye for now."

Martin knew he had to advise the Met's press office quickly, and get the release out. He should also contact some of the music staff, at least those who had worked with Petya. He called Marcie in, to go over the details. He decided to wait until the FBI had visited before he said anything else to anyone, except to Marcie.

Marcia Segarra had been Martin Schaeffer's Executive Secretary for over ten years. She was probably at least fifty years of age. She was short, with a plump figure slightly the worse for years of neglect. Her jet-black hair was what could best be described as hastily arranged, probably dyed. Her face had a dark, Latino pallor. She wore old-fashioned, butterfly frame glasses for reading, dating back to the sixties, and clothes in a style that mirrored Martin's own preferred mode of dress. She wore the same make-up and jewelry, day in and day out. Marcie lived for her job, for the Met. She knew everything Martin needed to know to do his job effectively. She was indispensable, discreet and reliable. Martin trusted her without reservation.

Martin told Marcie about the calls from Leo Connell and Geoffrey Wright. He also mentioned the meeting with FBI Assistant Director Novelli scheduled for the following morning.

Marcie thought for a moment, and then said, "Mr. Novelli called me back after you had spoken with him. It may not be anything, Martin, but he said not to bother you, and then he asked me whom you had spoken to in London. I said you were expecting a call from Mr. Wright. He then said that if it could be arranged, he would want to speak with Arnold Fischer about the Foundation, and with Petya Gubin's Attorney. He asked for the telephone numbers."

"That's OK, Marcie. I don't see a problem there."

"Except that I thought the FBI already had the numbers, from last year, when they were making those inquiries. I asked Mr. Novelli if I could call him back to confirm the numbers, and he said that wouldn't be possible. Strange, I thought. Not the way you would expect the FBI to work, especially at that very senior level."

"What are saying, Marcie? That you think this guy is an impostor! A bit melodramatic, isn't it?"

"That thought did occur to me, Martin, yes. I would be careful to check his credentials when he comes in tomorrow."

Chapter 5

Quentin parked the car outside the apartment in Oakley Street, just by the Albert Bridge. Alexandra owned a two bedroom, split level condominium, on the second and third floor of an old Victorian house, which Quentin thought was beautifully converted and surprisingly well appointed.

They went in. He offered to make a coffee. Alex said she would change into something casual.

As they entered the living room, Quentin said, "Oh, sorry, I forgot my bag with my clothes. I'll just go back down. Won't be a moment."

He descended the stoop to the pavement, and took out his phone. He quickly found Dominique's number from the missed call earlier, and pressed the call back button. It rang and Dominique answered immediately.

"Dominique, hello, it's Quentin. How are you doing?"

"Not good. Quentin, did you hear the news? I assume you did."

"Yes," said Quentin. "I got your voicemail message. I had to play it back to the Superintendent, when we were backstage in the conductor's dressing room. It was in front of Petya Gubin's body. Quite surreal. Alex heard your message too."

"You were in the dressing room?"

"Yes, we had to go back there to face some questions. He was just lying there, on the sofa. There was blood everywhere. Terrible."

Dominique started to cry. "I'm so sorry," she said, "It was unfair to make you go through such an ordeal. How is Alex? Is she coping?"

"Not well at all," said Quentin.

"This will be a very big strain for her, Quentin. You have no idea, I suspect. Is there anything I can do for you?"

"There may be, Dominique. Thank you. You're very kind. I am making this call from outside Alex's apartment and I have to go back upstairs now. She's expecting me."

"Just a minute. Quentin, I must tell you something. Alex would be even more upset if she knew what I am about to tell you, so please don't say anything."

"What do you mean?" asked Quentin.

"Petya and I were having an affair, you know. It was for over a year. I am expecting his child, in November. Alex has no idea about this. Please do not tell her, not yet."

Quentin could think of nothing helpful to say in response to this extraordinary confession. "That's a surprise," he stuttered. Then he suddenly had the image in his mind of Dominique bringing up Gubin's baby on her own. "My God, though, you must be totally gutted by Petya's death."

"What's that? Oh yes, of course. But I would like to meet with you, Quentin, as soon as possible. Just you, on your own, if you can manage that. Perhaps I can see you in your office, maybe? That way, Alex would not know. There are things I want to talk about. Important things, about Petya. Could we meet tomorrow afternoon? I will come to The Times office."

Quentin thought for a moment. He was very reluctant to deceive Alex further, but he thought he might learn something valuable from Dominique. "OK, get there around three. But call me first, just to make sure I'm there. See you tomorrow. Good night."

"Good night, Quentin. Thank you. I feel so much better now. You are a very nice man. So understanding. Sleep well, mon cherie, and try to get this terrible day out of your mind."

Quentin then got his bag from the car and returned to the apartment.

"You were a long time," Alex said. "Where have you been?"

"Getting the bag, " he said, blushing.

"You called Dominique, didn't you?" said Alex, raising her voice.

He could not lie. "Well yes, I did."

"What did she tell you?"

"Nothing really. Alex, don't you think it's you who should be telling me things. Not the other way round," he said, raising his voice. "Alex, bloody hell, you have to square with me, especially if you want me to understand."

"I can't say anything now. You'll just have to wait. Be patient, Quentin! Don't you realize what I'm going through?"

"No, I'm not sure I do, actually," he said a little sarcastically.

She then went upstairs to her bedroom, and slammed the door shut behind her, leaving Quentin in the middle of the living room, still holding his bag.

He thought he would change. He removed his daytime clothes from the bag, and undressed. As he did, he saw the CD in his dress jacket pocket.

Alex was probably going to stay upstairs for a while, he thought. Maybe the CD would explain everything, and they wouldn't have to suffer any more strained conversations. So he quickly finished changing and then placed the CD in the stereo system, which was in the cabinet by the fireplace. He pressed play. There was no sound track at all. Nothing. He realized it was probably a CD-ROM. He then moved into the office, adjacent to the living room, where there was a desktop computer. It was already turned on. He slipped the CD into the drive and found that there was just one folder on the disc, marked "Documents for London."

He opened the folder and found at least ten documents, all in Microsoft Word. Each was titled numerically, starting with "123", then "234", "345", and so on. He opened the first document, "123". It was partly in Russian. Or so he assumed. And there was some Arabic. There were diagrams, some map locations. Some of them appeared to be in the United States. He tried to study the contents.

Alex moved up behind him silently, stealthily, like a cat. "What the hell are you doing, Quentin?"

Quentin shot up from his chair. He instantly felt sick with guilt and embarrassment.

"I really don't know what to say, Alex."

"I think you had better give that to me now," she said, pointing to the computer.

Quentin removed the disc and gave it to her. She walked away and returned upstairs, shutting the bedroom door behind her.

Quentin swore to himself. What to do now, he wondered.

He decided to have something to eat. He was starving. He would then try again with Alex. Perhaps she would be in a better frame of mind in half an hour or so.

He went into the kitchen, and made himself a cheese and ham sandwich. He then turned the kettle on, and scooped some instant coffee into a mug. He noticed that it was a Metropolitan Opera House mug. As he ate the sandwich, the telephone rang in the living room. He assumed that Alex would answer the phone, on the line upstairs. But the phone continued to ring. He went to the phone to answer the call himself. He lifted the receiver, but heard in a fraction of a second that Alex had also lifted her receiver, simultaneously. He did not speak.

"Hello, this is Alex Matviyko. Who is this?"

He continued to listen.

"Hello, Alex. Leo here. How are you doing, my dear?"

"Not very well, Leo. Quentin is pressing me for explanations and I don't know what to say to him. He's getting really curious."

"Well, that's hardly surprising," said Leo. "You can't blame him. But be careful, Alex. You don't want to implicate him."

"I know. He called Dominique. God knows what she told him."

"Watch out for her. Talk about a woman scorned," said Leo.

"Quentin wants me to go to New York with him, for the Lincoln Center Festival. I've said I can't possibly do it."

"Alex, you must not do that trip. It would be a big mistake. I suggest you separate yourself from Quentin as much as you can. Now. He's becoming a real liability, and you're not doing him any favors."

"Leo, he's seen the CD that Petya gave me. He saw some of the documents. He took it out of my coat pocket when you and I were talking in the interval. I found him looking at it on the computer, here, just now."

"How much did he see? He cannot have understood that much."

"But Leo, the fact that he knows about it is serious. Very serious. What shall I do? Leo, you are so good at this kind of thing. Please tell me."

"OK. Here's what you should do. Tell Quentin he must go back to his place. He should leave you alone for a while. He should go ahead and arrange his trip to New York, without you. Go and see Roberts in the morning, but on your own. Tell him as little as possible. Then call me. And if Maria tries to contact you, avoid her at all costs. Maybe we could meet for lunch, after you have seen Roberts. And hide the CD, until Saturday, when we'll need to hand it over."

"Leo, you're amazing. You're so right, of course. To protect Quentin. It's in his interests isn't it? OK. I'll call you tomorrow morning. You're such a darling. Love you. Night night."

Quentin put down the receiver. He was stunned. He had rarely heard himself talked about in such a way before. And by his fiancée, in particular. He thought of leaving the apartment, now. That's what she wanted, after all. But then he reconsidered. He would wait for Alex to come down, and he would see what she would say about Leo's call.

A thought flashed through his mind. How the hell did Leo know about the meeting with Roberts? After all, Roberts had called him after they had left the opera house. Roberts must have spoken to Leo later. If so, why? What was going on?

Quentin sat on the living room sofa, waiting. There was no sound upstairs.

He switched on the TV and went to the CNN channel. Perhaps there would be something on Gubin's death. There was. They were doing a to-camera piece outside the opera house stage door. ".... there will be a press conference at nine o'clock in the morning, when a police statement is expected. CNN will cover it, live. Just to repeat, Petya Gubin killed by a gunshot wound this evening, right here in his dressing room at the Royal Opera House in London." Quentin had caught the tail end of the piece. He turned the TV off.

Multitudes of mixed up thoughts were going through his mind. Should he leave Alex alone for a while? But why? What should he do about New York? Should he see Dominique? What was she up to, anyway? And what was on that CD? Why had Alex written that message to go with the flowers? She must have planned the backstage meeting with Petya beforehand. Why hadn't she mentioned it until they were in the lobby, just before he went to change? And what were those voices he heard in the loo? Who were those men? And what about Leo. Could he be…..

Alex appeared in the doorway. "I'm so sorry, Quentin. You must think I'm horrible."

"I'm confused, Alex. To be honest, I don't know what to think."

"Quentin, we are supposed to see Roberts in the morning, right?"

"Yes, at eleven, I think."

"I don't want you to come, Quentin. I don't want you involved. This has nothing to do with you. I've been thinking. It's my problem, and I'll sort it out. I'll see Roberts myself. I'll say you're busy. At work, or something."

"I don't think that would be right, Alex. Roberts wants to see both of us."

"You're not coming," she screamed. "It's none of your business."

"I think it is," Quentin said quietly. "Very much so. Alex, if you and I have any future, I'm involved. With you."

"No, Quentin. We must be apart, at least for a while. It's for the best. You should not be here. And you should go to New York on your own."

"I'm not leaving you."

"You must, Quentin."

There was a long silence. Quentin remained on the sofa, and Alex sat on the floor in front of him, cross-legged.

She spoke again, deliberately. "This thing is, this is bigger than you realize."

"But what about little Q and A," Quentin said, trying to smile. She looked away. "What about all that openness there's supposed to be between us?

Can't we at least clear up some of the questions? I have to know, Alex."

"No, I've decided. I'm doing what's best for you, believe me."

"Alex, I'm not leaving you. I'm staying put. I don't care what you say."

Alex got up. She stood by the door. "Leave now, please Quentin. Please!"

"No, I'm staying. I want some answers."

"Then I'm leaving if you're not." Alex stormed upstairs.

Quentin remained motionless, hoping she would think again. Almost immediately, she returned. She was carrying a small bag.

"Quentin, I'm leaving now. You can stay if you want. But I'm leaving. I will call you at the office tomorrow."

"Alex, it's after midnight. Where will you go?"

"It's best you don't know." She slammed the door behind her.

Quentin instantly felt very nauseous. He thought for a moment that he would run after her. She would be getting a cab on the street corner, and he could easily catch her before she disappeared into the night. But he decided otherwise. He had never seen Alex like this. Distraught, and yet decisive. She didn't seem to want to give an inch. Totally stubborn. No point in chasing after her, he thought.

Where would she go? His thoughts went back to the call from Leo. She would go to Leo, that's right. Leo lived just off Baker Street, and she had stayed with him before, he remembered, before they had got engaged. He was her boss, after all, and he seemed to know a lot about what was going on.

Quentin went to the phone. He found the incoming calls list. There was Leo's number. He pressed the call button. There was a ringing tone, a delay, and then Leo answered. He sounded as though the phone had woken him.

"Hello, Alex. What is it?"

"No, it's not Alex. It's Quentin. Look, Leo, I'm sorry to bother you, but Alex is in a very stressed state of mind, and I'm terribly worried about her. She has just left here, and I wondered whether she might go round to your place?"

"Uhuh. So what's your point?"

"Leo, please, what's going on? What's Alex involved in? I'm very worried. Very worried indeed."

"It's OK. It will get sorted. Trust me. There's nothing you can do, Quentin. Really. Look, if she comes round, I'll say you called, and I'll get her to contact you tomorrow, when she's a bit calmer. She's in shock, you know. I must go now. It's late. Good night."

Quentin sighed. He was getting nowhere. He looked at the phone and starting to scan the call list. There were several calls from a 0207 number, central London. He did not hesitate. He pressed the call button again.

"Savoy, Can I help you?"

Chapter 6

Lord Jaeger and Maria Gubin arrived at his suite in the Dorchester Hotel shortly after midnight.

Maria had been very quiet in the chauffeur-driven car during the short journey to the hotel. She had been reprimanding herself for having lost her self-control with Alexandra in the opera house.

She had been greatly shocked to see Petya dead, with blood everywhere, but somehow the enormity of the situation had not yet sunk in. Her nerves were steady, she thought, and she was pleased to have the reassuring company of Lord Jaeger for the time being. She tried to put the horrific events of the evening out of her mind as much as she could.

"You are so kind, Ben. I could not have gone back to the hotel on my own."

"Think nothing of it," he said. "I'm pleased to be able to help. You can have the second bedroom and you'll be comfortable. Stay as long as you like. Would you like a drink?"

"Yes please," said Maria. "I'll have a brandy. Thank you."

He went to the cocktail cabinet and poured two large brandies.

Lord Benedict Jaeger had been Chairman of the Covent Garden Opera Board for just a year. He had given up the positions of Chairman and CEO of his own company when he had reached sixty, in January. His son was now heading the company, and he was pleased not to have the daily involvement any more. Jaeger International Enterprises had been a major sponsor of the arts for several years, and Lord Jaeger himself had become something of a legend, in providing millions of dollars for the performing arts. Now he could spend more time pursuing his passions, particularly politics and the world of opera.

Jaeger had taken the family title when his father had died. He had been just a teenager, still at Eton, when he inherited the estate.

He was a handsome man. He was over six feet tall, elegant, and had a natural, aristocratic air about him. His white hair contrasted dramatically with the black evening dress suit he was still wearing. He removed his jacket and sat on the sofa.

"Come here, Maria. Sit beside me," he said, patting the cushion.

Maria's gown was simple. Purple, strapless, with a flared skirt, knee length. She wore a diamond necklace and a diamond and emerald bracelet on her wrist. Her rings were diamond, emerald and jade. She had kept her youthful appearance. Her long dark hair, now dyed, was drawn back tightly and gathered into a tight bun, at the back of her head. She was slim, and petite.

She placed her handbag on one end of the sofa and sat beside him.

"I am so sorry about Petya, Maria." He took her hand. "What a tragedy. You know that I will do anything I can to help. Just say. Whatever you need."

"Thank you, Ben."

"You are bearing up remarkably well, if I may say so."

"Well thank you. And thank you for rescuing me this evening. I'm afraid I didn't behave very well. Seeing Alexandra there and hearing what she had written to go with the flowers was just too much. It is devastating about Petya, of course. The children will be mortified. They will be coming tomorrow night. I was able to get a call in to them before we left the theater."

"Good. But what about you, Maria?"

"I'm shocked, naturally. He would never have taken his own life, you know. Not Petya. Someone shot him. Most definitely. He was involved in so much. Sometimes, how shall I say, sleazy or even dangerous things. So I'm not altogether surprised. I never wanted to know the details. But the thing is, we were separated and were going through a divorce. I had decided to make my own future, without him. I came to that decision a while ago. So it's shocking, yes. But not so bad for me."

Lord Jaeger moved closer. "You are a brave woman. I admire that very much. Not many people could go through what you had to endure this evening, and recover so well."

"I know how to manage," Maria said. "I've had to suffer a lot in the past. In New York. Being with a famous person is never easy. Especially when they have an ego the size of Petya's."

"I can imagine. He was a wonderful musician though. One of the best. I know we shall miss him in the music world."

Maria shrugged. "He was what he was." She paused. "But how about you, Ben? What is going on in your life?"

"I have time to do the things I want to do. After Jocelyn died I threw myself into the company more and more, and it was good to be busy. Now I pursue my real interests."

"Ben, I envy you. I wish I could do that."

"But you can. Your children are off your hands, almost, aren't they?"

"They are, but I don't know what they will want to do now."

Ben put his arm round Maria's shoulder. She stroked his hand. She felt a throbbing desire, to be held tightly and caressed, but she told herself that she should avoid being impulsive, and not weaken in her state of shock.

Jaeger then took her face in his hands, and embraced her fully, on the mouth, breathing heavily. "You are a very desirable woman," he whispered. He then immediately backed off, saying, "I'm sorry, Maria, but I can't help it. You are irresistible."

She was moved by his passion, and she kissed him gently, on the cheek. "And you are a very desirable man, Ben."

He kissed her again, more passionately still. Now he stroked the back of her neck, and her shoulders.

"Let me take you to bed, my pretty one."

Maria could not resist.

She smiled. She removed her jewelry and placed it on the table next to the sofa. She finished her brandy, and shook off her shoes. She then removed some pins from her hair. She shook her head and her hair fell down, cascading around her shoulders. "Help me forget all of this, Ben."

Chapter 7

Quentin went upstairs to look in the bedroom. He checked to see if there was anything unusual of interest. Perhaps something to indicate where Alex had gone. He scanned the room for the CD but he could not see it.

He started to go through Alex's bureau, where he knew she kept some papers.

His eye was drawn to some bank statements. What astounded him was the balance on one particular statement. CHF 2,500,000. That's Swiss francs, he quickly thought. Must be over one million pounds.

He looked some more. The accounts were all in the name of Alexandra Matviyko, with a New York mailing address. He checked for any recent transactions. There was a deposit, dated just two weeks previously, for CHF 2,000,000.

*

He made a coffee, and sat on the sofa, pouring over the statements. Four of the accounts were held in New York, Geneva, London and Riyadh, respectively. There must be over three million pounds in all, he calculated. The deposits were all wire transfers, from the Anisimov Foundation in New York, spread over the past two months.

He went back upstairs, and looked into the bureau again. He found several papers that seemed to be legal documents, and took them back down to the living room. He made himself another coffee.

He found what seemed to be a copy of a will. There was a letter attached to it, from an attorney in New York. The letter was address to Gubin, dated this past April. He read the will, which he quickly realized was Gubin's. There were several attachments.

The will was long and intricate, and Quentin did not have any legal training. But he quickly gathered from the attachments that several insurance policies had been endorsed over to Alexandra.

The will benefitted Antonio and Chloe Gubin, with pecuniary legacies of two million dollars each. Then there were specific bequests, to Alexandra, Dominique Lieberman, Patricia Hanson, and three others, of five hundred thousand dollars each, and to Leo Connell, of two hundred and fifty thousand. There was a bequest of two properties to Maria Gubin, one in Paris and the other in New York City. There was also a million dollars to the Metropolitan Opera. Then a provision that the residuary estate be donated to the Anisimov Foundation, New York.

The letter was a copy, from a firm in New York, Frederick Ballard and Partners, Attorneys at Law. The letter was signed by Frederick Ballard himself. Quentin read that Ballard was confirming to Gubin that he would agree to act as executor, according to the terms of the will.

Quentin scanned some more documents. What caught his eye was an unheaded document, which was a schedule of payments to be made, including bank account numbers. The dates were spaced regularly over the following year, starting in July. Each of the payments was to be five hundred thousand dollars. There was a handwritten note at the foot of the document, which seemed to be in Russian. It was addressed to Alex, and was signed "Pet".

Quentin decided to put all the documents back in the bureau. He carefully replaced them, as he had found them. He then saw two folders of photos. There were several of Alex, with Gubin. In some of them they were smiling together and arm in arm. Quentin recognized some Manhattan scenes as he went through this first batch. He then turned to the second batch. Quentin saw that the photos had been taken in the kitchen and the living room in Alex's apartment, in London. There was a photo of Gubin, naked to the waist, lying on the bed. There was some handwriting on the photo, and some XXX's, It was signed, "Your Pet." The last photo in the batch was of Gubin and Leo Connell, arm in arm, taken in Alex's kitchen.

He replaced the photos in the bureau, keeping the shot of Gubin on Alex's bed, placing the photo in his wallet, in his pocket.

He then placed his dress suit and soiled shirt, with his bow tie and other accessories, in the bag he had brought from the opera house, and made a final check in the living room to see that he was leaving nothing behind. He made certain that he had his mobile phone in his pocket.

He then slipped out of the front door, bag in hand, walked to his car, and drove to his apartment in Wapping. It was now two thirty in the morning.

Chapter 8

Martin was sitting at his dining room table in his apartment on West End Avenue near the Lincoln Center, having a snack. He was eating a tuna melt, accompanied by a glass of white wine. His wife Emily was staying in Vermont with her sister for the early part of the summer.

The phone rang. "Martin, I apologize for disturbing you. Arnie Fischer here. I've just seen the news about Petya Gubin."

Arnold Fischer was President of Petya Gubin's Anisimov Foundation. He and Martin knew each other well.

"Hi there Arnie," said Martin. "That's OK. Yes, it's shocking. We don't have much in the way of details yet."

"Martin, was he murdered?"

"I have no idea, Arnie. That's pure speculation at this stage, I think."

Arnold continued. "Did you know that Petya had authorized several substantial grants to be made from the Foundation, over the last couple of months or so. They were all made over to Alexandra Matviyko. There's six million bucks, all told. I think we need to do some fast footwork here, if you know what I mean."

"Arnie, you are a good friend of mine," said Martin, "but really I don't want to get involved. The Foundation and the Met are not connected in any way."

"Well they are, Martin, because the link is Petya Gubin. Until recently he was having a lot of his fees deposited into the Foundation's bank account, including some from the Met."

"That may be so. But that was his affair."

"Martin, there's something important here. Let me get to the real point. Petya had a document drawn up by Fred Ballard. I witnessed it. It was a letter of understanding with Alexandra. If anything happened to him she was to pay the funds she received from the Foundation over to various bank accounts, in Riyadh and elsewhere. Immediately. My concern is that we have no guarantee she will do this."

"Were the grants made with the full knowledge of the Trustees, Arnie?"

"There are only five Trustees, apart from Petya. They are Fred, Fred's brother Sam, Maria Gubin, their son Antonio, and me. The grants were authorized by Petya."

"Did the other Trustees ratify the grants? Did you get everything written up, with formal Board resolutions?"

"Kinda."

"What do you mean? Did Maria know the details?"

"Not exactly. Well, I'm not sure. I sent her the Board resolutions but she never responded. And I never sent them to Antonio."

Martin asked, "What about the others?"

Arnold ignored the question. "But there's one other thing," he said.

"What's that?"

"Fred Ballard told me that Petya had recently changed his will. Alexandra is a major beneficiary, from the insurance policies as well. I'm really concerned about that girl. Especially with all the money she's holding."

"I'm not sure what you can do," said Martin. "But if I were you, I think I would get over to London as quickly as possible. And hire a lawyer there to help you."

There was a pause. Arnie then asked, "Do you trust her, Martin? Do you think Alexandra is on the level?"

"I wouldn't know," said Martin. "She was always OK as far as I was concerned, before she moved to London."

"Did you know she was seeing someone else? Some music critic guy?"

"Yes, I did know," said Martin.

"Is he kosher?"

"I have no idea, Arnie. I've never met him. You should check him out for yourself when you get over there."

"OK. Thanks, Martin. I'll keep you posted."

Chapter 9

FRIDAY

Detective Superintendent Tobias Roberts sat at his desk. It was eight in the morning.

He was puzzling over a fax he had received overnight, from the FBI in Washington. They had requested a conference call at one o'clock that day, to discuss the Gubin case.

He decided to ask his superior, the Deputy Commissioner, about it. He did not like any interference from anyone when he was on a case, especially from other law enforcement agencies. To him it was unwelcome and unhelpful. He did not know why the FBI should be involved. Gubin was an American citizen, of course, but that did not fully explain the FBI's immediate interest.

Toby Roberts was an unimposing man, at first sight. He was bald, short, and slim. He wore wire frame glasses, and combed his thinning hair forwards, greased down, to give the impression that he had more hair than he really did. He wore plain charcoal grey suits, always with white shirts, with detachable starched collars. His tie was from his alma mater, King's College, Cambridge.

He had risen rapidly in the ranks of the Criminal Investigation Department, the CID of the Metropolitan Police Force. He was known as an investigator with a razor sharp mind, a persistent and effective case solver. He was capable of being a bully, and he made no distinction between men and women in the way he handled them while pursuing his inquiries. He had never married, and remained a confirmed bachelor. He was cautious, sometimes to the extent of being pedantic.

He picked up his phone, and asked his Secretary to get him Deputy Commissioner Lanning.

The call came through immediately.

"Sir," said Roberts. "I have had a communication from the FBI in Washington, They want to discuss the Gubin case, later this morning. I am not sure that it's helpful, at this particular moment. What do you advise?"

"Really? I did not know they were interested," said Lanning. "There must be a good reason. I suggest you listen to what they have to say. Let me know, will you? I will want to keep the Commissioner informed. I have a telephone call into the American Ambassador right now, just as a courtesy. I believe you spoke to him last night, did you not? But I should ring him, for protocol reasons. Let me know as soon as you have a lead, Toby. What's the current status of the inquiry?"

"We have interviewed most of the back stage staff at Covent Garden who were on duty last night, Sir. Forensics is working on the crime scene. We do not have the murder weapon."

"Are you sure it's a homicide?"

"Yes, Sir. No question, because of the position of the body, no weapon, timing, and a lot of other reasons. But we have been careful not to say so publicly. We are having a press conference at nine, in half an hour. We will say nothing other than confirming the basic facts of Gubin's death."

"Any thoughts at this stage, Toby?"

"No, Sir. Gubin lived in the fast lane, that's for sure. There's a girl here in London he was involved with. A Ukrainian. She lived with him in New York, we believe. Gubin's wife is here too. Potentially tricky. I was able to get Lord Jaeger to take care of her, fortunately, as we had a developing situation with the Ukrainian girl right there in the opera house. Then there's the head of Gubin's agency, a man by the name of Connell. He seems to be anxious to help us in any way he can. He was trying to get information from us last night, about the investigation. Something not quite right there, Sir. I found him eavesdropping a couple of times, and had to ask him to leave. I have had the homes of the Ukrainian girl, her fiancé, and Connell under complete surveillance since last night. I am expecting the Ukrainian girl and her fiancé for further questioning at eleven this morning. We will continue with our inquiries as intensively as we can. I'll keep you informed."

"Thank you, Toby."

Roberts then walked over to the Scotland Yard Press Centre, where he coordinated the press conference. Geoffrey Wright joined him, but was not asked to participate. Roberts made a statement. He refused to answer any questions.

He returned to his office at ten fifteen. There was a voicemail message from Quentin Dart.

"Good morning, Superintendent. This is Quentin Dart. It is about nine thirty, and I am calling you on my way to my office. I very much regret that I will be unable to attend our scheduled meeting with you this morning. I have a number of pressing commitments, and will not be available. I am very sorry if this causes you any inconvenience. Please call me if you require my help at all in future."

Roberts was not pleased. He was not used to being treated this way, and he thought it was discourteous, not to say impertinent. He would go to see Mr. Dart later on, unannounced.

He then worked on his papers and prepared for Alexandra's visit.

*

Alexandra arrived at Scotland Yard at eleven fifteen. She was directed to an interview room, and asked to wait. Detective Superintendent Roberts entered fifteen minutes later, accompanied by two detectives.

"Good morning, Miss Matviyko. How are you this morning?"

"Well enough thank you. Mr. Dart will not be coming, Superintendent."

"Yes, I know. This is Detective Inspector Bartholomew and this is Detective Constable Trenton," he said, as the three men sat down opposite Alex.

Bartholomew and Trenton both got out their notepads. Roberts had his small black book in his hand already, and was now opening it.

"Miss Matviyko, may I call you Alexandra?"

"Yes, of course. Superintendent. Please do not involve Mr. Dart in all this. It has nothing to do with him."

"That is for us to find out, Alexandra. I will only keep you for twenty minutes. First, please tell me about your relationship with Mr. Gubin."

"We have been friends for a few years. We met in Kiev, and I went to work for him in New York, as his Personal Assistant. Then I moved to London and worked with the Connell agency. Petya Gubin is, or rather was, one of our clients."

"When did you move to London, Alexandra?"

"About two years ago."

"Was that your idea, or Mr. Gubin's?"

"Both really."

"What was the nature of your relationship with Mr. Gubin? Were you lovers?"

"I think that is private."

"It is not. At least not within the context of my inquiries. I repeat, were you lovers?"

"We shared an apartment."

"Let me put it another way, Alexandra. Was Mrs. Gubin happy about your relationship with her husband?"

"She and Petya had an agreement. They often went their own separate ways."

"Did Mr. Gubin support you financially, Alexandra?"

"He helped me out sometimes."

"I see. Where did you go immediately after you left the Royal Opera House last night?"

"I went home, with Mr. Dart."

"Where did you spend the night, Alexandra?"

"At home."

"What would you say if I told you that you were followed to Leo Connell's flat in Baker Street, and that you spent the night there?"

Alex had now gone deathly pale. What else did he know, she wondered.

"Oh yes, I forgot. I went over there to discuss some work things."

"At midnight, Miss Matviyko? Really?"

"Yes. He is my boss. I work unsocial hours."

"Alexandra, tell me what transpired in the dressing room before the performance yesterday."

"I met with Petya. I wished him good luck for the performance."

"What did he hand to you at that meeting?"

"Nothing."

"Did he give you anything at all?"

"I don't recall."

"Miss Matviyko, I must put you on notice that unless I receive your wholehearted cooperation I will have you arrested for impeding our inquiries. Not telling the truth. Be careful about what you say next, Alexandra. Very careful. Now, about the CD?"

Alex was shaken. She wondered how he knew.

"I'm sorry, I do remember, Superintendent. Yes, he did give me a CD."

"Why should he do that?"

"I don't know."

"Miss Matviyko, do you still have the CD?"

"Yes."

"Where is it?"

"At home, I think."

"Alexandra, you will be accompanied to your home, after this interview, by

Detective Inspector Bartholomew. Hand the CD over to him. You will cooperate. Do I make myself clear?"

"Yes." She thought about what how she would deal with that. Just play innocent when they got to the apartment, she supposed.

"One final thing, Alexandra. Who do you think murdered Mr. Gubin?"

Alex gasped. This was the first time she had heard Petya's death referred to as a murder.

"Was he murdered?"

"If he was, Alexandra, who do you think might have had the motive and opportunity to do it?"

"I really couldn't say."

"Are you aware of any problems he had experienced, during the time you worked for him as his Personal Assistant, or since?"

"No, I can't recall any."

"What about your fiancé, Mr. Dart?"

"That's absurd. As I said, he has nothing to do with all this."

"Then why did you insist that he accompanied you backstage last night, when you came round to the dressing room, at my request?"

"I was feeling very upset, Superintendent. I needed him to be with me."

"In that case why did you leave him at your flat last night, when you went to visit Mr. Connell? That's hardly consistent with your story, is it? My understanding is that you did not return home, at all."

Alex started to sob. "I decided late last night that we should ….that I should not involve him. Quentin, that is. It's nothing to do with him. My relationship with Petya is my business, and it's awkward, painful for Quentin having all this stuff dragged up."

"I see. What about Miss Lieberman, Alexandra. Where does she fit into the picture?"

"She is a friend."

"Really? Is that so?"

"Yes."

"Thank you, Alexandra. That is all for now. DI Bartholomew will now drive you to your flat and you will hand the CD to him."

Roberts indicated that Alex should now leave.

Chapter 10

Lord Jaeger wasn't there. No sign of him at all.

Maria looked at the clock. It was nearly lunchtime. Perhaps she would order room service. But where was he?

It had been a wonderful night. Full of passion. Ben had been a surprisingly attentive lover. But where was he now? She had woken at ten, and then soaked in a bath for at least an hour. She had then dressed and done her hair. Now she needed to get back to her hotel to change. What should she do?

She found the note. He had left it on the table by the entrance door to the suite.

"Good morning my treasure. You are a wonderful woman. Thank you for everything. I don't want to disturb you. You are sleeping so peacefully as I write this. I have to go to the office, and the police will want to meet again this afternoon. I will see you this evening, I hope. Please stay in the suite. It is yours to use as you wish. Why don't you check out of The Park Lane? Lovingly, Ben."

Ironic, she thought. A new man, on the same night that Petya had died.

Fate had dealt a strange hand. Petya was gone. How shocking, and yet she felt relieved. He had deserved a better end to his life, but on so many occasions he had flirted with disaster. What a waste of such a talent. She wondered whether she should give Fred Ballard, their attorney, a call. Maybe later. It was still very early in New York.

Her thoughts went to her children. Antonio would take it badly. She would have to spend some time with him. Chloe would cope better. When they arrived at Heathrow in the morning she would meet them. Around eight, she thought, but she would have to check the time again.

She decided to order lunch, and was about to call room service when the phone rang. Ben, she assumed.

"Good morning, Mrs. Gubin. This is Detective Constable Trenton, CID, Scotland Yard. Detective Superintendent Roberts would like to meet with you today, if that is convenient. Would you be able to see him, here at Scotland Yard, at five o'clock this afternoon?"

"Yes, I suppose I could," she said reluctantly. "Where should I go?"

"If it is more convenient, Superintendent Roberts could meet you at another location. At your hotel, perhaps, or at The Dorchester?"

"I would prefer to meet him here at The Dorchester. At five then. Good bye."

Ben must have told the police she was staying in his suite, she thought. She wondered whether it was wise to take Ben up on his invitation.

Chapter 11

Akbar Sattar was waiting for the call. He had parked the Mercedes and was reading the morning paper.

His mobile phone rang.

"Where are you?"

"Mayfair."

"Go to the address in Chelsea. You know what to do."

Chapter 12

It was now after twelve, noon. Leo Connell was in his office. He thought Alexandra would be finished at Scotland Yard by now. He would wait for her telephone call. Maybe she would come straight to the office.

The events of the night had changed things. He now had Alex to worry about as well as everything else. She had taken things badly, and Dart was now a real problem.

At least he had the CD. It was in the safe, in the apartment. It would be OK there, until it was needed on Saturday. After Saturday, things would get quieter.

He had lusted after Alex for the last two years. She had continued to hold a candle for Gubin. That was understandable. But she had also got involved with Dart, which had annoyed him intensely. It had been totally unexpected. Dart was no match for Alex. Beautiful Alex. Leo had never been convinced that Alex would marry that idiot. He was not sure why she had made the commitment at all. She would never go through with it, surely. Dart was such a wimp, he thought. Gubin still had a very strong hold over her, though. Well, up until now he had. Now, at last, he had his chance. Alex would now get more interested in him, maybe even sexually. He would convince her that she could not survive without him.

He remembered Petya telling him that he had met Alex in a nightclub, in Kiev. She was working as a prostitute, for God's sake. A hooker! Leopards never change their spots, Leo thought. Alex was basically capable of doing anything to suit herself, legal or not, and she was fundamentally promiscuous. She had no morals at all. He couldn't wait to make his next move with her.

Leo Connell's wife Dotty had left him years ago, when he had started the agency. She had run off with a Canadian concert pianist, when Leo had been sleeping with Rebecca. He loathed Dotty for the hurt she had caused him, and had looked for opportunities to avenge her. He owed everything to Rebecca. Rebecca Stein had worked with Leo for the Wigmore Agency, and she had suggested they started their own agency together. Rebecca had many good contacts and had put up most of the money. They successfully acquired most of the Wigmore artists. Then Rebecca had died. Poor Rebecca. Leo often anguished over this episode. She had loved him. And Rebecca had given him the opportunity to buy the agency, which had changed his life from that point on. After that he had channelled all his energies into the agency, and had worked hard to acquire the best conductors, instrumentalists and singers. He had surprised himself with his success.

He called Alex's home number. No reply.

He was getting agitated. She still hadn't phoned. Surely she had finished with the police by now. Maybe she was on her way.

Chapter 13

Roberts perused his notes on the meeting with Alexandra. She had not been cooperative. He would have to find a different approach. Connell was the key, perhaps. But he would get more facts together before interrogating Connell.

Roberts' Secretary called. "Mr. Mark Novelli on the line, Sir. FBI. Will you take the call?"

"Yes. Put him through."

"Good morning. Mark Novelli here. Assistant to the Director, FBI. Is it convenient, Superintendent?"

"Yes," said Roberts. "Who else am I speaking to? Your fax indicated this was to be a conference call."

"It will be just me, for the time being, Superintendent. May I ask you a few questions concerning your inquiries into the death of Petya Gubin?"

"What do want to know, Mr. Novelli?"

"The FBI believes that Mr. Gubin may have had some documents with him that were the possible reason for yesterday's events in the opera house."

"Please go on, Mr. Novelli."

"I'm saying that we, the FBI that is, are aware of certain documents that might possibly be a motive for the murder of Mr. Gubin. We are pursuing certain persons of interest in this case. It goes beyond the music world, Superintendent. Way beyond, if you understand me."

"Mr. Novelli, I really do not wish to discuss this on the phone. In any case we are at a very early stage in our inquiries here in London. I am not in a position to report on what the circumstances were, or might have been. Nor am I prepared to discuss any motive for homicide, if indeed it was a homicide."

"I understand. Quite right. But I have a specific question. Did you discover any of Mr. Gubin's documents in his dressing room, that might be relevant?"

Roberts was silent.

"Do you have any leads, may I ask?"

"As I say, Mr. Novelli, I am not prepared to speculate on the case at the present time. But I would ask you a question, in return. Please elaborate, if you are able to, on what you mean when you say you are pursuing certain persons of interest."

"We are concerned about connections Mr. Gubin may have had with individuals, or entities, overseas. More than that I am not prepared to say."

Roberts thought quickly. He decided to terminate the call.

"Thank you, Mr. Novelli. I will call you back if and when we have more information. Good day." He replaced the receiver.

Roberts then asked his secretary to ring the FBI office in Washington. "Ask if there is an Assistant Director there by the name of Mark Novelli, please."

She rang him back after a few minutes. "They have no Assistant Director in the FBI by the name of Mark Novelli. Not at the Washington DC office anyway, Sir."

"Get me the Deputy Commissioner, please. Straight away."

Lanning was on the line. "Toby, how are things going?"

"We have a situation with the FBI call, Sir. I am reluctant to say more at this stage, but I am certain the inquiry was not genuine. We appear to have someone in the United States who may be masquerading as an FBI agent, trying to get information."

"What do you mean?"

"We have checked and the person who called is not a bona fide FBI agent, at least not in their Washington headquarters. In addition, and possibly connected to this, there was a reference to other inquiries, involving what he called persons of interest. The caller wanted to know about certain documents he said Gubin had with him. That much is right, as we know. We are in fact trying to establish the link between a CD that we believe is now in Alexandra Matviyko's possession, and the possible motive for homicide."

"You're saying that this person who rang you knows that much. I see. First, trace the telephone number if you would, and second, we'll talk to the top brass at the FBI. I'll do that myself, once you have traced the phone call."

Roberts considered the situation. He was irritated by the call. And he did not want the FBI becoming involved in his case. On the other hand, the caller, whoever he was, had inadvertently given him a new perspective. It was all the more important to get hold of that CD, and investigate Gubin's background. It was becoming interesting, just the kind of case he loved to sink his teeth into.

Chapter 14

Quentin was thoroughly depressed. He might have lost Alex, he thought. She was in this thing so deeply that he didn't see how she could get back to any kind of normality in her life. Also, how could he ever trust her again? But then he thought of the power and magnetism of Petya Gubin, and he understood, to some extent.

He wondered how Alex's meeting with Roberts had gone. He hoped she was OK. He would call her later.

He had met with Jack Barker, his managing editor, earlier in the morning, to confirm the New York trip. He had decided to go through with it. He would leave on Thursday. Maybe the Gubin case would have settled down by then, and there would be some explanation he could accept for Alex's behaviour. He had not mentioned to Jack that Alex might go to New York with him.

He thought about Leo Connell. He wanted to tell him he knew what was going on. Give him a piece of his mind. Also make him see that Alex's personal loyalty was to him as her fiancé, first and foremost. They were engaged, after all.

The phone rang. It was Dominique.

"Hello Quentin. How are you today?"

"Not bad, thanks."

"Quentin, is it still OK if I come round to your office at about three, in an hour or so?"

"Yes, Dominique. I look forward to that. Bye bye."

Chapter 15

Detective Inspector Terry Bartholomew drove Alexandra to her apartment in Chelsea. The lunchtime traffic was very heavy, and it took nearly an hour.

During the journey they did not speak. Alex was going over her interview with Roberts, hoping that she had not upset him too much. She thought she had handled it quite well, in the circumstances. She had been feeling extremely nervous, yet she had managed to remain cool throughout the ordeal. She wondered when he would want to see her again,

She worried about Quentin. Was he still at the apartment? Would he be there when they arrived?

She thought hard about what she would say to Bartholomew when they got to the apartment. She would have to pretend to look for the CD. She would then tell him that it had been mislaid, although that might sound implausible.

Leo had to get rid of it as quickly as possible. It had to be handed over on Saturday. That was the deal. Except that Petya had told her he was having reservations. That had complicated things. She began to have doubts as to whether she should go through with it all.

Images of Petya lying on the sofa, blood all over his neck and shirt, kept haunting her. What had happened in that interval? Who had got into the dressing room?

Petya had seemed distracted before the show. Maybe it was because of the reservations he was having. Or possibly because he usually was distracted before a performance. His powers of focus and concentration as a conductor were legendary. Preparation time was when he shouldn't be disturbed. But he had been kind and thoughtful to her. They had kissed, and he had said they could meet on Sunday, at The Savoy. He had given her the CD. He said to keep it safe, and she would be told who to hand it over to, probably on Saturday.

What did he know? Had he realized he was in danger?

She suddenly remembered Roberts asking about the man called Bryce. Who was he? She worried that he might be the man to whom she was supposed to hand over the CD. Surely it couldn't be him. The contact guy would never have gone into the opera house. Far too risky.

She wondered what Maria was doing. Would the children come over? She was probably arranging that already. She hoped she didn't have to face her again.

Then she thought of Dominique. She had certainly charmed Quentin off his feet. No question. But she would be going back to New York. Would Quentin go to New York? If he did, would he get together with Dominique there?

She thought she would call Quentin later, after Bartholomew left the apartment.

Then she suddenly thought of Leo again. She had forgotten she was supposed to call him.

"We're here," said Bartholomew suddenly, as he switched off the ignition.

They went up the stoop, and Alex got out her keys to the building entrance. They climbed the stairs to the condo.

The first thing Alex noticed was that her front door was open. "That's strange," she said. Then she thought Quentin might still be in the apartment. She called out, "Quentin, are you there?"

She led the way into the entrance hall. It was immediately clear the place had been disturbed. She looked further, into the living room. It had been totally ransacked. Shelves were upturned, books and papers were on the floor, and even the sofa cushions were thrown down, by the TV and stereo cabinet. She went into the office. The computer was on the floor. Her disc box was open, empty. She looked for her floppy discs and CDs. They were scattered everywhere. Quentin's papers were also strewn all over the floor.

She pretended to search for the CD Petya had given to her.

Bartholomew said, "You have been broken into, Miss." He then started to make calls on his mobile phone. He was asking for assistance.

Alex went upstairs. The bedroom was a chaotic sight. The bureau had been turned over on its side. All the drawers were open, some on the bed, and others on the floor. The mattress was half off the bed and the bedclothes were on the floor. Files and papers, photos and many of Alex's personal items were everywhere, on the floor, on the bed.

"Is there anything missing?" Bartholomew had followed Alex upstairs and into the bedroom.

"I have no idea," she replied.

"Where do you keep jewelry, that kind of thing?"

"Under the bed, and in a locked cabinet in one of the other bedrooms," she said.

"Please check, would you?"

Alex went into the other bedroom. The cabinet had been broken open. Her jewelry case was there, open, and she checked the contents. "I think everything's there," she said.

She went back into her own bedroom. She looked under the bed. The various boxes she kept there were open, or disturbed, but nothing had been taken.

"It's all there."

"Miss, where is the CD I am supposed to take from you?"

"It was by the computer, on top of the disc box, in the office downstairs, I think," she quickly said.

"Would you please look for it, carefully."

Alex went through the motions, going into every room and deliberately studying each item that had been disturbed. She then spent some time looking in the office.

"It's not here," she said.

Bartholomew made another call on his phone.

Alex had returned to the bedroom. She was tidying and placing the drawers back into the bureau.

"Please do not touch anything. Our forensics people will be here shortly. We need to check for fingerprints. Leave everything as we found it."

Alex was stunned. She sat on the sofa in the living room. Who had done this? Had Leo, or someone else, decided to cover up for her and get her off the hook with the police? Or had someone really been looking for the CD? If so, who on earth could it be? She suddenly felt scared.

Her phone rang. "Hi, it's Quentin. I'm so sorry about yesterday, about last night. I feel dreadful. Can we meet, Alex? I really feel we should. I promise not to plague you with questions."

"Hi. That's OK. But it's not a good time to talk. The apartment has been broken into. It's a mess. The police are here now. Can we speak later? I'll call you. Are you in your office?"

"God, that's dreadful." After a pause, he added, "yes, I should be here in the office until about six. Perhaps we could meet for a drink somewhere. Ring me as soon as you can. So sorry about the break-in. Bye."

Alex rang Leo's office number. Bartholomew had gone upstairs.

Leo answered straight away.

"Hi, it's Alex. I've been delayed. I'm at the apartment. I can't speak now. Talk to you later."

Alex then tried to relax. Bartholomew returned from upstairs.

"We will have to remove some of the contents of your flat, Miss. Some papers, your computer, that kind of thing. Detective Superintendent Roberts is on his way. He will have a search warrant. It will be best if you give us total cooperation. He will be here shortly."

Chapter 16

Marcie Segarra got to her office at the Met at eight thirty in the morning. Her journey on the subway from the Bronx was usually an hour, door to door, and she had left at seven fifteen, to be sure to be there in time for the meeting Martin had with the FBI.

Martin arrived at eight forty-five. The walk from his apartment was barely ten minutes.

Marcie brought him a coffee. He was sitting at his desk, checking his emails, when Marcie buzzed and said, "Your nine o'clock is here."

Martin got up and welcomed Mark Novelli into his office. He invited him to take a seat on the sofa. Novelli sat down facing him.

"Thank you for seeing me at such short notice, Mr. Schaeffer."

Novelli was of medium build, with a sallow complexion, and receding black hair. Martin thought he was probably Middle Eastern. He was wearing a light tan suit, and brown leather shoes. He was expensively dressed. He had an attaché case, which he now opened.

"Not at all," said Martin. "Dreadful news, regarding Petya Gubin?"

"Yes, indeed." Novelli hesitated, and then said, "Mr. Schaeffer, can you tell me about Mr. Gubin's lifestyle, his financial circumstances, here in New York?"

"Before I do, Mr. Novelli, I wonder if you would be kind enough to show me some ID, some credentials. Just so that we have our cards on the table."

Novelli took a badge from his inside jacket pocket, and showed it to Martin.

Novelli was ten feet away, and Martin could not see the writing. "Do you have a business card, Mr. Novelli?"

"Yes, but I left them in my hotel. I'm sorry. I'm staying at Columbus Circle, nearby. I could drop it in later, if you like."

"Where exactly are you staying?"

"At the Trump Towers."

"OK. Well, I'm not sure that I can help you very much. Mr. Gubin's affairs in New York are looked after by his attorney."

"Who is his attorney?"

"Fred Ballard. I'll ask Marcie to give you his telephone number. He's here in the city."

"Did Mr. Gubin have an assistant? Would that be Alexandra Matviyko?"

"No she was his PA, but she's now in London with the Connell Agency."

"Doesn't she still work for Mr. Gubin?"

"Not, to the best of my knowledge. No."

"Mr. Schaeffer, are you aware that this might be a matter of national security? We are investigating some of Mr. Gubin's connections with organizations overseas, and we are following the money trails."

"I have no information on that. None at all. But if you want to ask me some specifics about Mr. Gubin's work here at The Met, I'll be happy to oblige."

"We believe Mr. Gubin had some information about some appropriations and other related security matters with him in the dressing room, in London, when he was shot. He would have taken that information with him to London, from here in New York. He would have had that data on a computer, probably in his office, here in this very building. Would you please ....."

Marcie then walked into the office. "Mr. Novelli, would you like some coffee?"

"No, thank you," he said.

Marcie moved to Martin's side of his desk and placed a piece of paper in front of him, folded in half. "You have this urgent message," she said.

Martin unfolded the note. Marcie had written, "Be very careful. Novelli is not who he says he is. I've just checked with Washington."

Novelli leaned forward. "You were saying, Mr. Schaeffer?"

Martin thought for a moment. He then said, "Mr. Novelli, would you be kind enough to hand me your badge. I would like to check it again, more closely."

Novelli then abruptly stood up, picked up his case, and said, "I'm late for my next appointment. I've just realized. I will get back to you." He walked out.

Martin thought quickly. He buzzed Marcie. "Come in, can you please?"

Marcie sat down on the sofa. She said, "He's an impostor, Martin. No doubt about it."

"Yes. Marcie, can you please get hold of security immediately. Tell them, from me, that I want Gubin's office sealed, double-locked, whatever, now. It's important that no one can get in. Then get me Fred Ballard on the phone. I have to speak to him urgently."

Marcie left the room. In only a few moments she buzzed him. "Martin, this is getting stranger by the minute. I have someone on the line who says he's from the FBI. He claims to be the Deputy Chief of Counter-Terrorism. He says he must speak to you."

Martin waited for Marcie to put him through.

"Mr. Schaeffer, my name is Franklin Stone. I am the Deputy Chief of Counter-Terrorism at the Bureau. In confidence, I must tell you we have received a report this morning that someone is masquerading as Assistant Director of the FBI, in an attempt to gather information relating to Petya Gubin, who was the subject of a suspected homicide at the Covent Garden opera house in London yesterday. We have been advised that this person, who uses the alias Mark Novelli, among others, has already attempted to get information from the police, at Scotland Yard. Mr. Schaeffer, if you are contacted by Novelli, please do not tell him anything, and immediately call my office to let me know."

Martin was taken aback by Stone's directness and the probability that this was a genuine call. He thought he should mention Novelli's visit. He said, "Novelli was here just now. He was asking for information, and when I requested he show me his ID, he left. Very quickly, in fact."

"Really. Well, you did the right thing. The FBI is in fact conducting inquiries into the death of Mr. Gubin. On that point, Novelli was correct. We will of course be tracking Novelli down, as quickly as we can. But in the course of those inquiries we are undertaking, we will be asking you for some information. I would be grateful for your cooperation. I will be flying up to New York this afternoon, and would like to meet with you later on, if I might. I will then be on a flight to London tonight."

"I understand. Yes, of course," said Martin. "May we call the FBI back in the meantime, just to verify your credentials? You'll understand how I'm feeling at the moment."

"Very much so. You should do that. Thank you. I will see you later. Would five this afternoon be convenient?"

"Yes. Come to the office at the opera house. Goodbye."

Martin buzzed Marcie. "Please check back with the FBI in Washington about Franklin Stone."

"I already did. He's the real thing. Martin, I have Fred holding on line two."

Martin was getting frustrated, upset as he was about Petya Gubin's death It was only nine thirty and this whole business was becoming more than a nuisance.

"Good morning, Fred. Sorry I had to keep you waiting."

"That's OK, Martin. What a terrible shock about Petya, isn't it?"

"You know already?"

"Yes, Maria called me just now, and told me everything. She is devastated, of course."

"You will presumably have to get his body back to the US, Fred. Isn't that the procedure? Was there a will? Were there any instructions regarding the burial, or cremation?"

"Yes, I'm the executor named in his will. By the way, you should know The Met is a beneficiary. I shall have to go to London. I'll get over there tomorrow night, and do what I have to do there. Do you have Alexandra Matviyko's current contact details? I do not want to ask Maria."

"No, that would be unwise. Marcie has her address and numbers, I think. I'll get her to email them to you. Failing that, contact Alex through the agency, you know, through Leo Connell."

"OK, thanks Martin."

"Fred, a word, very much entre nous. I was approached by a guy saying he was with the FBI, investigating Petya Gubin. It turned out he was a fake. But I suggested he should speak to you, before I realized he was an impostor. His name is Mark Novelli. At least, that was what he said it was."

"Thanks for the warning."

"One other thing. The FBI is involved. It actually is, and the Deputy Chief of Counter-Terrorism is coming in to see me this afternoon, before he goes on to London. What could they be interested in, do you think?"

"Sure beats me," said Fred. "Talk to you later. Thanks, Martin."

Chapter 17

Alex was in the kitchen, making a sandwich. She heard Roberts' voice outside. A shiver of anxiety took hold of her.

"Alexandra, we meet again, sooner than expected," said Roberts. He was accompanied by Detective Inspector Trenton, together with five other men she did not recognize. Four of the men carried large bags.

"Hello, Superintendent."

"Please wait while I take a look round, Alexandra. We have a search warrant, by the way, and we will be taking a number of items away for detailed examination."

Alex waited, seated on the sofa in the living room. She nibbled at the sandwich.

Roberts returned. "Well, you seem to have successfully lost the CD, don't you. Do you have any idea who could be responsible for all this?"

"No, I haven't a clue. I really haven't," said Alex.

"Very well. I will leave DC Trenton in charge. I will be in touch with you later." He left, taking one of the men with him.

Trenton, who had escorted Roberts and the other man to the door, exchanged words with Roberts in whispers, and then returned.

"I would make yourself comfortable, Miss. This is going to take a while."

Chapter 18

Quentin wondered when Alex would call him back.

He then looked up, and saw Dominique through the glass panel, standing outside his cubicle. She was waving, and smiling.

He got up and escorted her into his office, shutting the door, and he invited her to sit down.

"Dominique, I was shocked by the news you gave me on the phone last night. About the baby. Are you OK?"

"Yes, I'm very well. Thank you. What are you up to?" she asked, as she looked over his desk and around his office.

"Not much. But I've been making arrangements for a trip to New York. I'm covering the Lincoln Center Festival."

"Really, when you will be there? For how long?"

"I'm leaving next Thursday. Staying three weeks."

"Wonderful, Quentin! I'm leaving for New York myself, on Sunday. I am playing at the opening concert at Avery Fisher Hall, on Friday. And I will be there all July. Is Alex going with you?"

"Not as things stand at the moment," he said. "We'll see what transpires with the inquiry into the Petya Gubin thing. But I'll look forward to seeing your concert in New York in any event."

"You must come and stay with me. I insist. I have a nice little apartment on the Upper East Side, and it's very comfortable."

"Great. Thanks. But really, I don't think I could do that."

"Of course you can. If you come with Alex you can both have the spare room. If you come on your own, well, you can have the spare room all to yourself, if you want. Quentin, it will be my pleasure, really."

"Well, thanks again. I'll bear it in mind."

"How is Alex?"

"I don't know. She stayed at Leo's place last night, at least I think she did. We had a bit of an argument."

"Quentin, let me give some advice, as your friend. I know that you love Alex, and I would not want to hurt you in any way. But she's still deeply involved in Petya's affairs. She has been ever since she left New York. Everyone thought Petya had broken off with her when she came to London, but they were wrong."

Quentin noticed that Dominique was now quite tense, and that the knuckles on her hands had gone white. She continued, "Her life is, er, complicated, you know."

"Yes, I realize that. I understand."

Quentin looked up. He was stunned to see Detective Superintendent Roberts standing outside his office. "Oh my God, Roberts is here!"

Dominique stood up, concerned. "Who is that? What do you want me to do?"

"You had better leave. I'm so sorry, I really am. It's the police. Do you mind? I'll call you later."

Dominique and Detective Superintendent Roberts passed each other in the doorway, as Quentin beckoned Roberts into his office. Dominique disappeared into the outer office.

"Not interrupting anything, am I, Mr. Dart?"

"No, not at all."

"May I ask who that was?"

"Er …. That was Dominique Lieberman."

"Oh, really. I see. Well, I am sorry to burst in on you without warning, Mr. Dart, but I would like a word. I was sorry that you were unable to get to Scotland Yard this morning."

"Yes, I do apologize. I left you a message, Superintendent."

"Yes, yes. Now, Mr. Dart, what can you tell me about this nasty business?"

"Not much. I'm very confused."

"As well you might be. Please tell me whether you can think of any reason why anyone should break into Alexandra Matviyko's flat, and not take anything valuable away, except for a CD, possibly?"

Quentin blushed. "I couldn't say."

"Mr. Dart, you were at the flat last night, were you not?"

"Yes."

"And Miss Matviyko left around midnight?"

"Er, yes."

"Do you know where she went, by the way?"

"No, I don't."

"I see. While you were in the flat, did you see the CD that Miss Matviyko had with her, when the two of you left the opera house last night?"

Quentin was stunned by the question. How does he know all this, he wondered? What had Alex told him?

He quickly decided he would say everything he could about the disc, within reason. Alex had probably admitted having the CD, when she was questioned by Roberts earlier. "I did see the CD, yes. In fact I looked at it, just for a minute or so, before Alex left."

"What was on the disc?"

"It was difficult to understand any of it. There were several documents. The ones I saw were in Russian or Arabic, I think. And there were charts, plans, maps, that kind of thing. But I really couldn't make much sense of it."

"Mr. Dart, where is that CD now? Do you know?"

"No, I'm not sure."

"Did Alexandra take it with her, when she left the flat last night?"

"Yes, I believe she might have done."

"One other thing. Are you aware that the FBI is investigating this case?"

"Why would they want to do that?"

"Mr. Dart, we may be dealing with a highly sensitive security matter here. I should counsel you to be very careful indeed in how you conduct yourself in relation to this whole affair."

Roberts stood up. "I will now leave you to resume your work, Mr. Dart. I apologize again for the interruption. Thank you for your help. I will keep in touch, of course. Please let me know if you can think of anything else that might be of interest as we move forward with our inquiries. Good afternoon."

Quentin remained in his chair, shocked to the core. Then he wondered why he had volunteered to Roberts about Alex taking the CD to Leo Connell's apartment. Had he made things worse for Alex? And why were the FBI involved?

Chapter 19

Alex was waiting on the sofa. DC Trenton and their team were upstairs.

They had already taken an hour, and she was getting increasingly nervous.

There was a knock at the door. She opened it without thinking who it might be. It was Leo Connell.

"Leo, what are you doing here?"

"You didn't call back. I was worried."

Alex whispered in his ear, "Speak very very quietly. The police are upstairs. I had a break-in."

"You what?"

"The place was ransacked. Look! Everything turned upside down. I had the police with me when we discovered it." She lowered her voice even more. "They think the CD was taken from here. They don't know that you have it."

"OK. I should make myself scarce, before they come down."

DC Trenton was coming down the stairs. "Ah, I see you have company, Miss."

"Yes, he's just leaving."

Trenton moved nearer both of them. "Who are you, Sir?"

"I was just leaving," Leo said. "I came by to see how Alex was doing. Leo Connell. Nice to meet you," he said, holding out his hand.

Leo then left, as hastily as he had entered.

Alex was feeling more and more unsure of herself. Every move she made seemed to complicate things more with the police.

"I think we are through here, Miss. We will be taking three sacks of files and papers, your desktop computer, and a few other items," Trenton said. "We will document the items concerned and let you have a list as soon as it is prepared, and we have had it checked. Some time tomorrow, I would think. We'll be on our way, now. Thank you."

Alex looked around her. The mess in the apartment seemed even worse. What had they taken, she wondered? She had no way of being certain, because nothing was where it should be.

She went upstairs, and looked for the papers Petya and Fred Ballard had sent her. They were nowhere to be found. Had the intruder taken them?

Chapter 20

Fred Ballard sat in his Manhattan office, on the corner of 7th Avenue and Central Park South. It was a small firm. Just the two partners. His partner was on a golfing vacation in Florida all week, and their paralegal was off sick. He was the only person in the office.

The entrance door to the office, on the fourth floor, was equipped with a speakerphone.

He tried to absorb the news he had gathered from Martin Schaeffer. FBI investigation. Could be a complicated business, he thought.

He would have to get to Alexandra quickly, and to Leo Connell as well. He would try to leave JFK that evening. The London flights might be busy. Still, first class was usually available.

He wondered how the inquiries were going in London. Scotland Yard would not yet have any idea about the possible scope of the FBI investigation, and he would get there before they had come to any damaging conclusions, he was sure of it.

He turned to his computer and started to browse the airlines' web pages to find a suitable flight.

The office doorbell buzzed. He turned to the speakerphone on the wall immediately behind his desk. He lifted the receiver.

"Who is it?"

"Delivery. UPS."

"Just a moment."

Fred walked to the door, and looked through the peephole. All he could see was a man holding up a brown envelope. He could not see much more. He opened the door slightly, and peered round to see that it was the UPS man, just to be sure.

The door burst open, and Fred was forced back against the wall. He fell to the floor. There was now a large knife being held to his throat.

"Who is in the office, besides you?" the voice hissed. "Who?"

"My partner," stuttered Fred, lying. "He's there, in the back."

"Are you sure?" Go and get him, now!"

The man was now pointing a revolver at him and still holding the knife, now in his left hand. Fred noticed the revolver was fitted with a silencer.

Fred staggered to his feet. He went to go in the direction of his partner's office, and he heard the entrance door being slammed shut behind him. He felt an intense, sharp pain in his upper back.

Chapter 21

After sleeping on the news that Martin Schaeffer had given him the previous evening, Arnold Fischer had decided that he would definitely fly to London that night.

He would see Alexandra as quickly as he could, and meet with Maria as well. He would get the loose ends regarding the foundation funds tied up. That was the main thing.

He picked up the phone and called Martin.

"Martin, good morning. I appreciated having the opportunity to talk things over last night. You must be rushed off your feet right now."

"No problem, Arnie. Pleased to advise. Are you going to London?"

"Yes, I will try to get a flight out this evening. I called Fred Ballard just now, but couldn't get an answer. Do you know if he's in town?"

"Yes, I'm pretty certain he is. Have you tried his cell?"

"No, I'll do that. Any more news this morning?"

"Yes, Arnie, plenty. There is a new FBI investigation regarding Petya Gubin, and it's at a very high level indeed. I don't think it's linked to the business you had to deal with last year, but I couldn't be certain about that. There's also some guy going around impersonating a FBI Director. Really weird."

"Do you think I should put off my trip to London?"

"No. In fact I think you should get over there PDQ. I'm meeting the FBI, a very senior guy, this afternoon. I'll let you know if anything useful comes out of it, that I think you ought to know."

"Thanks, Martin, I owe you one."

Chapter 22

Akbar Sattar was lying on the bed in his small room in the Embassy Hotel, Bayswater. He was in his shirtsleeves. A gun, in its holster, two knives and a meat cleaver were on the bed beside him.

The phone rang. "Did you get it?"

"No. It wasn't there."

"It must have been. I was told she had it with her last night. Did you make a thorough search? Are you sure?"

"I turned the place over. It's not there. I'm sure."

"Where is she now?"

"She was still there, an hour ago. The police were all over the place. They've taken away papers, a computer, everything."

"You fool. Are you saying the police now have it? That would be a disaster. Especially for you."

"I am sure it wasn't there. Positive."

"We will need you to stand by tomorrow."

Chapter 23

Roberts was making his way over to The Dorchester hotel in a cab.

He was running late. He rang his secretary and asked her to re-arrange the meeting with Lord Jaeger for the following morning, Saturday, at eleven. At the opera house. He wanted to re-examine the murder scene.

He was happy with the progress he was making. DC Trenton had just reported that they had retrieved a lot of relevant papers from Matviyko's flat, or so he had said, and Roberts was looking forward to studying them later. Trenton had said he had run into Connell at Matviyko's flat. What was he doing there?

Dart had been helpful, and if he played his cards carefully, Roberts felt he could get a lot more relevant information out of Dart, particularly about Matviyko's involvement in the Gubin business.

The most important fact he had got from Dart so far was that Matviyko had apparently taken the CD with her over to Leo Connell's Baker Street flat. It was probably still there. He planned to call on Connell early the following morning. Surprise would be an important element.

He was pleased with himself for having Novelli checked out. It was not the first time he had correctly identified someone impersonating a law enforcement agent. He hoped the FBI would be able to track the man down. He had given the Deputy Commissioner the area code from which Novelli had made his call. New York City. Unfortunately they couldn't be more precise than that.

Apart from the Novelli call, he was very concerned that the FBI really was conducting an inquiry, as reported by the Deputy Commissioner. He tried to reason why it was the counter-terrorism branch that was dealing with it. He would have to ask. It would mean that the CIA would probably get involved as well, if it wasn't already. Controlling the inquiry would be a difficult challenge.

He thought about the circumstances that might have led to the shooting. It was strange that the man calling himself Bryce had not been seen exiting the theater. When had he left? Had Bryce concealed himself in the backstage area after seeing Gubin, before the performance, and then emerged in the second interval, and then shot him? What had transpired in the meantime? Had anyone been with Gubin in his dressing room in the first interval?

He thought about the call he had received from Trenton concerning the preliminary forensics report. The bullet had killed Gubin instantaneously. It had gone straight through his chest, and out through the nape of his neck, in one side and out of the other. There was no trace of the bullet at all, in the body, or anywhere else in the dressing room. Roberts had asked that they re-check the sofa, tear it apart if necessary, and re-examine every part of the room. There was no gun, of course. Blood had been found on the floor in several places, and there were fingerprints everywhere, but it would be difficult, if not impossible, to separate them. The dressing room was used by different sets of people every night of the week.

He got out of the taxi at The Dorchester. It was five thirty. He wondered how Maria Gubin was coping with the situation.

He was directed to the suite on the fifteenth floor, and he knocked on the door. Maria welcomed him, and invited him to take a seat on the sofa. She sat on a chair opposite him

"How are you, Mrs. Gubin?"

"I am doing quite well, in the circumstances, thank you."

"Mrs. Gubin, can you please tell me when you last saw your husband alive, apart from last night."

"It was in January, in Texas. We were with Antonio, my son, in Houston. Petya was doing "The Queen of Spades" there.

"Do I understand correctly that you and your husband were not on the best of terms?"

"Yes, that's right. We had decided to separate, on a formal basis. Antonio was in his final year at Texas A&M and I went down to see him after the New Year break. Then we both drove to Houston, and met Petya there. He and I then discussed the divorce. It was quite amicable, really."

"Did you meet your husband here in London, after you arrived?

"No. We spoke on the phone when I got here on Tuesday, but we did not meet."

"What was the position with the divorce?" Roberts asked.

"It was going through. Well, it won't now, of course. Our attorney in New York was dealing with it."

"Are you represented by different lawyers, Mrs. Gubin?"

"Yes, but Fred Ballard has been the family attorney for many years, and he has always handled Petya's business and legal affairs. I spoke to him earlier, in fact. He is flying over and will be here at the weekend."

"Are you familiar with what is in your husband's will, Mrs. Gubin?"

"No. I believe he changed it recently, and I was not involved."

"Mrs. Gubin, can I now ask you about the events of last night? I was at fault for inviting Miss Matviyko and Mr. Dart into the dressing room while you were still there, and for that I apologize."

"That's quite all right. Please go ahead."

"But it was an unnecessarily distressing thing for you, in the circumstances. I am sorry. Could you tell me, please, why your husband would have given Miss Matviyko a CD, when she went to see him before the performance?"

"No, I really have no idea."

"Was your husband computer literate, Mrs. Gubin? Did he use a computer?"

"Yes, he often did. At home and in his office."

"Mrs. Gubin, I am going to ask you to speculate on something. Just your own thoughts, if you would. We believe Miss Matviyko gave the very same CD to Leo Connell late last night. The CD apparently contained some important documents. Do you have any idea why she would do that?"

"No. Leo has been involved with Petya for many years, and he looked after his appearances in Europe. Alexandra works in Leo's office, of course, for the agency. But more than that I really couldn't say."

"Do you know what is on that CD?"

"No."

"Was Mr. Connell on friendly terms with your husband, do you know?"

"Yes, up to a point. But I believe Alexandra handled the details of the concert programs, and that she also did the scheduling. She left the paperwork to Leo, though."

"Do you know if Mr. Connell met with your husband this week, Mrs. Gubin?"

"I really don't know. Leo didn't mention it. I first saw him here when I arrived at Covent Garden last night. We were sitting together, but we didn't talk much."

"I see, thank you. Should I contact you here, if I need to ask you any more questions, Mrs. Gubin?"

"Yes, I suppose so."

"Are you staying here?"

"Yes, for the time being. Lord Jaeger has been very kind."

Roberts made his exit.

Maria then started to unpack her suitcases that she had arranged to be collected from The Park Lane hotel. They were on the floor by the sofa on which Roberts had been sitting. She had noticed that he made notes in a small book throughout the interview, and that he had looked at her cases quite closely.

The door opened and Lord Jaeger walked in. He moved towards her with his arms outstretched, smiling. He kissed her warmly, on the lips and on her brow.

"Maria, I have been distraught without you today. I have missed you so much. What kind of a day have you had? Are you well, my sweet?"

Maria was slightly overwhelmed, but very pleased to see him again. They sat down on the sofa, her hand cupped in his. "I'm fine. I hope this is all right, Ben, I have my things here now."

"Of course. That's what I wanted you to do. How delightful!"

"I spoke to Fred Ballard today, about the arrangements. He is coming over tomorrow and he will take care of everything. You know, he is our, my, attorney."

"Good. You shouldn't have anything to worry about, Maria."

"I have to go to Heathrow tomorrow morning, to meet my children. I will want to spend some time with them. I have arranged with The Park Lane hotel that the children will have my room."

"Let me know if there is anything I can do"

"Ben, I had a visit from the man from the CID just now. Roberts. He just left, actually."

"Really? What did he want?"

"He was very nice. He just asked me a few questions."

"What about?"

"Oh, about Petya. The divorce, you know. About last night."

"What did he ask you about last night?"

"It was strange, actually. He mentioned a CD, a disc that Petya had apparently given to Alexandra. He asked me why she should have handed it over to Leo?"

"Leo Connell?"

"Yes."

"I see. Well, let's not worry about all that now. I have plans for this evening, Maria. I want to take you to dinner, at The Ritz. We shall have a wonderful time. And then I shall escort you back here and make passionate love to you!"

"Sounds wonderful, Ben. Let me change."

Chapter 24

Marcie burst into Martin's office. "Fred Ballard is dead."

"What?"

"I've just heard it on the news. They found him in his office. Stabbed."

"That's terrible. Who could have done such a thing? "That's unbelievable."

"Martin, we were just speaking to him earlier this morning."

"I know. He was leaving for London today, or maybe it was tomorrow, I can't recall. We were talking about Petya Gubin's death and the arrangements he would have to make in London. I was telling him about the FBI."

"The FBI?"

"Yes, I warned him about that guy Novelli."

"Martin, I think you should tell the police. That's just too much of a coincidence for my liking."

Chapter 25

Arnold Fischer had also picked up the news about Fred Ballard, and he was very distressed.

Ballard was a good friend of his. They were both on the Boards of Trustees of a number of not-for-profit organizations, and Ballard was a key person on the Anisimov Board.

The news flash had said he had been stabbed.

Marcie Segarra then telephoned him. "Have you heard about Fred Ballard, Arnie?"

"Yes, I just saw it on TV," he said.

"Arnie, Martin will be talking to the police about it. It's connected to Petya Gubin's death, he thinks. In fact, he is certain of it. He asked me to call you, to tell you to leave the city now, to get over to London as soon as you possible can."

"I'm leaving tonight."

"Yes. But you should leave your office now. Immediately. Go somewhere, anywhere, until you have to be at JFK to check in. You could even make for the airport early. Martin says it's for your own safety."

Chapter 26

Quentin looked at his watch. It was six fifteen. Alex had not been in touch again. He tried her number, but got her voicemail. He did not leave a message, and rang off. He decided to drive over to her apartment.

He was feeling extremely anxious, as he pondered over the events of the last twenty-four hours. There was so much he hadn't known about Alex previously. But he felt a lot of warmth towards to her, and believed he had to make one last effort to get her to talk to him.

He thought about Dominique's visit to his office. He wondered whether her motive in flirting with him was to get back at Alex. Dominique was probably annoyed if or when she had found out that Petya had not broken off from Alex totally.

The Friday evening traffic was just as bad as it had been the night before, and it was an hour before he got to the apartment. He decided not to use his key, and he pressed the button on her speakerphone. Alex answered.

"Hi, it's Quentin."

"Come up," she said straight away.

She had left the apartment entrance door open.

Alex ran to him as he entered, and hugged him. "It's good to see you," she said, sobbing. "I'm so scared, Quentin."

Quentin was surprised that the apartment was in such disarray. "I'm sure it will all be OK," Quentin said reassuringly, as he took her by the hand into the kitchen. "Let's have some tea."

"This is such a mess. What can I do?"

"Just try to relax, my darling. It will be all right." He kissed her, saying "You know how much I love you."

"I know you do. Me too." After making a pot of tea, she said, "Quentin, the police took away so much. So many papers. Even my computer."

"They are investigating a possible murder. They have to do that. They have to be very thorough," he said.

"But they will think I had something to do with it. I know it. Roberts gives me the shivers. He's so suspicious."

"That's his job," Quentin said. They took their tea into the living room, and sat down together, on the sofa.

"Alex, I have to tell you, Roberts came to see me this afternoon. At the office. He was testing me, in a way. Against things you had obviously told him this morning."

"I didn't tell him anything, really I didn't," Alex protested. Then she said, "But I do think they've been tapping my phone, and I'm sure they are following me."

"Well, he's clever. And the tapping and other surveillance would explain a lot," said Quentin. "Anyway, one of the things he mentioned was about the CD. He knows that you gave it to Leo. You did, didn't you?"

"Oh Christ, Quentin! I told him it was at the apartment, and that I would give it to them. Then we got here and the break-in had happened. Now he knows I was lying. Oh my God! No wonder he's treating me so suspiciously."

"Why did you give it to Leo?"

"You had seen it and I didn't want you involved. I had to keep it safe, away from here, away from you. Also, I didn't know when I would be coming back to the apartment. The CD is now secure, in Leo's apartment."

"There's another thing. Alex, the FBI are involved now. Why are they, do you think?"

"They were looking at everything last year, including Petya's Foundation. They didn't find anything. I don't know." She looked away from him.

"I think there's much, much more that I don't know, that's what I think. But Alex, I want to help. I really do. You're going to have to level with me."

"I'm trying. I am, believe me!"

"Alex, as far as you and I are concerned, the issue is simple. Can I trust you?"

She tried to interrupt him. He gently raised the palms of his hands towards her. "No, let me say this. I want to be very serious now. You've obviously still got a thing for Petya. And you've been seeing him, even though you didn't tell me. I found enough stuff upstairs in your bureau after you had gone last night, to realize you're moving money around for him or something. But the main thing is, can you and I stay together, and move on from this?"

"Oh, Quentin, I hope so." She nestled her head against his stomach.

He felt a deep sense of desire. They caressed, and he said, "Let's go upstairs."

"No, it's a mess up there. Let's stay here."

They made love, there on the sofa, and he felt a huge sense of relief. Everything would work out. After all, she hadn't committed murder.

Chapter 27

Detective Superintendent Roberts was settling down at his desk. It was ten o'clock. It was dark outside.

Bartholomew and his team had done a good job with the material from Matviyko's flat. They had sorted it into batches, had put each batch into a box file. One box was labelled "Gubin will and associated financial papers". Another was "Matviyko and Gubin – photos, letters, etc."

Roberts started to look in the Gubin will box. Bartholomew interrupted him. "Dart is with Matviyko, Sir. He's been at her flat for three hours."

"That's all right, Terry. If I am a good judge, I think he will stay there for the night. I will not be finished here until late. I want you to come with me to Baker Street first thing in the morning. We should take Trenton with us, and a uniformed officer as well. The main objective will be to get the disc. Why don't you go home now, and get some sleep. I'll see you here at seven thirty in the morning."

"Very well, Sir."

"Oh, Terry, one other thing. I have a meeting with the Deputy Commissioner at noon. He has been talking to the FBI in Washington. There's an important development. If we don't have enough time, I may ask you to take over for me with His Lordship."

Roberts then returned to the will and financial papers box. He let out a tiny gasp. "Goodness me," he said to himself, "what do we have here?" He had in his hand a batch of statements from a number of banks. One in Riyadh, another in Geneva. One in Paris. Attached to letters were copies of bank mandates. Some were dated over a year ago. Others were more recent. It was the names of the co-signatories on the accounts that had his attention.

Chapter 28

Alex woke first. She heard the phone. It was just before eleven in the evening. She must have been sleeping for a couple of hours, she thought.

Quentin awoke. "Don't answer it," he said.

"I should. It might be something important."

She picked up the telephone. "Alex, it's Leo. Hi. I've just got in. Sorry I had to rush away earlier but I didn't want to get involved with the police. How did it go?"

"Oh, they took things away. The place is still a mess."

"Alex, come round, if you would. We have to talk. I can make things easier for you."

"But I really don't want to do that now, Leo, if you don't mind. I am very tired. Perhaps in the morning."

"Alex, it can't wait. Arnold Fischer will be here tomorrow. He's flying over tonight. We have to get things straight before then."

Alex thought for a moment. She didn't see that she had any alternative. "OK, I'll be there in less than an hour. Bye."

"What's going on?" asked Quentin, still drowsy.

"That was Leo. I'm going over there. I don't want to go, really I don't, but I have to. I'll only be a couple of hours. You go back to sleep, my darling."

"Must you?"

"I won't be long. I'll just get dressed."

Chapter 29

Martin had called the police. An Officer from the NYPD would be round shortly, he had been told.

He wondered whether poor Fred Ballard had indeed been killed by Novelli. Fred's ordeal must have been horrific. He hoped Arnie had got away, and was safe. He wondered what Novelli had been looking for.

Stone was late. Would he turn up at all? And just then, Marcie called to say he had arrived. She opened the door into Martin's office.

Franklin Stone was a large, slightly overweight man, with a military bearing. He had white hair, styled in a crew cut, and a full white beard, cut short. He was wearing a dark charcoal grey suit. He was carrying a large brown suitcase and a black leather computer case. He asked Marcie if she would look after the suitcase for him. She indicated that she would and that he should sit down on the sofa, opposite Martin. She left and closed the door behind her.

Stone shook Martin's hand. Martin winced a little with the strength of his handshake.

"Thank you for your time, Mr. Schaeffer."

Stone then took a laptop computer out of his case, and put it on his knees. He started to type as he spoke. Martin could not see what he was doing, or what Stone was looking at.

Stone then took a badge and visiting card out of his pocket and, stretching across to Martin, said, "This is who I am."

Martin noticed that his title was "Deputy Chief of Counter-Terrorism".

"You have an awesome responsibility, Mr. Stone," he said. "What can I do for you?"

"Mr. Schaeffer, what I am about to share with you is under a high level security blanket. That means you are not permitted to repeat any of what I say, to anyone. Is that understood?"

"Yes. Of course."

"Mr. Schaeffer, did you know that Gubin was funding terrorist cells in Chechnya, and the Middle East?"

Martin choked. Recovering, he managed to stutter, "No."

"Gubin had his reasons, no doubt. In the past, some funds were channelled through banks in Riyadh, Geneva, and elsewhere, from the Anisimov Foundation. We believe that a new, much larger, parcel of funds may be laundered through these same channels shortly. A very substantial amount of money. It is imperative that we lose no time in stopping it. We have been putting the pieces together, and are planning to make our move next month, before the state visit by the Russian President."

"You mean the state visit to the US?"

"Yes. The administration wants to be able to put on a good show for the Russian President, if you get my meaning."

Stone continued, "We tracked previous funding to over twenty cells. To fund terrorist activity, Mr. Schaeffer."

"Where? What cells are those?"

"Some we now know are linked to Al Qaeda."

"You cannot be serious."

"Our investigations have been going on for over two years now. But it was only recently we began to get the real evidence. Our friends in the CIA have been helping us to establish the links from these cells to regions where there are significant, escalating degrees of insurgency."

Martin weakly said, "Is there anything you want me to do, Mr. Stone?"

"Yes. I need to have access to all Gubin's personal papers. His computer, his documents, anything you have here at the opera house, in his office. I need to arrange that with you now."

"That will be perfectly OK," Martin said. "I have had Gubin's office secured already, in fact, and I can arrange for you to have access whenever you want."

"Good. We are also doing a search in his Manhattan home over the weekend."

"But on one thing I am not at all clear," said Martin. "Petya Gubin died yesterday. Doesn't that clear the problem up for you?"

"No. Not at all. It is possible he was murdered to insure that the planned flow of funds was not impeded in any way. Or he may have been killed by those attempting to break the chain down. We don't know. That's why we have to establish who killed him. We want to ascertain where his funds came from, every single cent, and where they went, or are intended to go. His income from conducting, concerts, operas, recording contracts, and royalties, must have been in excess of twenty million dollars a year alone. But there were additional funds from other activities. We want to make sure we have the whole picture. Our financial experts are working with the IRS on this."

"I'm astounded."

"But the really important, critical issue, that is very time sensitive, is that we believe the funds may be used to procure chemicals and equipment to build WMDs. Weapons of mass destruction, Mr. Schaeffer. There is a strong likelihood that these WMDs will be used against allied targets, including some belonging to the United States."

"I cannot take all this in, Mr. Stone. It's just too extraordinary."

"Indeed. So if you would now please open up the office, I will take a look, and then arrange for my people to come in over the weekend, if that is all right."

"Of course. I will show you to Gubin's suite myself. One other matter, if I may ask?" The visit I had from the man called Novelli. What was that about?"

"Novelli is not his real name, of course. He has several aliases. He is an Iranian, with a known record. He has been in the United States for over a year, we think. We have been on his trail, but recently we lost track of him."

"Well, I think he may have had something to do with the death of someone I know. Fred Ballard. Fred was stabbed in his office, this morning, soon after

Novelli came here to see me. And Ballard is, or I should say was, Gubin's attorney.

"You're ahead of me there, Mr. Schaeffer. I did not know that. Allow me to make a couple of calls if I may, before we go to Gubin's office."

"I called the NYPD myself, a while ago. They're coming in, to get a statement from me."

"My own people will want to talk to you, as well."

"I am concerned about Arnold Fischer, Mr. Stone. He would also have had documents of interest to Novelli, concerning Petya Gubin's affairs. He is the President of the Anisimov Foundation."

"We know Fischer."

"He is on his way to London. Flying out of JFK tonight, I believe."

"I will see if I can have my people intercept him at the airport."

"Mr. Stone, why would a guy like Novelli want to do this? Kill Fred Ballard."

"Destroy the paper trail? Maybe protect the network and those in the chain? We'll have to see."

Chapter 30

Alex sat in the cab on her way over to Baker Street.

She was pleased that she and Quentin were now together again. He had been so gentle, so loving. She hoped that the rest of the story about her past would not prove to be too much. But she was feeling more optimistic.

The taxi drew up outside Leo Connell's building.

There were four apartments in the building, one on each of four floors. Leo's apartment was on the ground floor. It had its own front door, to one side of the building entrance lobby.

Alex rang the doorbell. Leo came to the door. He was wearing a silk dressing gown.

"Great you could come. Let's go in. Make yourself comfortable."

"So what is happening, Leo?"

"This and that. But let's have a drink first. Martini?"

"OK, I guess so. Thank you."

Leo went to the bar and made the drinks. He returned holding two glasses. He offered her one. "Cheers!"

"Cheers," said Alex quietly.

"Let me put some music on," he said.

He returned, with Brahms now playing in the background. He sat next to Alexandra, on the small sofa. She edged away slightly.

"What's up, honey? You feeling off?"

"No. I thought you wanted to talk about the CD."

"How much have you told Quentin?"

"Quentin and I sort of made up," she said. "He is back at the apartment now, probably asleep."

"I see." Leo's eyes narrowed. "I think there should be a distance between you two. I told you that last night. Didn't you listen?"

"Yes, I know. But he's being really understanding. He's being great."

"Alex, my dear, I can do so much for you. Don't let that idiot get implicated. It will not help. And it could make things worse for you."

"I'm not sure about that."

Alex took sips from her martini. It was very sweet. She suddenly sensed a heavy drowsiness coming on. She was so tired, she would have to concentrate. Get this chat with Leo over with, and then get back to Quentin.

Leo was now fondling her neck, her breasts and her legs. "You are the most stunning girl I've ever known. I've wanted you so badly."

He then started tearing at her blouse, at her skirt, and pushing his hand up her thigh.

Alex was now feeling as though she was about to pass out. So tired.

Leo then pulled off her skirt. He tore down her tights. He then straddled her, pulling at her blouse again. He removed her bra and was kissing her breasts.

He took off his dressing gown, and she noticed in her delirium that he was naked.

"My Alex, my dearest Alex ………"

Chapter 31

Arnold Fischer was now at the British Airways ticket desk at JFK. He handed the clerk his passport and credit card. He placed his suitcase down on the floor, to one side of the desk.

"London, Heathrow. The nine-thirty flight, please. Arnold Fischer." He spelled out his last name.

The clerk scrutinized her computer. She then picked up a list and ran her finger down it.

"Ah yes, Mr. Fischer. Wait a moment, please. Just stand to one side, if you would."

Arnold waited ten minutes. What could be wrong, he thought.

Finally, two airport security men approached him. "Mr. Arnold Fischer?"

"Yes", said Arnold.

"Can we see some identification please? Your passport?"

Arnold went back to the clerk, and she returned his passport and credit card. He handed the passport to one of the two men.

"Thank you, Mr. Fischer. Where are you travelling to, this evening?"

"London, Heathrow. I'm on the nine-thirty."

"Please come with us."

"What's this all about?"

"Just a routine procedure, Mr. Fischer. It shouldn't take long. Bring your bags with you."

The two men escorted Arnold to an office up two flights of stairs. He noticed the sign on the door. "FBI".

One of the two men opened the door, and indicated for him to enter. He saw that the room was equipped with three desks. A large, dark-suited man got up from one of the desks.

"Ah, Mr. Fischer. I'm Franklin Stone. Nice to meet you again."

Chapter 32

Alexandra Matviyko's naked body was lying prone on the small sofa. Her ankles were raised up over the armrest at one end. She was still. There was a trickle of dried blood on her neck.

Leo was now in the bedroom. He removed a framed print from the wall. There, revealed, was a large safe, with a dial on the front. He dialled five times, clockwise, and then counter-clockwise, and so forth. He opened the safe door. He took out a CD and a number of documents, and then placed them in a briefcase. He put the briefcase back in the safe, and dialled several times, clockwise. He replaced the print on the wall.

He returned to the living room, and carefully collected Alex's clothes together. He laid them neatly beside her. She stirred a little. He looked at her body. She was so ugly, he thought. So different. He noticed the blood, and then he saw his sperm on her upper thigh. He took a wet cloth from the bathroom and carefully wiped it over her face and body.

He went to a closet in the bedroom and took out a bed cover. He unfolded it and placed it over Alex's body.

He picked up the phone, and dialled. It was several seconds before Quentin answered.

With nothing much more than a grunt, Quentin struggled to say, "Hello".

"Hi Quentin. Sorry if I disturbed you. I just wanted you to know that Alex has gone to bed here. She was exhausted. I don't think I should disturb her for a while. Let her sleep on for a bit, don't you agree? She should be OK by the morning. Good night."

He then checked the living room. He noticed the glasses that he and Alexandra had been drinking out of earlier. He washed them, and put them in the kitchen closet.

He then went into the bedroom, and lay down on the bed. He looked forward to the morning's events.

Chapter 33

Franklin Stone was questioning Arnold Fischer. "I want you to know that we will require access to all your records straight away, Mr. Fischer. We intend to work over the weekend."

"But I have to be in London tomorrow."

"I regret that you will not be flying to London tonight, Mr. Fischer. In fact, you will not be flying anywhere. You will be accompanied back to your home by an FBI agent, and tomorrow morning you will allow two of them full access to your office, and to your records."

"But I have to attend to matters following Mr. Gubin's death. This is urgent. I am expected in London tomorrow."

"Who is expecting you, Mr. Fischer?"

"A number of people. I cannot leave this any longer."

"I see. Well, you will be able to contact these people in the morning, and advise them, whoever they are, of the delay."

Chapter 34

"Marcie, I'm not allowed to say anything, to anyone, about what the FBI is doing. But I want you to know that as soon as I can, I will give you the whole story."

"I understand, Martin."

"It's huge. You cannot imagine what Petya was involved in. Terrifying."

"Martin, Stone said he was going to London tonight. Arnie is also on his way. Don't you think we should warn Maria Gubin? She must be going through a nightmare over there. And I expect she has the children to take care of as well. She has more than enough on her plate. Shouldn't we contact her?"

"We should, Marcie."

"You can speak to her as a friend. Just say that Arnie is flying over, and that he may want to see her. In any case you really should give her our condolences, from The Met. You haven't spoken to her since her husband died."

"You're right. See if you can find out where she's staying, if it's not too late over there by now."

*

Maria and Lord Jaeger had returned to his suite in the Dorchester.

The evening at the Ritz had been special. They drank champagne, followed by wine with dinner.

They slept, content in each other's arms.

*

Marcie called The Park Lane hotel, and was told that Mrs. Gubin had checked out. She was now at The Dorchester, they said. Marcie called The Dorchester. "Mrs. Maria Gubin, please. She is a guest at your hotel."

The receptionist was unable to trace the name. "I am sorry but we don't have any record of that person staying at the Dorchester."

"Are you certain?"

"Yes, I'm sorry."

Marcie went back into Martin's office. "Martin, I don't know where she is. She checked out of her hotel. They say she is at The Dorchester, but The Dorchester has no record of her."

Chapter 35

SATURDAY

Roberts was at his desk when DI Bartholomew interrupted him. It was seven fifteen.

"You're early, Sir."

"I have been here all night. I've been going through the documents we obtained at Matviyko's place. This is a major case, Terry. The stakes are very high indeed."

"Shall we be off then, Sir? DC Trenton and Police Constable Freeman are waiting downstairs."

"Yes. I need a few more minutes."

The traffic was light. It was only fifteen minutes later when the car stopped in Baker Street, near Leo Connell's apartment.

"This may be messy, Gentlemen. Connell may resist. Terry, do you have the search warrant?"

There was a pause. Bartholomew said, "No, Sir. We don't have it. You didn't mention that you wanted one."

Roberts exploded. "I cannot believe you have been so incompetent, Inspector. You surely would have anticipated that we would need it."

"Very sorry, Sir. Shall we delay?"

"No", said Roberts. "We will go ahead. But call in now and get it sorted. I shall speak to you later about this."

Bartholomew made the telephone call.

The four men entered the building lobby. Bartholomew, Trenton and Freeman then stood back while Roberts knocked on the door. There was no response. Roberts then knocked loudly. The sound reverberated around the lobby. Bartholomew then spoke. "Police! Mr. Connell, open the door!"

The door opened. Leo was in his silk dressing gown, under which he was wearing pyjamas. His face was ashen. Although only half awake, he understood that he was about to have to think on his feet, quickly.

"Come in, Gentlemen. I'm sorry, but you woke me up."

Roberts spoke. "This is DI Bartholomew, DC Trenton, and this is PC Freeman."

As they entered the living room, Leo was surprised to see that Alexandra was not on the sofa, and that there was no trace of her clothes or the bed cover.

"Yes. In fact Mr. Trenton and I met yesterday, briefly. What can I do to help you?"

"Why don't you dress, Mr. Connell. We will wait," said Roberts.

Leo went into the bedroom. He closed the door behind him. Alex was crouching on the floor behind the bed, by the French doors. She had dressed.

"The police are here. They want to talk. Leave now, through there," Leo whispered, pointing to the French doors. "That leads out to a yard, and round to the side street. I'll change and get rid of them as soon as I can."

Alexandra opened the doors. As she did, she managed to stutter, "They know you have the CD."

Leo was dumbstruck. He closed the doors, dressed, and returned to the four policemen.

"Mr. Connell," said Roberts, "I would like to ask you some questions about a CD that I believe Miss Matviyko handed over to you last night. Do you have it here?"

"I'm not sure I know what you mean."

"I am not a patient man," said Roberts. "We will shortly have a search warrant and we will find it."

Leo said, "Alex and I are always giving each other documents and so on. She works for me. She has often given me CDs."

Roberts said, "Mr. Connell, we are going to take you in for questioning. We believe you have had, or currently have, information that is pertinent to the investigation we are undertaking in connection with the death of Petya Gubin. You will now be taken to Scotland Yard, and we will carry out a search of your apartment here. Is that clear?"

"Yes, I suppose so," said Leo.

"We will find the CD, if it is here," said Bartholomew.

Chapter 36

Roberts told Bartholomew, Trenton and Freemen that he wanted them to drive back to Scotland Yard, taking Leo Connell with them. They were to hold Connell for questioning while he would meet with Lord Jaeger at Covent Garden. They should take care of the search warrant. He would go to his meeting with the Deputy Commissioner at Scotland Yard after meeting with Jaeger, and after that he would conduct the search at the Connell apartment. He would then tackle Connell himself. Roberts prided himself on his flexibility.

He looked around the apartment. He wondered whether Connell might have removed the CD and put it somewhere else, safe. Maybe he had got rid of it already?

He made his way out, and decided to walk over to Covent Garden. He needed to think, particularly about the contents of the documents that had been retrieved from Matviyko's apartment.

He had walked as far as Holborn, when his mobile phone rang. It was Bartholomew. "Something you ought to know, Sir. I have just received a report that Matviyko left her flat shortly after eleven last night. No report of where she went, except that she took a telephone call from Connell beforehand. Our man in Chelsea saw her return to her flat this morning, at eight thirty-five. I thought you ought to know."

"Why wasn't I told this before?"

"They do not always report everything straight away, Sir. I only heard this when I got back to the Yard just now."

"This isn't good enough. I want to know about every move, as soon as it happens. Check again to ascertain if and when Matviyko arrived at Connell's flat, and if she was there, when she left. Also double check with Oakley Street, to see whether Dart left at any time. Get back to me as soon as you can. I am not a happy man, Terry."

Chapter 37

Alex arrived back at her apartment and let herself in. She was relieved to find that Quentin was still asleep on the sofa in the living room.

She made some coffee, and decided to run a bath.

She went into the bathroom with her coffee, and undressed. She noticed some bruising on her thighs she had not seen before. And looking in the mirror, she saw that there were some scratch marks on her neck. Puzzled, she sat on the edge of the bath, going over the events of the night before. Quentin was a considerate lover, very gentle, and she could not remember him being rough with her. Her thoughts then went to Leo. She could not clearly recall what had had happened at Leo's apartment. She had become very tired. She then suddenly remembered the martini. My God! Had he laced the drink? What had he done to her? The scenario gradually became clear. She started to cry. Loud, agonized cries.

"Are you OK in there?" Quentin's voice interrupted her.

"Yes. I'm fine. Just having a bath. Be out in ten minutes or so."

Alex lowered herself gently into the still hot bath. She wondered whether Leo had actually penetrated her. She felt instinctively that he had.

*

Quentin made breakfast. Cereal, orange juice and toast.

Alex entered the kitchen, wearing a bathrobe.

Quentin stood up and embraced her. "How are you this morning, my darling?" he asked.

"I'm fine," she lied, sitting at the table.

"It was good, last night, wasn't it?" he said.

"Yes. Wonderful."

"What time did you get back from Leo's?"

"Oh, I don't know. Not too late."

"That's good. Actually I remember Leo calling at some stage. He said you were sleeping. Come to think of it, he said he would let you sleep on."

"Really?"

"Did you go upstairs to bed when you came in? I was still on the sofa when I woke. I must have been exhausted."

"Yes."

"So what are your plans for today, my darling?"

Alex slumped forward on to the table, her head in her hands, crying uncontrollably.

Quentin took her in his arms, consoling her.

She remembered that they were supposed to hand over the CD today. Presumably, Leo would take care of it, if the police hadn't found it. She decided to put it out of her mind. She recovered her composure.

"Quentin, please don't leave me today."

Quentin continued to caress her. "I will have to desert you later, darling. I'm so sorry. I forgot to tell you last night. Covent Garden announced yesterday afternoon that they are going ahead with the performance of "Onegin" tonight. I shall have to go. They've managed to get Guido Farinelli to take over. He's rehearsing the company this morning."

"Must you? Can't someone else cover it for the paper?"

"No, not at such short notice. I have to go. I promised Jack I would. They want the review in the paper on Monday, because they're doing a follow-up news item on Petya Gubin at the same time. You needn't come with me, though. In fact I don't suppose you would want to."

"No, I don't. OK, I'll stay at home. Let's have dinner before you leave, around six, and I'll do some more cleaning up while you're out."

"You sure you'll be OK?"

"Sure."

"There's another thing I should mention. I'm booked on a flight to New York next Thursday. For the Lincoln Center Festival. Have you thought any more about coming with me?"

"Not really. But it sounds like a nice idea now. Let's talk about it tomorrow."

Chapter 38

Maria was waiting at international arrivals at Heathrow. Lord Jaeger's chauffeur had dropped her off at Terminal Four, and he would keep circling, waiting for her to return, with her two children.

It was a busy morning at Heathrow. Antonio and Chloe's flight was late, but it had landed and their bags were now in the baggage hall. Antonio had traveled up to New York from Texas the previous morning, and then they got the BA overnight flight together out of JFK, at nine-thirty.

They had business class seats and had been reasonably comfortable, but had not slept much during the flight. They had talked about their father's death, and how they felt about the news from London.

Antonio Gubin was twenty-two years old. He was a masculine, tall, slim man, with his father's good looks. He wore his hair long, in a ponytail. It was jet black. He had some of his mother's Italian style and elegance.

Chloe had just turned eighteen. She was shorter than her mother, but was otherwise like her in so many ways. When Maria had been a little younger, three or four years previously, they had sometimes been mistaken for sisters. Her hair was also dark, but styled short, in a bob. She tended to wear loose fitting casual clothes which did not do full justice to her trim figure.

Antonio had been close to his father when he was younger, but they had since grown apart. Petya Gubin's lifestyle was hectic, and had kept him from seeing much of his son for eight or nine years. Antonio did not share his father's knowledge or tastes in music, which had been an obstacle in sustaining a close relationship.

Chloe felt she did not know her father at all. She had not seen much of him since she was ten. From that time onwards she had been training as a ballet dancer. She hoped to audition for the American Ballet Theater in the fall. Maria had always encouraged her with her dancing, and was quietly ambitious on her behalf.

Antonio felt anguished by his father's death, mainly because he regretted that they had not been closer. He was proud of his father's achievements on the international music scene. But he much preferred to spend his own time in the pursuit of young women, and enjoying popular music and sports.

Chloe had not outwardly reacted to the news of her father's death. She was even a little frustrated that they would now have to spend some time in London. She wanted to get back to New York and her ballet classes.

She and Antonio had talked during the flight of their family vacations with their parents on Long Island, and their visits with them to Moscow, Munich. Milan, Vienna, Paris and London, when they were much younger. They both felt a little nostalgic as they talked about their childhood together.

Antonio said that he hoped his mother would not be too affected by their father's death. Chloe replied that she felt certain that they had been planning to get divorced. Everyone knew that they had in fact been living apart for some time.

The two of them were a handsome young couple, as they walked through customs with their luggage. Chloe spotted Maria beyond the barrier as they emerged from the customs area. She abandoned Antonio and ran to her mother. When Antonio joined them, the three of them stayed in a long embrace.

"How are you bearing up, Mom?" asked Antonio.

" Well, thank you," she said, stroking his cheek.

"Mummy, you look wonderful," said Chloe. "I expected you to be an a terrible state. You're positively glowing!"

"I'm fine, my dear. We have a limo taking us into town. A very good friend of mine, Lord Jaeger, has kindly allowed us the use of his car and chauffer, and the driver should be outside."

"Who is Lord Jaeger, for heaven's sake?" asked Antonio.

"He's the Chairman of the Royal Opera House. We have become quite close. In fact I am staying in his Dorchester hotel suite. You are both booked into The Park Lane hotel, in the suite I had reserved for myself. We'll go there now."

"You're something," Chloe said. "I can't leave you alone a minute and you're up to no good."

Maria smiled. "It's all quite innocent, I assure you. Ben, Lord Jaeger that is, was very kind to me on Thursday night when this dreadful business happened."

Maria then led Antonio and Chloe out to the pick-up area, just as Lord Jaeger's chauffeur drew up in the Rolls Royce.

*

Franklin Stone emerged from the arrivals area a little after the Gubin family had left the airport. He was greeted by FBI agents, and taken to a meeting room, where they discussed the latest news from DC, and Stone's proposed itinerary in London.

Stone was advised that he had a noon meeting with Deputy Commissioner Lanning, at Scotland Yard. He said that he would like to go to his hotel first.

"Where have you booked me?" he asked.

"At the Connaught, Sir. It's very comfortable."

Chapter 39

Akbar Sattar called the number he had been given. A different number. He had parked just off Baker Street. He was supposed to wait for news, but he was getting agitated.

He said, "Connell has been detained by the police. I saw him being escorted out of the apartment earlier."

"Go in there now. If the CD is there, get it. Make certain you are not seen."

"What about the girl?" asked Sattar.

"Don't concern yourself with her. Not yet. If the CD is not in Connell's place, you will be given new instructions."

Chapter 40

Roberts arrived at the stage door of the Royal Opera House. He introduced himself to the doorkeeper, and said he would like to meet Lord Jaeger in the conductor's dressing room. He had an appointment with him, at eleven.

It was now ten twenty-five. He was asked to wait.

After fifteen minutes, Lord Jaeger emerged from the backstage area. He greeted Roberts warmly.

Roberts said, "Shall we go to the conductor's room, Your Lordship?"

"Oh, please, call me Ben. No need for all that."

Jaeger then escorted Roberts to the dressing room. It had been cordoned off, with tape across the door. Jaeger removed the tape, and unlocked and opened the door.

As they entered, it seemed to Roberts that it was exactly as they had left it on Thursday night, except of course that Gubin's body had been removed. There was now a large sheet over the sofa where he his body had been lying. The bouquets and greeting cards were still in the room.

"Superintendent Roberts, I'm afraid we're very busy here this morning. I shall only have a few moments. We are rehearsing "Eugene Onegin" for tonight, with a new conductor. There was a full cast call for ten o'clock this morning."

Roberts could hear the rehearsal through the speaker, on the wall. "I'm surprised you're doing it at all," he said.

"Well yes, it was a difficult decision. But we have a responsibility to our patrons, and we felt we should go through with the second scheduled performance. Please sit down."

"I see. Actually, Lord Jaeger, I would like to take another look at the scene here. If you would like to leave me to it, alone, I shall be quite happy."

"That's perfectly all right. I do have a little time."

"In that case, permit me to ask you a few questions. Did you meet with Petya Gubin before the performance on Thursday?"

"Yes, I did. I called in to wish him good luck just before curtain, around seven forty-five."

"Did you notice anything significant? Anything out of the ordinary?"

"Nothing at all. Gubin was getting ready for the performance, so I did not stay long."

"Did you see any other visitors?"

"No, I didn't."

"Did you see the man who called on Gubin before the performance? He had announced himself to the stage door keeper as Bryce."

"No, not at all."

Roberts now became more persistent. "The stage door keeper did not see Bryce leave the theater on Thursday evening. Is there anywhere in the vicinity of the conductor's dressing room where Bryce could have concealed himself, once the performance had started? He was described as a very large man, wearing evening dress. He would have stood out, surely?"

"Not necessarily. The stage area was very busy. We have a large company for "Onegin." And the male chorus wears modern evening dress for two of the scenes in the opera. He might not have been noticed, assuming he was here at all."

"Were you aware that Alexandra Matviyko had visited Gubin? It must have been just before your saw him yourself."

"No, not until it emerged later, when we were all in here together."

"How do you feel, Lord Jaeger, as the Chairman of Covent Garden, given that a likely murder was committed in the opera house? Before your very eyes, so to speak?"

"Upset, of course, especially if it was a murder. Was it, do you think?"

Roberts looked directly into Jaeger's eyes. "Did you have any reason to suspect that Gubin's life was in danger, Lord Jaeger?"

Jaeger hesitated. "No, none. Why? Should I have?"

Roberts ignored the question. "What is the nature of your relationship with Mrs. Gubin?"

"I resent that question, Superintendent. That's my own business. And Mrs. Gubin's business."

"Wouldn't a casual observer think it odd, almost inappropriate perhaps, that the wife of someone who dies in very suspicious circumstances should later that same evening go to the hotel room of another man?"

Jaeger stood up. "That's outrageous. As you well know, I offered to help Maria Gubin when she became upset on Thursday night, after the scene with Alexandra Matviyko. It was quite natural that I should give her moral support by escorting her to her hotel. In fact, because she was so distraught, I offered her the use of a bedroom in my Dorchester suite. An offer that she gladly accepted, but only as a temporary measure."

"Lord Jaeger, please sit down. How long have you known Petya Gubin?"

He sat. "Difficult to say, offhand. Several years."

"And Mrs. Gubin?"

"I think we first met when Gubin conducted "War and Peace" here. That was about five years ago."

"How would you characterize your relationship with them both?"

"We were on good terms."

"I see. Thank you. Now I would like to study the scene here, alone, if I may."

"Please go ahead." Lord Jaeger remained in his seat.

"You may leave, Lord Jaeger."

Jaeger quickly left the room.

Roberts first took a close look at all the walls. Then he looked under the sofa, and then under the sofa cushions.

His eye was then drawn to the hinged, fabric-covered, screen standing against the wall behind the sofa. There were clothes on two hangers, hooked on to the top of the screen. He removed them. He immediately saw what seemed to be a small hole in the screen. There was something inside, reflecting the light from the lamps in the room. He then examined the clothes he had removed. There was a dogtooth check-patterned jacket, and a bathrobe. Roberts noticed a small tear in the sleeve of the jacket, almost invisible to the naked eye. He then moved the screen out from behind the sofa, and turned it round. There, just protruding through the rear of the screen, was the tip of a bullet.

He picked up his phone, and called Bartholomew. "I am in the conductor's dressing room at the opera house. I have found the bullet, Terry. It was in the screen behind the sofa, concealed by a jacket. Send forensics back straight away. I don't understand why they missed it the first time. I must get back to the Yard quickly, or I will be late for the Deputy Commissioner. I am leaving everything as it is. Oh, and get a detailed description of the man called Bryce from the stage door keeper, will you?"

Roberts then replaced the clothes on the hangers, the hangers on the screen, and the screen behind the sofa. He inspected the scene, then left, locking the room behind him. He replaced the tape, and went to the stage door.

He spoke to the stage door keeper, on his way out of the theater. "Here is the conductor's dressing room door key. Please do not give it to anyone."

Chapter 41

It was six thirty in the morning in New York City.

Novelli entered the lobby of the building on the Avenue of the Americas and West 51st Street. The night porter was at his desk, watching television.

Novelli approached. "I have been asked by Arnold Fischer to get some things from his office. I am doing some work for him, for the Anisimov Foundation that is, over the weekend. I have a key."

"Yes, Sir, I believe Mr. Fischer is in London. You'll find the office on the third floor. Please sign the book, if you would, Sir."

Novelli signed the visitor's book, and took the elevator to the third floor.

He exited the elevator and quickly found the Anisimov office. There was no one around.

He took a crowbar out of his bag and forced open the door.

He entered the office and began to go through filing cabinets, desk drawers and boxes of documents on shelves. He worked for an hour. He selected a number of documents, placed them in his bag, and returned downstairs the way he had entered.

Chapter 42

Roberts arrived for his appointment with the Deputy Commissioner just over fifteen minutes late. He was annoyed with himself for not being on time.

Lanning's Secretary showed him into the large, well furnished office.

Deputy Commissioner John Lanning and one other man were talking to each other in one corner of the office, sitting on opposite sides of a conference room table.

Lanning stood up. "Detective Superintendent Roberts, I'm glad you're here. This is Mr. Franklin Stone, Deputy Chief of Counter-Terrorism of the FBI. Franklin, Toby Roberts here is handling the Gubin case for us."

Roberts and Stone shook hands. Stone and Lanning then resumed their seats, and Roberts joined them at the table, sitting next to the Deputy Commissioner.

"I apologize for being late, Sir. I was over at the opera house. I was reviewing the crime scene. In fact I found the bullet, I'm pleased to say, embedded in the screen behind the sofa. Forensics should be over there by now, following up."

Stone nodded in approval. "What's the status of your investigation, Toby?"

Roberts was surprised by the familiarity.

He thought for a moment. He got out his notebook, and referenced it at frequent intervals as he spoke.

"Mr. Stone, we have already undertaken extensive inquiries, and interrogated a number of persons of interest, including Alexandra Matviyko, her friend Quentin Dart, Petya Gubin's wife Maria, and Lord Jaeger, Chairman of

Covent Garden. There was a man by the name of Bryce, so called, who visited Gubin on Thursday evening at Covent Garden, before the performance. We have no information concerning when he left the opera house. So he could have been there in the interval, when Gubin was shot, or maybe he had already left by then. We don't know."

Roberts referred to his notes again for a moment. He continued, "We have taken Leo Connell into custody for questioning, and we have a search warrant to examine his flat and the contents. We believe we will locate a CD there, with certain information on it. This CD was handed to Matviyko by Gubin on Thursday evening, just before the performance. Matviyko then took it to Connell, late that night. We know that the CD contains some documents, in Russian, and other languages, with maps, drawings, and diagrams. Dart, who briefly saw the CD when he was at Matviyko,'s flat, on Thursday evening, has mentioned that he thinks the maps might show some locations in the United States."

Roberts paused and briefly looked at his notes. "I have been reviewing the documents we retrieved from Matviyko's flat, after a break-in there. By the way, we assume that the break-in was an attempt to get hold of the CD, which by then had been handed to Connell by Matviyko. The documents are of extreme interest, and of the utmost importance. They give us a good indication of the movement of funds between Gubin, the Anisimov Foundation in New York, and bank accounts in Matviyko's name, in Riyadh, Geneva, Paris and London. We have a copy of a schedule of payments that are supposed to be made out of those accounts, starting shortly. The co-signatories on the accounts are Matviyko and Connell. We also have a copy of Gubin's will. The beneficiaries under the will include Matviyko, Gubin's wife, the children, and several women. Also Connell, the Metropolitan Opera House, and the Anisimov Foundation. He changed his will quite recently. It will be a substantial estate."

"That's all very useful, in fact," said Stone. "You've done well in such a short period of time. It fully supports the scenario that the FBI has put together, with assistance in the field from the CIA."

"Mr. Stone, it would help me if you could explain exactly what that scenario is, if you don't mind," said Roberts.

"Yes, of course. Call me Frank, please. This is a matter of the utmost importance. A security issue beyond any other that currently affects both our countries' interests."

Stone told Canning and Roberts that Petya Gubin was believed to have been funding terrorist cells in Chechnya, and in the Middle East. These funds had been remitted to banks in Riyadh, Geneva, and elsewhere, through the Anisimov Foundation. He said that a new, much larger parcel of funds was believed to be ready to be laundered through the same channels, very soon, as the documents Roberts had referred to verified quite clearly.

Stone explained that the FBI and CIA had already tracked previous funds from the foundation, indirectly, to over twenty organizations overseas. He said that some of these organizations were now known to be closely linked to Al Qaeda. He said that investigations had been going on for over two years, but it was only recently they had begun to prove the links with proactive terrorist activity.

Stone speculated on whether the motive for Gubin's murder might have been to insure that the planned flow of funds was not impeded in any way, to be followed by a massive cover-up. Alternatively, he said, Gubin might have been killed by those attempting to break the chain down. That was why the investigation into Gubin's murder was so important.

Roberts was now writing notes even more hurriedly than before.

Stone added that the most critical, time sensitive, issue was that the new funds were possibly earmarked for the procurement of chemicals and equipment to build weapons of mass destruction. He said the FBI and CIA believed there was a strong likelihood that the weapons would be used against western targets. He said that was the reason why it was important to get hold of the CD as soon as possible, and why Gubin's records and computers in New York were being checked out over the weekend.

Canning and Roberts had both been listening attentively, occasionally expressing surprise and deep concern.

Canning said, "Frank, please continue with what you were saying to me before Toby came in, about what the FBI is doing in New York."

"When I met with Martin Schaeffer yesterday afternoon, he gave me access to Gubin's office suite at The Met. I was able to take a quick look. I did not have the time to examine the computer files in any detail. So I have arranged for two of my agents to spend this weekend going through those computer files and the other documents that are there, in the office. I have also organized a similar operation at the Gubin home, in Manhattan."

Stone continued, "As you know, there is a man known as Novelli, presenting himself as an FBI agent. He is strongly suspected of having been responsible for the killing of Frederick Ballard, Gubin's attorney, yesterday morning. Ballard was fatally stabbed, in his own office. The NYPD reports that a number of documents appear to have been removed from the office."

"Extraordinary. I spoke to Novelli only yesterday," said Roberts. "He rang me, saying he was Assistant to the Director of the FBI. He was asking a number of questions. I was on to him immediately, of course."

"Novelli is more dangerous than you would think. He is a trained assassin, and he does not hesitate."

Stone then said, "Today, as we speak, another two of my agents are examining Fischer's papers at the Anisimov Foundation offices. Anything material will emailed to me here at once, so that we can cross-reference that information with what is being retrieved from the Gubin office and home in New York, and what has been collected from Alexandra Matviyko's home here. Toby, I would appreciate having a dossier on the Matviyko material as soon as possible, please."

Roberts was truly impressed by Stone's detailed update. He was also taken by surprise at the apparent scope and scale of the crimes involved. But his mind quickly switched back to his own inquiry, and pursuing his own investigations. His job was to find Gubin's killer.

Roberts got up from his chair, and said, "Thank you, Mr. Stone. What I have learned has been very useful to me. It gives me a good perspective for the inquiry I am conducting into the Gubin homicide. I trust that we can continue to work together. It has been a pleasure meeting you."

Stone now also stood up, to his full six feet four. "Toby, let me make this clear. What we are dealing with here is a matter of international security, of the gravest and most serious kind. Many innocent lives will depend on a timely, clean and effective conclusion to this business. Not to mention the international relations that are involved. The CID in the UK must, I repeat must, collaborate with the FBI, the CIA, and all other law enforcement and surveillance agencies involved, to the fullest possible extent, in order that we bring all those responsible to justice as soon as possible. We must break up these terrorist cells that are being funded by the Gubin network."

"I understand, Franklin, totally, absolutely," said Lanning.

"Good. We are of one mind on this." He pointedly looked at Roberts. "That's right, isn't it, Toby?"

"Yes," said Roberts, quietly. He then placed his notebook in his pocket, and made for the door. As he did so, he whispered to himself, "Bloody FBI."

Chapter 43

Arnold Fischer did not sleep well.

After being forced to abandon his flight to London, he had been escorted back to his apartment by the FBI.

He made himself some breakfast, and at eight o'clock the doorbell rang. The two FBI agents told him they wanted him to go with them to the foundation office.

Arnold had intended to call Alexandra and Leo in London but now it would have to wait. He did not want to speak to them while FBI agents were around, listening.

They arrived at the office fifteen minutes later. The weekend porter met them at the door. "I was about to call you, Mr. Fischer. I am afraid you have had a break-in."

They took the elevator to the third floor. The door to the office was ajar. Arnold noticed that it had been jimmied open.

The FBI agents took the situation in swiftly. Neither spoke to Arnold. One started to examine the files and papers thrown on the floor, and the other was making a phone call. "Mr. Stone, we are at the Anisimov office. It seems someone beat us to it. There has been a forced entry." He then listened, occasionally acknowledging that he understood the various instructions Stone was giving him.

He now turned to Arnold. "Please try to identify what is missing. We will want a detailed list."

Chapter 44

Maria, Antonio and Chloe were in the room at The Park Lane hotel.

The phone rang. Antonio answered. He held the receiver out to Maria. "It's for you, Mom. It's Lord Jaeger."

"Hello Ben."

"My dear, I wanted to make sure everything is going well. How are the children?"

"Fine. Their flight was OK, and we are just getting settled in. Thank you again for the use of the car."

"Not at all. I'm at the Garden. Rehearsals here are just finishing. I have a few things I have to do, but I would like to invite you, and the children of course, to have tea with me this afternoon. I thought we could go to Fortnum and Masons. Would that be all right? Around three thirty, perhaps? We could meet at Fortnums."

"We would love to, Ben. Wonderful. See you there."

Chapter 45

DI Bartholomew had invited Leo Connell to join him in the interview room. "We will require your front door key, Sir. We have a search warrant."

Leo reluctantly gave Bartholomew his key. He thought to himself that even if they found the safe they would probably not be able to open it, not without an expert.

He was advised that he would be interrogated further later.

*

Roberts joined DI Bartholomew and they were driven to Baker Street. Roberts decided not to say anything to him about the FBI meeting with the Deputy Commissioner. As annoyed as he was about the potential for interference in his handling of the case, he fully appreciated the need for total confidentiality at this stage.

"Oh, I got that information you wanted, Sir," said Bartholomew. "Matviyko left her flat just after eleven last night. Our man in Baker Street did not see her or anyone else go in to Connell's place after Connell had himself entered earlier in the evening. Matviyko was seen arriving back at her own flat at eight thirty-five this morning. Dart arrived at Matviyko's flat yesterday evening, at about six-thirty, and has not left, as far as we can tell. We believe he and Matviyko are still there."

"There's something missing, Terry. Where did Matviyko go last night? Didn't you have her followed?"

"No, Sir. We know she had a telephone call from Connell around eleven, and that she then intended to go to his flat. We tried to alert our man at Baker Street, but without success. Nevertheless, we still believed we had the situation covered. She was not seen there at any time last night."

Roberts snapped. "It's as plain on the nose on my face that she went to see Connell. Why was that missed, for heaven's sake? Why was there no record of her arriving at, or leaving, Connell's flat? Was an officer on duty there or wasn't there?"

"There was, Sir. But he took a short meal break around ten thirty. He could have missed her. But he assures me that he was outside all night, and that he did not observe her enter, or see her leave. She could well have gone somewhere else for the night, couldn't she, Sir?"

Roberts ignored the question. "Why did he take a meal break? Did he have a replacement?"

"No, Sir, I'm afraid not."

"Why on earth not, Inspector? That's not acceptable."

"We don't have the manpower, Sir."

"Inexcusable!"

They arrived at the apartment and let themselves in.

Everything was as he had left it earlier, thought Roberts. "Inspector, you take the living room, I'll search the bedroom."

Roberts was dismayed at what he saw in the bedroom. A breeze was blowing into the room through the French doors, which were partially open.

"Inspector, come in here."

Roberts said, "Did you know there was a way in through these doors?"

"No, Sir, I didn't."

"Why not? Didn't we have the location thoroughly checked before placing a surveillance officer here?"

"It's not obvious from the back street that there is a way in through the French doors, Sir. Not clear at all."

Roberts was now so livid he could barely speak. He had lost the initiative, purely because of the incompetence of his men, he thought to himself.

"Prepare a full schedule of known movements and telephone calls for Matviyko and Connell over the last twenty-four hours. I want a report from you on my desk, by tomorrow morning. No, by six o'clock this evening."

"Yes, Sir."

His phone rang. It was DC Trenton. "Yes, what is it?"

"We have a development, sir. Forensics is at Covent Garden. They say there is no screen in the conductor's dressing room. No sign of it, Sir."

"That's ridiculous. It was there earlier. I locked the room myself when I left. I gave the key to the stage door keeper. It must be there."

"It's not, Sir. In fact I gather the room has been stripped. There is nothing in there at all."

Chapter 46

Quentin and Alexandra spent part of the morning tidying the living room. Alex said she would deal with the bedroom while Quentin was at the opera, later on that evening.

They talked over lunch but avoided any references to Petya Gubin. Several times Alex wondered how Leo was dealing with the CD, but she decided to leave it until he contacted her.

"Curtain up is seven thirty," Quentin said. "I ought to leave at six thirty."

Alex nodded. "Maybe we should delay having something to eat until after you get back. There really isn't time before you have to go. Anyway, I'm feeling a bit tired. I'd like to take a nap, if you don't mind."

"That's OK. I'll get a snack there. I'll leave in two hours or so. I won't disturb you if you're still asleep."

He kissed her gently on the cheek. She smiled, and went upstairs.

He decided to read for a while, and settled on the sofa.

He started to feel drowsy. He thought that he should not go to sleep or he might not awake in time to get to the opera house. He decided to go to his apartment in Wapping, check his mail, and change there. He quietly let himself out.

Chapter 47

Akbar Sattar made a telephone call.

"There's a safe there. I couldn't open it. Shall I blow it?"

"No. Not yet. Too dangerous. Was anyone there? Any sign of the police?"

"I went in the back way, through the French doors. Connell wasn't there. I didn't see the front of the building. Didn't notice any police."

"Maybe Connell's still with the police, or with the girl. You have to get the safe combination. Go round to the girl's place. Force it out of her, or Connell if he's there. You know what to do."

Chapter 48

Roberts sat at his desk. He considered the situation.

He was extremely disappointed with the lack of thoroughness concerning surveillance at the Matviyko and Connell flats. There had obviously been a breakdown in communication between the telephone monitoring and the surveillance. That should never have happened.

He wanted to interview Lord Jaeger again, at the opera house. He needed to get to the bottom of the mystery surrounding the sudden clearance of the contents of the conductor's room. Stripped bare, apparently. He would speak to the staff there. He would get a full description of Bryce from the stage door keeper.

He needed to interrogate Connell thoroughly. Where was the CD, he wondered?

He decided to go back to Covent Garden first, and he telephoned Jaeger's office. A secretary answered. He introduced himself and asked to speak to Lord Jaeger. The secretary said, "I'm afraid His Lordship is out for the afternoon. Call back at seven, if you would, Sir. No later than that, because there is a performance at seven thirty tonight."

Roberts looked at his watch. It was just after three o'clock.

He elected to go to Covent Garden anyway. He would talk to the stage door keeper, and then perhaps catch Lord Jaeger as soon as he returned to the opera house. That was assuming the secretary had told the truth, and that he had gone out, of course.

He instructed DI Bartholomew and DC Trenton to interview Connell while he was gone.

He would have preferred to talk to Connell himself, but he had to delegate. He couldn't do everything.

He ordered a car, and made his way back to the opera house.

On the way, his telephone rang.

"It's DI Bartholomew. Forensics will not be at the Baker Street flat until later on this afternoon. They are short-staffed, because it's a Saturday. The only available team has to come down from Nottingham, where they were working earlier this morning. They are on their way, Sir, but it may be a couple of hours."

Roberts snapped, "I thought there was a forensics team at Covent Garden earlier. Send them round to Baker Street. What's the problem, Inspector?"

"They are now off duty, Sir."

"Tell those bastards from Nottingham to get there as soon as they can."

*

Roberts arrived back at the opera house. He questioned the stage door keeper, "Did anyone ask you for the keys to the conductor's dressing room, after I returned them to you?"

"No."

"Who has a key to the conductor's room, other than yourself?"

"The Head of Music Staff, the two General Directors, of the Opera and the Ballet companies, and … let me see…."

"There are others?"

"Yes. The Head of Security."

"Anyone else?"

"Well, there's the Chairman's office. They have master keys for the whole building."

Roberts sighed. "Are any of those you mentioned here in the opera house today?"

"Yes, Sir. The Head of Security was in earlier."

"I see. Is Lord Jaeger in the house?"

"No, he isn't. Oh, I gave your Inspector a description of the man who was here on Thursday night, sir."

"Thank you. I would like to go to the conductor's room now, please."

The stage door keeper said, "There's nothing in there."

Roberts quickly walked along the corridor. The tape had gone from the door, which was unlocked. He opened the door. The dressing room was entirely empty.

He went back to the stage door. "When was the dressing room emptied, please?"

"Earlier this afternoon, Sir."

"Who by?"

"By the Head of Security and two of his staff. We have another dressing room now being used for the conductor."

"Who gave the Head of Security those instructions?"

"I'm not sure, Sir. The Head of Security said that the police had given the all clear to have the room emptied."

"Where are the contents of the dressing room?"

"Locked away, by the Head of Security."

"I would like to see the Head of Security right away."

"I'm afraid he's not in the house. He'll be back at seven."

"Why did you not tell me all this when I arrived?" he asked the stage door keeper.

"You didn't ask me."

Roberts felt that the case was slipping away from him. The day had been a disaster.

He decided that he would discuss the unauthorized clearance of the dressing room with Lord Jaeger. He was the person ultimately responsible for what went on in the opera house. He would wait for him. Someone would have to take the rap for interference with a crime scene. That was a serious charge. Jaeger, Wright, or someone. At that moment he really didn't care who it was, as long as he could get to the bottom of it.

He asked to be escorted to the Chairman's suite. There he was met by the Chairman's secretary, who invited him to wait in the outer office.

Just after he had sat down, his phone rang. "Franklin Stone here, Toby. I would like to meet with you later on this afternoon, if it's convenient. Maybe at five thirty, in the Deputy Commissioner's office?"

Roberts thought for a moment. He didn't want to miss Lord Jaeger. But on the other hand he couldn't afford to get on the wrong side of Stone, with all the things that had gone awry.

"Yes, I'll be there," he said.

Chapter 49

It was now three forty.

Akbar Sattar had changed into casual clothes, and was wearing sunglasses.

He rang the buzzer on the phone by Alexandra's door. There was no answer.

Sattar took a credit card out of his pocket and forced the street door open, as he had the previous day. He slipped into the lobby. He silently climbed the stairs. He listened carefully for other occupants. He did not want to be observed. Using a small, thin chisel, exactly as he had before, he swiftly and skilfully forced the entrance door to the apartment open.

He quickly scanned the entrance hall and the entire downstairs level. The living room had been cleaned up, he noticed. He went upstairs, and into Alexandra's bedroom. She was sleeping on the bed. She was wearing a knee length T-shirt.

He shook her shoulder. She woke up immediately. She screamed, and fell off the bed on the other side from where Sattar was standing.

"You won't be hurt if you cooperate," he said. "Go downstairs."

She stumbled down the staircase. Sattar followed. "Sit down," he said, pointing to the sofa.

"Where is Connell?"

"I have no idea," she said.

"Where is he? Tell me!"

"I don't know. At his apartment, perhaps?"

"He's not there. Do you have the combination to his safe?"

"No I don't," she said.

Sattar took a knife out from under his belt, and held it to Alex's neck. "What's the combination?"

"I promise you, I don't know. He never told me what it was. Anyway, he's always boasting that he changes it all the time."

"Wait there. Don't move!"

Sattar went into the office. Standing where he could still see the back of Alexandra's head, he pulled out his mobile phone, and dialled a number.

"I'm at the girl's apartment. She 's here, but Connell isn't. She says she doesn't have the safe combination. She says Connell keeps changing it. She doesn't know where Connell is."

"Do you believe her?"

"Perhaps. Shall I do a search here? Shall I hurt her?"

"No, go back to Connell's place as quickly as you can. Blow the safe, but be very careful."

Sattar then made for the door. "You don't know how lucky you are," he said.

Alexandra remained seated on the sofa for several minutes, sobbing hysterically. She cried out, "Quentin, where are you when I need you?"

She slowly recovered. She then noticed Quentin's mobile phone that he had left on the seat beside her. She picked it up, and dialled his home number. There was no answer.

She then thought about what had just transpired. She decided that she would leave the apartment. It was too dangerous to stay.

She went upstairs to change. She would go to the opera house. She would meet Quentin there.

Chapter 50

Maria, Antonio and Chloe had rested. Maria had encouraged Antonio and Chloe to have a nap. She had remained with her children all day.

They arrived at Fortnum and Masons a little early, a few minutes walk from their hotel, and waited at their table for Lord Jaeger to arrive. He swept in just after four o'clock, and they ordered their sandwiches and cakes.

The conversation flowed. Lord Jaeger told the three of them about plans for the next season at the Royal Opera House, and he chatted about his country home, near Gloucester. Jaeger asked Antonio about his college activities, and Maria proudly spoke of Antonio's many sporting achievements. Petya Gubin's name was not mentioned at any time.

Jaeger then temporarily left them, to take a call on his mobile phone.

While he was away from the table, Chloe said, "He's really nice. He's obviously nuts about you, Mummy. He can hardly keep his hands to himself."

"You're very naughty," said Maria, smiling "He's just being attentive, that's all."

Chloe then looked at her brother. "What do you think of him, Tonio?"

"He's a bit stuck up if you ask me. But he must have plenty of dough. Did he know Dad, by the way?"

Maria paused. "That's a good question. I never actually asked him. I just assumed they knew each other. After all, your Dad conducted here before, more than once."

Chloe said, "Mummy, invite him to Long Island for a visit in the summer. Maybe he could get me into the Royal Ballet School if the ABT doesn't want me, you never know."

"You're not to mention it, Chloe," said Maria, wagging her finger at her.

Jaeger returned to the table. "Sorry about that. Now, does anyone want some ice cream?"

"I would, please," said Chloe.

"Good. I'll order some," he said, beckoning to the waiter. "You'll forgive me if I leave you soon. I really don't want to, but I have to get back to the Garden. I have to entertain some people before the performance tonight. We are doing "Onegin". I'm sorry in a way. It would have been better to keep the house dark for a few more days, in memory of your dear father. But the Board wouldn't see it that way, and so we decided to go ahead. We got Farinelli in to conduct. It won't be quite the same, of course."

"Did you know my father well, Lord Jaeger?" asked Antonio.

"Yes, very well. He conducted here many times, and we had some good times together. A wonderful man, your father."

"Ben, do you know Fred Ballard?" asked Maria. "He is our attorney. He has been a friend of the family for many years?"

"No, I don't think so. Why?"

"Oh no reason really. But he's here in London. He should have arrived this morning from New York. I wondered if he had gone to the opera house."

"Well, tell him from me that I'll have best seats for him if he would like to attend the performance tonight. Or at any other time," said Jaeger.

"Thank you," said Maria, suddenly looking perplexed. "Oh, I've just realized that Fred won't know to contact me at The Dorchester. I never told the opera house that I had moved from The Park Lane. Tonio, if Fred has left a message for me at The Park Lane, do pass it on, won't you, dear. Maybe you could call him if he has left a contact number, and tell him to get in touch with me at The Dorchester, in Lord Jaeger's suite."

"No problemo, Mom," said Antonio. "Actually I'm suddenly feeling very tired. Chlo, do you mind if we go back to the hotel? I think I have to crash."

Maria held Antonio's hand. "You should both get some more sleep. Ben, thank you so much for this. It has been delightful."

"My pleasure," said Jaeger. "I must run too. I'll deal with the bill on my way out. Well, I hope to see you tomorrow. Maria, I will catch up with you at The Dorchester, later. I will probably not stay for Act II. So I'll see you about nine."

He then stood up, bent over Maria, and kissed her. He held out his hand to Chloe, and then Antonio, in turn, and said, "I have enjoyed meeting you so much. You are both such a credit to your wonderful mother. Good bye."

"Wow, Mummy. What a gent!"

"He's nice, isn't he?" she said. "Now you two get back to the hotel. I'll call you in the morning."

Chapter 51

Roberts arrived at the Deputy Commissioner's office at five fifteen. He had waited for Lord Jaeger at the opera house until four thirty, but had decided he couldn't wait any longer. He did not want to be late for Stone a second time.

He sat and waited outside Lanning's office. At five forty, Franklin Stone emerged from the office and invited him in. Roberts noticed at once that Lanning was not there.

"The Deputy Commissioner was good enough to let me use his facilities over the weekend. Welcome, Toby. What sort of a day have you had?"

"So so," said Roberts. "How can I help you?"

"The first thing I should mention is that Arnold Fischer's office in New York was turned over last night. Any documents that might have been of interest to us, I suspect, have been removed."

"Any idea who was responsible?" asked Roberts.

"Yes. We have a description. It looks like the work of our friend Novelli."

"Not him again."

"I'm afraid so. It means that those documents you have obtained are all the more critical, Toby. I would like you to bring them over to this office for me tomorrow morning, and I'll go through them with you. Would seven thirty work for you?"

Roberts stuttered, "Yes." He preferred not to work on Sundays, but this was an exception he thought. He felt growing resentment towards this man from the FBI. He's going to hijack my evidence, he said to himself.

Roberts' mobile phone then rang. Stone said, "Go ahead and answer that, Toby."

Roberts answered. It was DI Bartholomew. "Sir, I have some bad news."

"What is it, Bartholomew? Spit it out."

"We have just had a report from Connell's flat in Baker Street, Sir. The forensics team is there."

"Yes?"

"Sir, there's a safe in the bedroom. The safe door has been blown open. Apparently there's nothing left inside."

"What?"

"Yes, Sir. Bad situation."

"It's more than bad, Inspector."

"Sir, together with DC Trenton, I interviewed Connell. He admitted he had a safe, but he said that he could not remember the safe combination, and that the numbers were hidden in his desk at the flat. He claims he changes the numbers every week or so."

"It hardly matters now, does it, you idiot! Where is Connell?"

"Still here, sir."

"I'll be with you in thirty minutes. Send Trenton round to Baker Street. Get a report on my desk in an hour. Together with that other report, I requested earlier."

"Yes, Sir."

Roberts stared into space.

Stone broke the silence. "Bad news, Toby?"

"Yes. A safe in Connell's flat has been blown. I suspect we have lost the CD."

"That's more than unfortunate. Well I can see you have plenty to do. Why don't you meet me here in the morning? Let me know in the meantime if you feel the need to give me an update. I'm staying at The Connaught," he said.

Roberts went back to his own office. He had to think things through.

Should he go back to the opera house, and tackle Lord Jaeger? Or interrogate Connell? Or should he just release Connell and have him tailed. It was possible there was someone working in tandem with him. Maybe he would lead them to whoever else was involved.

He decided he would not detain Connell any further, and that DC Trenton would be delegated to tail him. He would get over to the opera house as quickly as he could. It was now after six o'clock.

Chapter 52

Quentin parked his car in the same car park he had used on Thursday evening, and walked to the opera house.

He entered the lobby, and was taken aback to find Alex waiting for him. She ran towards him, and threw herself into his arms.

"Quentin, where were you? Why did you leave?"

"What do you mean?"

"This huge guy broke into the apartment. He threatened to kill me!"

"Oh my God! What did he want?"

"The combination for Leo's safe. I don't have it. I never did have it."

"What happened?"

"He seemed to believe me when I said I didn't have the combination. He wanted me to tell him where Leo was. I didn't know. Then he made a phone call, and then he left, suddenly."

"Oh, you poor darling." He smothered Alex with kisses. "Thank God you're OK."

Alex, standing there, cradled in Quentin's arms, thought of Leo. She hoped he was suffering. He deserved nothing less, the lecher. At that moment, she hated him. She wished she could tell Quentin what had happened the night before, how Leo had drugged her and then raped her. But she couldn't. It would have to remain her secret.

"Let's eat," said Quentin. "Do you want to stay for the performance?"

"Not really. But I don't want to go home either. Not without you. The front door to the apartment is not secure, and anyone could walk in. I don't want to be there on my own."

"OK. Let's go over to Café Rouge. It's just across the street, here in Bow Street. We have time before the opera."

They went to the restaurant, and sat down at a table by the window.

"Alex, what did this guy look like? The one that threatened you?"

"Dark-skinned. Probably Saudi. Or maybe he was Iranian. Or Lebanese. I don't know. He was very fat though, and tall. He was wearing dark glasses."

"Don't you think you should tell the police, tell Roberts?"

"I suppose I should. I don't really want to see Roberts again, unless I have to. I'll think about it."

"If you're going to report it, I think you should do it now. But I don't have my mobile phone on me."

Alexandra thought for a moment. "I'll call him first thing in the morning."

They enjoyed their meal, and watched the crowds gathering outside the opera house, and going in for the performance.

Alexandra then pointed in the direction of a taxicab that had drawn up outside the opera house. She shook Quentin's arm. "Look, there's Dominique! I didn't know she was coming this evening."

Quentin blushed. He felt a little guilty for having befriended Dominique without telling Alex, and for not saying anything about Dominique's visit to his office.

"She has offered us the use of her apartment in Manhattan. That is, if you go with me for the Lincoln Center Festival," he said. "It's only five days away. You should decide whether you're going with me."

"Maybe I will come with you, if I can. I don't want to be here on my own."

They finished their meal, and made their way over to the opera house.

Chapter 53

Maria sat on the sofa in the suite at the Dorchester. She watched TV, pleased to be on her own for a while. She was relieved that Antonio and Chloe had not reacted badly to Petya's death.

The telephone rang. "Mom, it's Tonio. Chloe is asleep. I'm just going to crash myself. You had two messages waiting here when we got back. One from Arnold Fischer. He says it's urgent he speaks to you. He's at home in New York. Said to call him back, and that you have his number. The other call was from Martin Schaeffer's office, at The Met. They said they had tried The Dorchester and asked if you would call them as soon as you can."

"Was there a message from Fred Ballard?"

"No. Mom. There wasn't. Just the two."

"OK, honey. Thanks. Sleep well."

Maria decided to call Martin Schaeffer's office first. Marcie answered.

"Hello Marcie. Maria Gubin here. I believe Martin left a message for me to call him back. Is he there?"

"No. He's at home. Maria. He wanted to say how shocked we all were to hear about Petya. We're thinking of you."

"Thank you Marcie. Yes, it has been quite an ordeal."

"How are you bearing up?"

"Fine, thank you. The children are here. And people are being very kind. Lord Jaeger has given me the use of his suite at The Dorchester. And everything is OK, in the circumstances."

"Good. Martin wanted to give you a heads up that Arnie Fischer was flying over, and that he would probably want to meet."

"He's been in touch, actually. He wants me to call him back. He's in New York, I think."

"No, he was definitely due in London earlier today."

"How strange."

"There's something else, Maria. I don't know whether you know ….. have you heard about Fred Ballard?"

"No. What?"

"He was killed yesterday. Stabbed. In his office."

"Oh my God! That's terrible."

"Yes. They think the person who did it was someone impersonating an FBI agent. The same man came to see Martin at the office, in fact."

"That's awful."

"Fred was also going to fly over to London, to see you, and make all the arrangements for Petya's funeral. Deal with the will, that kind of thing. I guess Petya's body has to come back to the States now."

"I'm shocked by the news, Marcie. I'll have to think about what to do."

"OK. Let us know if you want us to help in any way. I know Martin would like to do everything he can."

"Thank you, Marcie. Please tell Martin I called."

"Of course."

Maria assumed Arnold had delayed his flight and stayed in New York because of Fred being killed. She would need another attorney. She knew Petya's affairs were complicated, and that she would have to get professional help, fast. She hadn't even seen the will. That would have been in Fred's office. Maybe there was a copy in Petya's desk at home. Or at The Met. Her thoughts then went to Lord Jaeger. Maybe he would help. He would know what to advise. And she would call Superintendent Roberts. But that could wait until Monday.

She picked up the phone, and dialled Arnold Fischer's number.

He was at home. "Oh, thank you for calling back, Maria. I was so sorry to hear about Petya."

"I've just been speaking to Marcie Segarra. She told me about Fred. It's terrible news. One thing after another."

"I know. Maria, there's some sort of operation going on here. My office was turned over last night. There are a lot of documents missing. Papers concerning grants from the foundation. You know, quite sensitive material."

"Really? I don't like the sound of that. Not at all."

"Absolutely. And another thing, I was stopped from getting on the plane last night when I was going to London. The FBI wouldn't let me board. They insisted on going to the office this morning. That was when we discovered it had been broken into."

"Arnie, I don't know what to say. It is all getting very worrying. Scary, in fact."

"Let me know if there's anything I can do, Maria. I don't know when I'll be able to get out of here. I'm hoping maybe Monday. I'll let you know. Good bye."

Maria decided that she would ask Lord Jaeger to handle everything, as far as he possibly could. That would be a load off her shoulders. Also she would meet with the children in the morning, and see if Antonio could help as well.

Chapter 54

Roberts had arrived back at the Royal Opera House stage door at six forty-five. The stage door keeper asked him to wait. Lord Jaeger would come down as soon as he could.

He was just about to insist on going up to Jaeger's office, after waiting fifteen minutes, when he appeared. He was wearing a dress suit.

"Ah, Superintendent. Nice to see you again," he said. "I'm so sorry you've been kept waiting, but I have guests."

"Lord Jaeger, I need some more of your time, please. I have to ask you some questions."

"Yes, delighted to help. Let's go upstairs to my office. I'm afraid I'll only have five minutes or so. I'm sorry, but the performance is about to start, and I should be in my seat in the theater."

They sat in Jaeger's office.

"Lord Jaeger, did you give instructions to have the conductor's dressing room cleared? Would you explain that to me, please?"

"Er, yes. Well our Security Chief did. We thought your people had finished. No one told us that the dressing room had to remain locked. Unless I am mistaken, you did not say anything this morning yourself, about the room having to remain secure."

"I left the key with the stage door keeper, with specific instructions that he was not to give it to anyone. When I met you in the dressing room this morning, Lord Jaeger, the tape was still on the door, which was locked. You received no authorization from me, or anybody on my behalf subsequently, that you could empty the room. I want to be clear about this. It was, it is, a crime scene. You have committed an offence by interfering with it. It's a most serious matter, Lord Jaeger."

"I see. I had no idea. Well, if I'm at fault, I am sorry. What can I say?"

"Where are the contents of the conductor's dressing room now?"

"In another part of the house."

"I would like to see that area now, please."

"I'm afraid that will be difficult. They're in a storage room by the stage, and that area cannot be accessed during a performance. Perhaps I might suggest you come back tomorrow, in the morning, and I'll arrange for you to see the items then."

"That is not good enough, Lord Jaeger. I will return after the performance this evening, with a search warrant if necessary, and you will then give me access to the room where those items have been stored."

"As you wish, Superintendent. Whatever you say. May I suggest you return at about eleven? As soon as we strike the Act III set you can be given access. Now if you'll excuse me, I have to go. Shall we?" Jaeger pointed to the door.

Roberts seethed. He had been to that bloody place four times in one day, he thought to himself. And what had been achieved?

After leaving the theater, he called DI Bartholomew. "Are those reports on my desk, Inspector?"

"Not yet, Sir. Half an hour."

"Is Connell being tailed by DC Trenton, as I requested?"

"Yes, Sir. He has gone back to his flat. Our officers are there, at the front and the back. Dart drove away from Matviyko's flat earlier this afternoon, and she subsequently left, as well."

"Let me know if there are any further developments. I have to be back here at the opera house at eleven, after tonight's performance. The conductor's dressing room has been cleared. It's totally empty. I have put Lord Jaeger on notice that we regard this as interference in a crime scene."

"Will that be all, Sir?"

"For the moment, Inspector."

Roberts then walked round to the entrance lobby. He watched the crowds for a while, and then decided to have something to eat. He went into "Café Rouge."

Chapter 55

Maria had fallen asleep on the sofa.

Lord Jaeger sat down beside her, and kissed her on her brow. She awoke.

"Ben, how nice. What time is it?"

"Just after nine. I didn't stay for Act II. I wanted to get back to you."

"That's wonderful. In fact, I need to talk to you."

"What is it?"

"Ben, there has been a murder. A stabbing. In New York. A man called Fred Ballard. He's Petya's attorney."

"Really? How awful."

"Yes. Fred has been our attorney for a long time. He was planning to come over to London to help deal with Petya's affairs. You know, to get his body returned to the States, that kind of thing."

"Do you want my help, Maria? I will do anything I can. Just tell me what you need."

"Thank you. I would like your help in finding an attorney, a solicitor, here in London, to deal with everything. Can you suggest anyone?"

"Yes, I believe I could do that. Anything else?"

"Petya's financial affairs. I want Antonio to take on some responsibilities, but he will need some guidance."

"He's a sharp young man. I'm sure he'll be able to cope. Why don't we get him over here in the morning, and we can go through what you need him to do?"

"Ben, could you also contact Martin Schaeffer at The Met, please? I think some of Petya's papers are there, or else in the house in Manhattan. Martin can work with you and Tonio on getting a number of things sorted out. The FBI is investigating Petya's affairs, but ……."

"The FBI?"

"Yes, apparently."

"Why?"

"I have no idea, Ben. But I have to go ahead with certain arrangements. There will have to be a funeral. A memorial service. It should be in New York."

"Of course. I'll do whatever I can."

"Thank you. I don't know what I would do without you."

"My pleasure. By the way, has Superintendent Roberts been bothering you?"

"No, not really. Why?"

"He has been at the Garden today, three times, would you believe. He's annoyed that we cleared the conductor's dressing room. He says we shouldn't have done that. That it's a crime scene. I don't think he's very effective, if you ask me. Might I suggest that you refer him to me, if he contacts you again? I don't want you bothered any further."

"Thank you, I'll do whatever you advise."

Chapter 56

Leo Connell was feeling exhausted. He had never experienced police detention before, and he didn't like it. Also, he was worried that he hadn't been able to deal with the CD, and hand it over.

He opened the door to his flat. He went into the bedroom to change, and immediately noticed that the safe was open. And that it was empty. Had the police opened it perhaps? No, surely not. He looked more closely and saw that it had been forced open, not by using the combination. A feeling of terror overtook him. He thought the police would really be after him now. And especially the others. But why had the police agreed to release him? Why hadn't Roberts interrogated him further? He reasoned the police would never have blown the safe. They would be hoping he would implicate himself further, perhaps by leading them to the others who were involved. He would have to be careful.

He thought about Alexandra. He checked his telephone. No messages. He considered contacting her, but decided he would not, at least not until he was feeling better. He would leave it until the morning. The telephone rang.

"We have the CD."

He relaxed a little, relieved that the CD was now in the right hands. But the voice continued.

"Where were you? We had to blow the safe."

"I was detained. I would have got it to you."

"The money has to be moved. It's needed, now."

"It's not just up to me, you know that. Mine is not the only signature required."

"You and the girl will have to attend to it on Monday. No later."

Chapter 57

Roberts reflected on the possible motive for removing the contents of the conductor's dressing room.

Had he missed something? Was there more evidence that was being concealed?

It did not make sense.

Connell was acting most suspiciously, he thought, but the fact that his safe had been blown while he had been in custody was interesting. Who had been responsible for that?

Matviyko had been in her flat all day, but where had she gone last night? To see Connell? If so, why? Were she and Connell having an affair? Probably not, he thought. It had to be something to do with the CD, and the information on it that was clearly of critical importance. Why had Gubin given Matviyko the CD? Why hadn't he given it directly to whoever he was working through? Probably because he decided to use Matviyko as a cover, he thought. But why not just give it to Connell? What was Connell's role? He must be the key. He decided that he would interview Connell if he didn't lead them to anyone within twenty-four hours. He would tackle him tomorrow evening.

Roberts made his way back to the stage door as the performance finished. Crowds were starting to emerge from the theater exits.

He asked for Lord Jaeger, and was told he had left the theater earlier. He explained that he had arranged with Jaeger that he would be given access to the storage area by the stage, and he asked to see the Stage Director. He was told to wait.

The Stage Director, Ronald Grainger, appeared after a delay of ten minutes. Roberts recounted his earlier meetings with Lord Jaeger. "Why was the conductor's dressing room cleared this afternoon?"

"You would have to ask Lord Jaeger that question," said Grainger. "Come with me, if you would, and I'll show you the storage room." They made their way to an area by the back of the stage, and Grainger took some keys from his pocket, and unlocked the door.

Roberts entered, and immediately noticed that the furniture from the conductor's dressing room was neatly stacked in one corner of the room, at the back. He then spotted the screen that he had examined earlier, and he looked for the bullet. It had been removed. He turned to Grainger, and said, "I have reason to believe that criminal evidence has been removed from here. I will see Lord Jaeger about this."

"Lord Jaeger is not here."

"I know. Who has access to this storage room, Mr. Grainger?"

"Almost any member of staff who works backstage in a supervisory capacity, Superintendent. You would have to check the key lists."

Roberts stormed out of the theater.

Chapter 58

Quentin and Alexandra arrived back at her apartment after the performance.

Quentin had spotted Dominique at a distance during the second interval, but thought Alexandra had not, so he decided that it would be inappropriate to approach her. He said nothing to Alex.

Alex checked her phone messages. There was one. "Arnold Fischer called while we were out," she said.

"Who is he?"

"He is the President of the Anisimov Foundation. I had better call him back. It might be something important."

She went into the office, and dialled Fischer's number. Quentin sat on the sofa.

"Arnie. I'm glad you're there. We were out when you called. Quentin and I were at Covent Garden."

"Alex, I was supposed to be in London today, but the FBI detained me. I won't go into that now. I must ask you about the funds."

"It's difficult right now, Arnie."

"Alex, you don't get it. Those funds have to come back to the foundation. Immediately."

"No, I am supposed to make the payments as detailed in the schedule, as you know. But all in one lump sum, now. I really can't talk about it any more at the moment," she said, worried that she was probably being overheard by the police.

"Alex, I implore you. You and Leo have to remit those funds back. We will all be in the most terrible trouble with the FBI, and God knows who else, otherwise. Now that Petya is dead, the police in London, and the FBI, will not leave a stone unturned."

"I'll have to talk to Leo. I'll call you back."

"When, Alex?"

"Well, we can't do anything until Monday, when the banks open. I'll call you tomorrow."

Alexandra returned to the living room, and sat down next to Quentin.

He spoke quietly. "Alex, tell me about the payments."

"They are wire transfers I am supposed to make from various banks, for Petya Gubin. That's all."

"What did Arnold want?"

"The funds originally came from the foundation, among other places. I am responsible for making these payments. But Arnold Fischer wants the money back. It's very difficult for me."

"I see. What has this got to do with Leo? You said on the phone to Arnie that you would have to speak to Leo."

"Leo is a co-signatory on the accounts. Petya and Fred Ballard set it up that way. It's not my money."

"If Arnold says it has to go back, shouldn't you send it back, straight away, as he says?" asked Quentin.

"Maybe I should. Arnie says the FBI is looking into it, so perhaps I should. Petya said things might be getting too difficult. I don't know what to do."

"Send the money back, Alex. You have to. You mustn't get into trouble with the FBI. You've already got the CID here looking at you suspiciously."

"It's so difficult. I don't want to do anything Petya wouldn't have wanted." She started to cry.

"What did Petya say to you on Thursday, Alex? Why did he give you the CD?"

"He was having doubts about the timing of the money. He mentioned something about it becoming too hot. But stupidly I didn't ask him why he said that."

"If he was having doubts, surely that's another reason for sending the money back. But you didn't answer my question about the CD?"

"Petya said I was to hand it over to someone. That person would make contact with me, supposedly today."

"Well, that's out of your hands now. Why do you think Petya was murdered, Alex?"

"I don't know. He was involved in so much. So deeply into things that had got far too complicated."

"Alex, I saw the will on Thursday night. When you went over to Leo's apartment, I looked upstairs. I saw a lot. I know that you're a beneficiary under the will, and from Petya's insurance policies. The police will think you had a motive for killing Petya. You have to do the right thing. You have no choice about the money. Petya's dead now. You must take care of your own interests. Alex, I saw the documents, all the figures. I know how much is involved. Send it back to the foundation, all of it. You have to do that."

"I'll call the bank on Monday, and fax them instructions. I will. OK. But I'll need Leo's agreement, his written authorization. He is a co-signatory."

"Alex, you have to do it. First thing Monday morning. And I think you should tell Roberts you're going to do it. Tell him everything. Make a clean breast of it."

"You're right. Let's talk about it more tomorrow morning."

"Alex, another thing. I saw the photographs." He showed her the photo of Petya on her bed that she had kept in the folder in her bureau, and that he had put in his wallet.

"I found this. And others. I know he was here, in the last few months."

"Oh Quentin, I've been so mean to you. I really didn't want all this to come out. I just want to forget it all. And be with you."

Quentin tore up the photograph. "That's what I think of that. Let's leave it at that, for now."

Chapter 59

SUNDAY

Roberts had not slept well. He had not slept at all the previous night. He was beginning to feel unwell. He was running a temperature, he thought.

He arrived at his office at seven fifteen. He collected the box files, and made his way over to the Deputy Commissioner's office.

Franklin Stone was already seated at the conference room table. He stood up, and held out his hand. "Good morning, Toby. How are you?"

"Good morning. Not well, not really. I have a lot on my mind at the moment."

"Quite so. Shall we get down to work? Let's go through what you have here," he said, turning to the box files.

They spent thirty minutes examining the documents. Stone occasionally checked points against his own computer files, working quickly and efficiently.

"Well, there are a few surprises," Stone said finally, "but nothing that causes us to go back to square one."

Roberts cleared his throat. "Mr. Stone, I should tell you that there has been serious interference with the crime scene, at Covent Garden." He then recounted the events of the previous day, in chronological order. He concluded by saying, "Lord Jaeger is being cavalier about this, and I believe he may be turning a blind eye to what is going on there, or even worse."

"I see. Here's what I suggest. You should see Lord Jaeger, at his home in London. Today. I will come with you, but don't tell him I'm joining you. The element of surprise might well be an advantage, in the circumstances, given my position with the FBI."

"That's an excellent idea, Mr. Stone. We can see him at his suite at The Dorchester, this morning. What time will be convenient for you?"

"Make it around eleven. I'll catch up with you around ten thirty. Will that work? Give me a call to confirm."

Roberts returned to his office.

He then started to read the reports Bartholomew had left on his desk. He felt his blood pressure climbing.

The phone rang. It was Bartholomew. "Sir, you asked me to let you know as soon as we have any new information."

"I'm going through your reports, Inspector. I do not like what I am reading."

"Yes, Sir. Dart and Matviyko returned to her flat just after eleven last night. She then made a telephone call to a number in New York City. She addressed the gentleman as "Arnie." They discussed the movement of funds. It may be important, Sir."

"I see. Let me have a transcript on my desk as soon as you can. Then I will want you to accompany me to The Dorchester this morning, to interview Lord Jaeger. We will leave the Yard at ten thirty. We will be joined by the FBI. That information is not to be repeated, Inspector."

Roberts then dialled The Dorchester. He was put through to Jaeger's suite. "Good morning, Lord Jaeger. I am sorry we missed each other after the performance last night. If I may, I would like to continue our discussions. Will you be at The Dorchester all morning?"

"Yes, I will. Until about noon."

Chapter 60

Alex awoke first. She felt better for having slept well. Quentin had also slept soundly. Overslept, in fact.

She went downstairs, to make some coffee.

The phone rang. It was Leo Connell.

"We should talk, Alex. But not on the phone. Can we meet later?"

"Yes, but I am not prepared to see you on my own. Quentin and I will meet you at your apartment, at two."

"You shouldn't involve him, Alex. It's too complicated. Dangerous even."

"Quentin will be with me. That's how it is from now on."

Quentin joined her in the kitchen. "I heard that. Thanks for nothing!"

"I am not going to do anything without you from now on. I made up my mind about that before I went to sleep last night."

"I was kidding. That's great. Good decision."

"I am just going to call Roberts. I'm going to tell him about the funds. OK?"

"Absolutely. Also tell him about the guy who broke in yesterday."

She dialled his number. "Superintendent Roberts, good morning. This is Alexandra Matviyko."

Roberts was momentarily surprised by the call, and he hesitated, before saying, "Good to hear from you Alexandra. Why the phone call?"

"There is something you should know." She then told him the story of the break-in the previous afternoon.

"I am pleased you have reported this, Alexandra. We will need you to give us a detailed description, as soon as possible. What did he look like?"

Alex briefly described the intruder.

Roberts said, "It sounds to me as though your man could be the same individual calling himself Bryce who was at the opera house on Thursday. It is important that you work with one of our artists to get a good likeness of the man. Bryce is sought for questioning in relation to Petya Gubin's death."

"Really, Superintendent? Perhaps I could do that tomorrow. But I must also tell you that I have been talking to Arnold Fischer in New York. He heads up the Anisimov Foundation, you know. I have been holding some …. er, Mr. Gubin arranged for me to receive some funds into various bank accounts, mainly from the foundation, and I was supposed to forward those funds to certain places, over a period of time. There was an understanding that if anything happened to Petya I was to move all the money at once. Make a lump sum payment, immediately. But Mr. Fischer has requested that I return those funds to him in New York, and I have agreed. I will be doing that tomorrow."

"That's very good. Thank you for telling me."

"I will need Leo Connell's authorization to do this, because he is a co-signatory. I am meeting him today, to get his agreement."

"That's understood. Is there anything we can do to help?"

"No, I don't think so. Mr. Dart will be with me. I think it will be all right."

"When are you seeing Mr. Connell?"

"At two this afternoon."

"Do you think he will give you the agreement you are looking for?"

"I hope so, Superintendent."

Quentin hugged Alex as she replaced the receiver. "Well done, my darling. That was fabulous."

Chapter 61

Antonio and Chloe arrived at Lord Jaeger's suite at The Dorchester just before eleven.

"Join us for brunch," said Maria, greeting them both. "Ben and I were just going to order room service."

"OK, thanks," said Antonio. "Did you manage to get back to Martin Schaeffer and Arnold Fischer last night?"

"Yes, I did," said Maria. "Bad news, I'm afraid. Fred Ballard has been killed. His body was found in his office on Friday."

"Oh my," said Chloe. "Why on earth would anyone do that?"

"I don't know," said Maria. "Tonio, I need you to do some things for me. Ben will give you all the expert help you need. I've decided that I will engage a lawyer here in London, and I want you to get hold of your father's will, somehow. Maybe there's a copy in his office at The Met. You could ask Marcia Segarra to help you. Call her tomorrow. We will have to make arrangements to get Petya's body back to New York. We should aim at having the funeral by the end of the week, by Friday, at the very latest."

Jaeger said, "You will have to speak with Scotland Yard about that. They won't release the body if they are still dealing with some key questions relating to your husband's death. I don't know for certain, of course. But I think you should ask first."

"Yes, we will," said Maria. "We'll get round to doing all these things tomorrow. Tonio, Ben is going to recommend a lawyer. We will want to get that done quickly. Can you be ready to see whoever it is tomorrow morning? I will join you if necessary, of course."

"Yes, I guess so."

The telephone rang. Jaeger answered it. He listened for a moment, and then said, "Send them up."

"We have some visitors, I'm afraid."

"Who is that?" asked Antonio.

"Detective Superintendent Roberts, and he has Detective Inspector Bartholomew with him. I will take them into the small bedroom, and in that way you will not be disturbed."

There was a knock at the door. Lord Jaeger opened it, and he invited Roberts to enter. Roberts spoke first. "Lord Jaeger, this is Detective Inspector Bartholomew. He is working with me on the case. Inspector, this is Lord Jaeger."

Franklin Stone then emerged from behind Roberts and Bartholomew, taking Jaeger by surprise. Roberts said, "This is Mr. Franklin Stone, of the FBI."

By this time, Stone, Bartholomew and Roberts were standing face to face with Lord Jaeger, Maria, Antonio and Chloe. "Ah, I see you have visitors," Roberts said. "Good morning, Mrs. Gubin."

Maria held out her hand to Roberts. "These are my children, Superintendent, Antonio and Chloe." Turning to Stone, she said, "I am pleased to meet you. Mr. Stone. May I ask where you are from?"

"From Washington DC," he replied.

Antonio was studying Stone. He asked, "What is your position with the FBI, Mr. Stone?"

"Counter-Terrorism. I'm the Deputy Head."

There was an uncomfortable silence. No one spoke for several seconds.

Jaeger then said, "Well, goodness me, Superintendent. You've certainly brought out the big guns this morning. Might I suggest I take the three of you into another room, and we will leave Mrs. Gubin and her children to enjoy their brunch."

Roberts started to speak, but Stone interrupted him. "If I may, Toby, I would like to offer an alternative. I would not want to spoil your morning, of course,

Mrs. Gubin, but why don't we all sit down here and have a chat, first. After all, we're being informal, aren't we?"

Antonio sat between Maria and Chloe, on the sofa. Lord Jaeger and the three visitors sat opposite them. Lord Jaeger took the chair nearest Maria.

Antonio spoke first. "What exactly is your interest in my father's affairs, Mr. Stone?"

"That's a fair question." Stone chose his words very deliberately. "The FBI has recently been undertaking some inquiries into certain international security matters, and we have discovered that Mr. Gubin may have had some information that is relevant, and useful to us."

"Linked to counter-terrorism?" asked Antonio.

"I could not say at this stage. Nor would I wish to, even off the record."

Maria spoke, now gripping Antonio's hand firmly. "Superintendent Roberts, can I ask you a question? Do you think Petya's death might be linked to what Mr. Stone is telling us?"

"It is too early to form an opinion, Mrs. Gubin. But we are not ruling anything out. Lord Jaeger, do you have any questions for us, or for Mr. Stone?"

Jaeger was taken off guard by Roberts' sudden question. He hesitated, and then said, "Quite frankly, I am totally confused by the whole business. I have no idea about any of this. All I want to do is to make sure that Mrs. Gubin and her children are comfortable and that they have everything they need. I desire nothing other than that, and to assist in getting over this awful event."

Roberts leaned forward in his chair. "But Lord Jaeger, you have not been assisting us, have you? Why is that you were instrumental in interfering with crucial evidence at the crime scene at the opera house? Why was the dressing room cleared without the knowledge and prior agreement of the police? Why was that, Lord Jaeger?"

"Oh, that's all in the hands of our Head of Security. I am the Chairman of the Board, Superintendent. I do not get involved in day-to-day matters. I explained that to you yesterday."

"Forgive me," interrupted Stone, "but this is an important and sensitive matter, and it is perhaps inappropriate to discuss it any further in the present circumstances. It is the subject of a formal CID inquiry, after all. Lord Jaeger, might I suggest that you accompany the Detective Superintendent to Scotland Yard, so that discussions can be continued there. I would also like to ask you some questions myself, but that can wait until later. In the meantime, I would like to remain here with Mrs. Gubin, Antonio and Chloe, if that is acceptable to you, Maria? I would like to hear more about your husband."

Maria nodded in agreement, looking at the two children as she did so. Stone then added, "Toby, why don't you and Lord Jaeger leave now?"

Jaeger was now standing up. "I really don't think that is necessary. In fact it is not convenient. I have another appointment at noon, as I said earlier to the Superintendent."

Stone got up from his chair, and Roberts also stood, next to him. Both of them looked at Lord Jaeger, as Roberts, speaking loudly and deliberately, said, "Lord Jaeger, you will please accompany me and DI Bartholomew to Scotland Yard. We are taking you in for questioning." He then addressed Maria. "Mrs. Gubin, I look forward to our next meeting. Mr. Stone, I expect I will see you later."

Jaeger had now become angry. "I must protest. This is quite ridiculous. I shall have to contact my lawyer about this, immediately."

"You may do that when we reach Scotland Yard," said Roberts.

*

Stone now resumed his seat immediately opposite the Gubin family. Maria was looking concerned.

"Well, I am sorry you had to witness that, Maria," Stone said. "It was not very pleasant."

"I don't know what to say, Mr. Stone, I had no idea there had been any difficulty. I'm sure it can all be sorted out amicably."

Stone grimaced. "I certainly hope so. Now, Maria, tell me about your late husband, if you wouldn't mind".

Room service then called. Maria requested that brunch be brought up straight away.

The meal arrived and it was set out on a small table.

As they ate their meal, Maria told Stone a little of the story of her life with Petya.

A doctor and his wife raised Maria as their only child. They lived in Pesaro, a small town on the Italian Adriatic coast. Pesaro had originally been just a fishing community, but it had since gained some renown as a center for music, due to the fact that the composer Rossini had been born and raised there, and that he had made it his home. There was now a diverse program of music in the schools and Conservatorio in Pesaro, and Maria was encouraged to play the piano as a young girl.

She showed considerable promise with the piano, and her teacher suggested that she might have a future as a concert pianist. Maria was happy to pursue it, although she was not particularly ambitious on her own behalf. Her parents wanted to send her to the Conservatorio in Milan, so she applied, and was accepted. In Milan, she spent her time happily with other students, although she did not always take her piano studies as seriously as she should. She spent increasing amounts of time with one student in particular. He was a young Russian, Petya Gubin, who had graduated at the Moscow Conservatoire, in piano and conducting. He was in Milan to study the Italian baroque composers such as Corelli and Vivaldi, and the works of Bellini, Donizetti and Verdi. He was sponsored by the Communist Party and was one of the first musicians to be allowed to travel and study outside the Soviet Union.

Maria fell in love with Petya, and he invited her to join him in Moscow for a summer vacation. There she met his mother. His father had died in a boating accident when he was a young boy. Petya had no brothers or sisters.

Petya had some radical political views that Maria did not fully understand or agree with, she said, but she was happy to be in his company, and to enjoy watching his growing talent for music making. He was becoming more interested in conducting than piano, and when they returned to Milan from Moscow, he spent more of his time concentrating on studying to become a conductor. He was intensely ambitious, and really needed no encouragement, from Maria or anyone else.

Petya entered an international conducting competition, which he won, and he began to attract interest from concert promoters and agents. By the time he and Maria had finished their studies in Milan he had some professional engagements, and it was widely believed that he would have a spectacular career ahead of him.

Before he returned to Moscow they spent the summer in Pesaro, and Petya proposed marriage. She accepted, with her father's blessing, although her mother had doubts, and some regrets. Maria thought this was because her mother realized she would see very little of her only daughter in the future, but she learned in later years that her mother had some anxieties about Petya's character, even then. They were married the following spring, in Moscow. They made their home there, in a spacious apartment near Red Square.

In Moscow Petya was appointed Assistant Conductor at the Bolshoi, and he was beginning to get engagements for concerts, and operas, in East Germany, Hungary, and Poland. Because news of his successes spread, he was soon invited to conduct in Berlin, Geneva, Paris and Vienna. Maria remained in Moscow and did not often travel with him. She missed her parents and her life in Italy, but Antonio and Chloe were born and she dedicated herself to raising the children.

When the children got older she sometimes took them with her to Petya's concerts. She particularly enjoyed the operas, but for those Petya was often away for a month at a time, and it was not practical or desirable for the children to be away from school for long periods.

When the Soviet Union broke up, there were increasing numbers of engagements and recording contracts that Petya could accept in America, the United Kingdom and France, and the family sometimes traveled together to New York, London and Paris.

Petya soon leased apartments in New York and Paris, because he said it was better than living out of suitcases and just staying in hotels.

Maria much enjoyed staying in these apartments whenever she could get away from Moscow, and she began to desire to live in Europe or the United States permanently. Her parents had both died by this time, and she decided that she would find schools for Antonio and Chloe in New York, and settle there, in the apartment Petya had leased.

Franklin Stone had been listening intently. He said, "You tell the story well, Maria. Did you know very much about how Petya spent his time when he was away, when he was not in the concert hall, the opera house or the recording studio?"

"Not really," she said. "It got to the point that we saw so little of each other, and we never seemed to have the time to talk about what each of us was doing. I shouldn't think I saw Petya for more than fifty days a year. He was so busy. We were really living separate lives."

Maria then said she knew that Petya had love affairs. He was a very attractive man, and he found it easy to seduce younger women. She said she accepted that it was almost inevitable that there would be these digressions. She was deeply unhappy about it at first, but in due course it became easier to endure. Petya was careful to hide details of these relationships from her and the children. Sometimes she just did not know which women he was spending his time with, but she suspected that most of the relationships were short-lived.

Chloe then said, "But Mummy, he did have that long affair with Alexandra, didn't he?"

Maria blushed. "He did, and I never understood why."

"Well, it was because they were always together," said Antonio. "She ran his office in New York, and they often traveled together. He was dependent on her. Also, she was Russian, or Ukrainian, and they had that in common."

Maria blurted out, "She was, she is, a very selfish young woman. I don't want to talk about her, if you don't mind."

Stone nodded sympathetically. "Maria, I understand. Just one question though. Do you think Alexandra was deeply involved in his financial affairs, professional and personal?"

"I do. She is a young woman, young enough to be his daughter. She is impressionable, and he would have found it easy to get her to do what he wanted. He could be very persuasive, and she fell for him hook, line and sinker."

Stone then said, "I want to change the subject, if I may. Maria. What can you tell me about Lord Jaeger?"

"Very little. I think I must have met him before, but I can't remember exactly when. We were together in the theater for "Eugene Onegin" last Thursday, and when the performance was stopped I went backstage with him."

"Who asked you?"

"Lord Jaeger did. He was very kind. He looked after me, and then he offered to bring me back here. I really didn't want to go back to my room at The

Park Lane, on my own. I was a bit in shock, I think."

Stone leaned forward. "Do you know much about him, Maria?"

Maria looked embarrassed. "I don't, I have to say."

Antonio then put his hand on Maria's. "Mom, I think you've got to be a bit careful with that guy. I didn't like the way he responded to the questioning from the detective just now."

"I agree. Your son is absolutely right, Maria," said Stone. "I would counsel you not to have anything to do with him, at least for the time being, until the inquiry is over."

"But he has offered to stand by me and he is going to help me find an attorney here. I agreed that he would to that."

Stone raised his voice. "As I say, Maria, keep your distance from him, for now."

*

Lord Jaeger was escorted to Scotland Yard, and Roberts asked him to take a seat in his office. Bartholomew joined them.

Roberts was pleased that Stone had come up with the idea to take Jaeger by surprise. It was an obvious ploy, but clever. It had enabled him to get Jaeger in for questioning, and put him under pressure. Perhaps things were looking up.

Roberts sat behind his own desk. "Lord Jaeger, I regret to tell you that we are still not satisfied with the explanation you have given us for the interference with the crime scene at the Royal Opera House."

"I am sorry, but I have told you all I know."

Roberts shook his head. "That is not good enough. How do you account for the fact that a bullet was removed from the screen that was in the conductor's dressing room? The bullet that we believe killed Petya Gubin."

"I can't. I have no idea about that."

"Lord Jaeger, I put it to you that you do know, and that you are being evasive."

Jaeger chuckled. "You may think that, Inspector, but you are wrong."

Roberts now became angry. "I do not think I am wrong. You are lying, Lord Jaeger!"

"I have had enough of this. I am not prepared to continue without my lawyer present."

"Lord Jaeger, it would be much easier for you, for everybody, if you just told us the facts."

"I am saying nothing more, nothing at all, unless I have my lawyer here. And I want you to know I shall be speaking to The Commissioner about this. He is a personal friend of mine. I have several good friends in the Home Office, in fact."

Roberts halted the questioning. He thought for a moment, and then asked Bartholomew to join him outside for a private word. He said, "This is a member of the House of Lords we're dealing with here. We have to be cautious. And he may well know The Commissioner. I wouldn't be at all surprised. I think we should either release him and put him under close surveillance, or allow him to bring in his lawyer, and continue with the questioning. What do you think, Terry?"

Bartholomew was taken aback to be asked for advice by Roberts. He was flattered. He thought carefully for a moment, and then said, "What evidence do you have to back this up, Sir? Are you sure that Lord Jaeger did this himself, or did others remove the dressing room items, and the bullet from the screen?"

"I don't know, Terry, that's the problem. We haven't yet interrogated the other staff at the opera house about that. We must do so. The Head of Security, and all the stage workers who have access to that storage area."

"In that case, Sir, I think we should let him go. Have him closely watched, and then bring him back in, but not until we have conducted further inquiries at the opera house and interviewed everybody in question. He can bring his lawyer with him then, if he wants."

"Terry, I agree. That's a good compromise. But I want the very best surveillance, mind you. Monitoring of phones, staking out his suite at the Dorchester, his home, everything. I don't want any mistakes, Terry."

"Very good, Sir. But it will take some doing. Tapping the phone at the opera house may be difficult, unless he has his own line. And it is Sunday, Sir. It will take time to set it all up."

"Do it, Terry. As fast as you can."

"Yes, Sir."

"Don't let him go without taking a statement. Take him to your office."

"But he may refuse. He will say he won't do that without his lawyer present."

"So be it. But don't let him go for an hour or two. Give yourself time to get the surveillance orders into place."

Chapter 62

Quentin and Alex arrived at Leo's apartment. It was two in the afternoon.

Quentin put his arm round Alex's shoulder as Leo answered the door.

"Come in," he said, not looking at either of them.

He invited them into the living room, and indicated to the sofa for them to sit down. Alexandra declined, sitting in an armchair. Quentin sat on the floor beside her. Leo sat on the sofa.

Alex spoke first. "Did you get rid of the CD?"

"Yes. It's gone, replied Leo."

"Good. Leo, we have to sort out the money arrangements, now. Quentin knows everything, by the way, so we can speak freely."

"OK. Yes, I agree. I am under a lot of pressure to get the funds transferred."

Alex said, "The funds have to go back to the Anisimov Foundation. Petya said as much on Thursday."

"No! That's a lie, Alex! Petya and others went to a lot of trouble to set this up, and much depends on it. We both know that."

Alex shook her head. "We have to do what Petya would have done if he was still here. He wouldn't have gone through with this if it was too risky, and it is too dangerous. He said something to me about it getting too hot, on Thursday, as a matter of fact. And the police are all over this, Leo."

Leo was getting angry. "That's bloody nonsense. He gave you the CD and he didn't say anything to me about aborting. If he was thinking about changing his mind, he would have told me."

Alex shook her head again. "Not necessarily. He could well have said to others that he was having reservations about the timing, as he did to me, especially if he knew the FBI was making inquiries."

Quentin interrupted. "I think you may have hit on a possible motive for Petya's murder. Perhaps he was killed because he did indicate to others that he wanted to cancel, or delay, and they knew that with him out of the way, everything could still go ahead. The money was already in Alex's bank accounts, and all set to be transferred."

"That does make sense, I have to admit, but it's only a theory," said Leo. He continued, "But even if, and it's a big if, that theory is correct, you and I are still safe, Alex. We're necessary to the whole operation, because we're the signatories on the accounts."

Quentin shook his head vigorously. Looking at Alex, he said, "You're only necessary until you get the money transferred. After that you're both dispensable, in fact a huge exposure as far as the people who are behind this are concerned. You know far too much. So you're at risk whether the funds are transferred or they go back to the foundation in New York, either way."

Alex was shivering with fright. "God, that's right," she said. "Leo, we can't go through with the transfers. The money has to go back to New York. We have to get out of this. And find a way of staying safe ourselves."

Quentin continued, now looking at Leo. "Here's what you can do. Agree to transfer the funds back to the foundation, and in the meantime ask for police protection. If the police, and the FBI, think they can get to the people who are behind all this, with your help, surely they will be pleased to give you, both of you, a measure of security. They will do that, won't they?"

"I don't think we should go to the police," Leo said.

"I already have," said Alex.

"You've what?"

"I told Roberts that I was going to wire the funds back to the foundation. The police know that's what I want to do."

"And they also know we're round here with you, right now, Leo," added Quentin.

Alex got up and leaned over Leo. "So you, see, we have no choice."

"And you have to do this tomorrow morning, as soon as the banks open," said Quentin. "I recommend that after that, you both go to see Roberts, together."

Leo felt cornered. He was half convinced that Alex and Quentin were right, but he was scared of what might happen to him. He felt he was in a catch twenty-two situation. After a long silence, he said, "You've set me up. I'll have to think about it. I don't know."

"Let's meet early in the morning, at the bank in Berkeley Square, near the office," Alex suggested. "We can do the wires from there."

Leo said nothing for a moment. Then he sighed, and leaning back on the sofa, with his hands clasped behind his head, whispered. "OK, I guess."

"Good, that's great," Alex said. But then she suddenly thought of the break-in to her apartment and the subsequent police visit. "Leo, bring the details of the bank accounts with you, and the amounts we have to transfer, assuming you still have your copies. Mine were all taken from the apartment. You do have yours, don't you?"

"Yes, of course I do. They are in my safe, at least they were in my safe. Before."

"Why? What's the problem?"

"The safe was blown. I didn't tell you. The CD was taken. All my documents were taken as well."

"What? Who blew the safe?" asked Quentin.

"I think it was the people I was supposed to hand the CD over to in the first place. I was at Scotland Yard at the time."

"Who else has copies of the documents?" asked Quentin.

"No one, except the CID," said Alex. "I'll have to call Roberts later and get the details from him. I hope he has them. Leo, be there tomorrow."

*

Quentin then escorted Alex back to her apartment. "It's a worry about Leo's safe being blown, but otherwise that went well," he said.

"Yes. Quentin, don't forget you've got to write your piece for the paper. It's supposed to be in by tonight, isn't it?"

"Oh, you're right! I had forgotten all about it. Well that will take care of the rest of the afternoon."

"I don't have the computer. The police took it."

"I'll just have to write it out in longhand, and then I'll fax it in," he said.

Chapter 63

Lord Jaeger returned to his suite in The Dorchester. He thought about the explanation he would give Maria.

He saw the hand-written note that had been left on the table by the door.

The note read, "Dear Ben, I have decided to go back to The Park Lane hotel with the children. I will be staying there, with them, for the time being. They need me to be with them. Thank you for everything. Fond regards, Maria."

He went into the bedroom, and noticed that she had removed all her clothes and other possessions. The cases were gone, everything. "Blast the stupid woman," he said out loud.

He poured himself a large whiskey and soda.

Chapter 64

MONDAY

Alexandra woke up early, and made a cooked breakfast for Quentin. She had called Roberts the previous evening. He had the relevant papers to hand and he gave her the bank details she wanted. It occurred to her that it was indicative of the pressurized and dangerous situation they were in, that all these break-ins had taken place. She would be pleased to put the whole business behind her.

The telephone rang. "Roberts, here, Alexandra. How are you this morning?"

"Well, thank you."

"I just wanted to get your confirmation that you are wiring the funds back to the foundation today."

"Yes. I am going ahead with it. I am hoping that Leo Connell and I can meet with you, after we've finished at the bank. Will that be convenient?"

"Yes, of course. I'll see you then."

Quentin was helping Alex to wash the breakfast dishes in the kitchen. "Do you think you should call Leo now, just to make sure?"

She dialled Leo's number. "Hi Leo. Is everything OK for this morning?"

"What's that?"

"You'll be at the bank, right? At ten?"

"I guess so. Bye."

After Alex had replaced the receiver, Quentin asked, "Does he still agree to do it?"

"Yes, I think so," said Alex. "He's obviously not certain though."

Chapter 65

Roberts called DI Bartholomew into his office.

"Terry, is the surveillance in place for Jaeger?"

"Yes, Sir. And we have a tap on his direct line at the opera house."

"Good. I reviewed your reports by the way. There are some lessons to be learned there, Terry, key lessons."

"Yes, Sir."

"I am expecting Alexandra Matviyko, together with Connell, at around eleven o'clock this morning. Would you make yourself available? I want you to put out an APB on Bryce. We will need to give Alexandra some time with an artist, and then I want you to ask the stage door keeper at the opera house to verify it. Then I want to give the Deputy Commissioner an update."

"Yes, Sir."

"By the way, you can redeploy the surveillance officers from Baker Street and Oakley Street now, Terry, especially if you want to use them for Jaeger. I don't think we need to maintain surveillance with Connell and Matviyko any longer, now that they are keeping us informed of their activities." He corrected himself, "I should say, now that Miss Matviyko is keeping us informed."

Roberts' telephone rang. "Good morning, Toby. Franklin Stone here. Let me have a short report on your interrogation of Jaeger, will you? You detained him, I assume?"

"No, we didn't. We had to let him go. He wanted his lawyer here, and quite frankly we weren't getting anywhere. We have heightened surveillance on him, and we are obtaining detailed statements from individuals at the opera house. Jaeger says he's a friend of the Police Commissioner, so we have to be prudent."

"I agree, Toby, how far have you got with your inquiries with Alexandra Matviyko?"

"She has decided to return the funds to the foundation. She has Leo Connell's agreement, she thinks, and they are going to the bank together this morning. Also, she has given us a description of Bryce, whom we believe is the man at the opera house on Thursday night. He broke into her flat, and threatened her, on Saturday afternoon. I think Alexandra and Leo Connell will ask us for some security, some measure of police protection."

"Well, I am sure you can arrange that. That's all good news. Excellent. By the way, if Jaeger is a buddy of The Commissioner's, shouldn't you give your boss, his Deputy, the heads up?"

"Yes, I will be meeting with the Deputy Commissioner later this morning."

"Good. Make certain you keep me in the loop, Toby. I'll probably join you for that meeting."

Chapter 66

Alexandra and Quentin arrived at the bank in Berkeley Square at ten o'clock. Leo Connell joined them shortly afterwards

They met with the Assistant Manager, and Alexandra advised him that she wanted to make a number of urgent transfers of funds from certain banks overseas, and that she and Leo Connell as her co-signatory would sign the documents. The Assistant Manager said that he would be pleased to fax signed authorizations to the banks requesting that the wire payments be executed immediately. He cautioned that they should allow for time differences, and that funds might not be in the New York account for at least three to four working days, maybe longer.

Alexandra gave the Assistant Manager the details of the bank accounts and the amounts that she had obtained from Roberts. The documents were prepared, and then signed, by both Alexandra and Leo. Photostat copies were handed to each of them.

Standing outside the bank, Alexandra said, "Leo, shall we go over to Scotland Yard now?"

Leo said, "I have some business to attend to first. I'll meet you there in an hour. See you then, OK?"

"See you there," said Alexandra, as she and Quentin set off for Scotland Yard.

They arrived just before eleven, and were escorted to Roberts' office.

Roberts welcomed them and invited them to sit down. Alexandra advised Roberts of what had transpired at the bank, and she said that Leo Connell was expected shortly.

Roberts asked to see copies of the signed authorizations, which she gave him.

Roberts said he had an important meeting with the Deputy Commissioner, and that he would have to leave them shortly. He invited Alexandra to work with the artist on a description of Bryce. He requested that after the sketch was completed, she and Quentin should wait in the outer office, until Leo Connell arrived.

As they were leaving Roberts' office, Franklin Stone approached. "Ah, I was looking for you, Toby. Are you on your way to see John Lanning now?"

"Yes, very soon."

"And who is this?" Stone asked, looking at Alexandra.

"Mr. Stone, this is Alexandra Matviyko, and this is Quentin Dart. As you know, they are assisting us in the Gubin case." They each shook hands with Stone.

"Good to meet you," said Stone.

Quentin noticed Stone's American accent. "And what are you doing in these parts, if I may ask?"

"I am with the FBI, in Washington."

"Really," said Alex, "in what position?"

"Counter-Terrorism. Taking care of a few nuts and bolts, that's all," Stone joked. "Nice to meet you both. We should sit down and have a chat some time soon."

Roberts then left them in the hands of his secretary. Alexandra spent twenty minutes with the artist, and they were then escorted to the waiting room.

*

The Deputy Commissioner invited Roberts into his office, together with Franklin Stone and DI Bartholomew. They sat at the conference table. "Frank, I hope my office was to your liking. You were here over the weekend, I am told."

"Yes, everything was fine, John. Thank you. Incidentally, I have just met two of our protagonists. Alexandra Matviyko and her friend Quentin Dart."

"Really," said Lanning, "and what are they doing here?"

Stone and Roberts then briefed the Deputy Commissioner on the events of the weekend and that morning.

After asking a few questions, Lanning said, "I am extremely concerned by what you have told me regarding Lord Jaeger, Toby. I hope there won't be any difficult repercussions. I'll speak to The Commissioner as soon as I can. I am aware that Lord Jaeger and The Commissioner are connected. The Commissioner is a patron of the opera house."

Roberts then mentioned that further inquiries would be made at the opera house. "One of the remaining issues, now that the funds are being transferred back to the foundation, is to try to establish who blew Connell's safe."

"That's only a small part of it, if I may say so," said Stone. "We have a lot of work to do in getting to the intended recipients of the funds. And Toby, you should try to bring Bryce in, and establish whether he was responsible for killing Gubin, as soon as possible."

Roberts was annoyed with Stone, and he considered responding. But his mobile phone rang, interrupting his train of thought. He answered the caller in monosyllables, and then said, "Let me have a detailed description, and keep me informed." He rang off and replaced his phone in his pocket.

"That was our officer in Covent Garden, Gentlemen. He has been observing Lord Jaeger. Jaeger has just arrived at the "Orso" restaurant, in Wellington Street. He has met with an unidentified man there, and he has handed him a brown envelope. We're getting a description of the man."

*

Quentin leant over to Alexandra. They were still in the waiting room. "It's been over an hour," he said. "Leo isn't coming, is he?"

Chapter 67

Leo Connell was sitting on his sofa at home. He didn't know what to do next. He thought he had been weak to agree to the transfer of the funds back to the foundation. In addition, he was afraid that Alexandra was setting a trap for him with her proposal that they should go to Scotland Yard together. He wandered whether she remembered the events of Friday night, when he had sex with her, and if she was feeling resentful and angry towards him. If so, it would explain why she was now trying to set him up.

He was interrupted by a sound from the bedroom. Someone had come in through the French doors.

Akbar Sattar entered the living room.

"Stay there," Sattar said. "Have the funds been transferred?"

Leo went to move away. He looked terrified. "Yes."

"Give me documents to prove it."

"I don't have them. Alexandra Matviyko has them"

Sattar lifted Leo off the sofa and threw him to the floor. He took a meat cleaver from under his jacket, and held it to Leo's neck. "Where are the documents? I am supposed to get them from you."

"They are with Alexandra," Leo repeated.

Sattar ripped the jacket off Leo's shoulders, and went through the pockets. He found the copies of the faxes and the documents that Leo had brought back from the bank. He examined them for several minutes, going over the same pages repeatedly. "These say the funds are being transferred to accounts in New York," he said, accusingly

Leo stuttered, "No, you're mistaken. They ….." He struggled to get the words out. "They are being wired through a bank in New York. Everything is correct, I assure you."

"It doesn't look that way to me." Sattar then pulled a mobile phone out of his pocket, and spoke to someone in a language Leo did not recognize. He appeared to be reading from the bank documents. Leo caught the reference to New York.

Akbar Sattar then replaced the phone in his pocket. He removed his own jacket, and rolled up his shirtsleeves. He then grabbed Leo and heaved him into the kitchen. Leo's feet did not touch the ground. He shoved Leo on to a chair by the kitchen table, and pinned Leo's left wrist on the table with his left hand. Leo could not move.

Leo called out. "What are you doing? Please!"

Akbar Sattar held the cleaver in the air over Leo's left hand.

He then chopped down onto the hand, and sliced through the fingers. The tips of each of four fingers rolled across the table. Leo yelled out in agony. Blood poured from his hand.

"You now know we are serious. You will cancel the transfers. Or else you will lose a lot more than the fingers of one hand."

Akbar Sattar then wiped the cleaver on a cloth hanging over the stove, and went into the living room. He replaced his jacket, and left by the French doors.

Leo lay slumped on the kitchen table, moaning, in terrible agony.

Chapter 68

Roberts returned to his office after his meeting with the Deputy Commissioner. He had detailed a junior security officer to be deployed outside the flat in Oakley Street, and if requested, to accompany Alexandra everywhere she went, over the next seven days, or until further notice. He wrote his report for the Deputy Commissioner on his interrogations of Lord Jaeger, and he included a briefing note for The Commissioner as well. It would be John Lanning's prerogative as to what to send to The Commissioner. He delegated DI Bartholomew and DC Trenton to spend the afternoon and evening at the opera house, to get statements from all those staff with authorized access to the stage storage area. He would now have some time to work on a strategy for finding Bryce and maybe identifying Gubin's killer.

His telephone rang. It was DI Bartholomew.

"Sir, we have identification of the man Jaeger met at "Orso". We have a photo of the two men leaving the restaurant. We know who it was with Jaeger."

"Who was it?"

"He's a member of the Government Opposition front bench. It's the Shadow Foreign Secretary, Derek Grant."

"Terry, get that photograph to me pronto."

Roberts thought for a moment, then picked up his telephone, and asked his Secretary to get him the Deputy Commissioner.

The call went through quickly. "We have a development, Sir. The man Lord Jaeger was seeing at lunch was Derek Grant."

"The Shadow Foreign Secretary? The Commissioner himself will have to handle this. I'll let you know what he recommends. Thank you, Toby."

Chapter 69

Maria was having lunch with Antonio and Chloe, at The Park Lane hotel. Chloe asked Maria how she was going to deal with Lord Jaeger in the future. She said that she would be courteous but that she would try to avoid him as much as possible.

Antonio reported that he had made some preliminary inquiries about engaging a lawyer, and he said he had an appointment with Henry Walton, of Walton, Perkins and Partners, near Liverpool Street, at four o'clock. That would hopefully give him time beforehand to obtain information regarding his father's will, from New York, he said. Maria suggested he contact Detective Inspector Roberts, concerning the status of his father's body.

Antonio had purchased a mobile phone that morning, and he called Scotland Yard straight away, asking for Roberts.

Roberts told him that his father's body was still at Scotland Yard, in the police morgue, and that he would try to give Antonio and his mother an indication about a likely release date for shipping the body back to the United States as soon as possible. He advised that it might be several days, however, before he would get clearance. Roberts then asked Antonio whether he had seen his father's will.

"I have a copy of a recent will. I assume it's the latest. You presumably know that your mother, your sister, and you are all beneficiaries," Roberts said.

"No, we have no details," Antonio said. "We have been trying to find out how we might be able to obtain a copy, following Fred Ballard's death. In fact, I want to get a copy over to Walton, Perkins and Partners this afternoon. I am seeing Henry Walton at three."

Roberts said he would be pleased to help, and that he would courier a copy over to him within thirty minutes.

*

Maria asked Antonio whether he had heard from Arnie Fischer about foundation matters. "You know you're a Board Trustee, Tonio, don't you?"

Antonio shrugged, and said, "I have never received anything from Arnold Fischer. Why?"

"Oh, it's just that I recall receiving something from him recently about some grants, that's all. I never replied," she said blandly.

"Well, if he is coming over to London, we'll be able to get an update from him pretty soon," said Antonio.

*

The three of them were having coffee on the hotel patio, when the envelope from Roberts arrived.

Maria opened it, and started to read. She studied the pages for several minutes, and then said, "This is very shocking. Your father has left money to Alexandra Matviyko, and a number of other women. Quite a lot of money. The will leaves me with the properties in Paris and New York, but little else, it seems. You both get some money, and the rest goes to The Met in New York, and the foundation. Oh, and some money to Leo Connell."

She handed the document to Antonio, and he and Chloe looked through it.

Antonio was angry. "You have to contest this, Mom. This is a disgrace. You and Dad were still married and you have certain rights."

"Maybe." Maria stifled a tear.

"Are there any insurance policies?" asked Chloe.

"I'm not sure," said Maria. "I think so. We'll have to find out."

Antonio said, "With Fred Ballard's death, there is no executor. I didn't see any provision in the will for an alternate. So that's an issue straight away.

Then the police inquiry could make a difference too, if it's found that something illegal was going on."

Maria had now started to sob. "This is all very unpleasant. I'm so sorry, for both of you, that we have to deal with this."

Antonio said, "Why don't we ask Franklin Stone to advise us?"

Chloe nodded. "That is a good idea. Let's all go and see Henry Walton together, and see what he says. Then we can go to Stone. Great, we have a plan. Cheer up, team! Mom, that's good isn't it?"

Chapter 70

Quentin and Alexandra returned to her apartment in Oakley Street. They were concerned that Leo hadn't turned up at Scotland Yard.

Alex rang Leo's numbers, but there were no replies.

Quentin suggested to Alex that they now booked her ticket for the flight to New York. She readily agreed. Quentin telephoned British Airways to get another seat for Alex on the same flight as his, but it was full. He then rang several other airlines but there was no availability for Thursday. "It is the height of the season, after all," Alex said.

"Any reason why we shouldn't try for Wednesday, instead?" Quentin suggested.

This time he was luckier, and he managed to book two business class seats on Virgin Atlantic, leaving Heathrow at eleven thirty, Wednesday morning.

Alex felt happier. Although she was grateful to Scotland Yard for providing a security officer, she still felt she was at risk, and that in New York she would be safe.

"We should tell Roberts we're leaving Wednesday," said Quentin. "Let's leave it until the last moment, though. I don't know why, but I think that might be wiser."

Quentin then went into the kitchen. Without looking at Alex, who was still in the living room, he said, "Shall we take Dominique up on her offer to stay at her apartment in Manhattan?"

"No, I'd rather not," was the prompt reply.

Quentin was disappointed, but nevertheless relieved that he and Alex had re-established their relationship. He still felt betrayed by her, but he believed there was compensation in the fact that she would surely be true to him in the future. There could not possibly be any further disclosures about her past life. And she was going to New York with him. He felt the happiest that he had been for several days.

His mind went back to the events of the previous Thursday, when Alex had left him to go back stage, to see Petya Gubin. He suddenly remembered the conversation he had overheard in the toilets, when he was changing.

He said, "Shit, I've suddenly thought of something that may be important."

Quentin recounted what he had heard. Alex listened closely.

"You have to tell Roberts."

"OK. I'll call him shortly. He's becoming quite a chum, isn't he!"

Chapter 71

Leo Connell hailed a taxi in Baker Street and asked to be taken to St. George's Hospital, Casualty Department.

He was still bleeding when he arrived. He had wrapped his left hand in a clean dishcloth, which was now soaked in blood. He had put his four severed fingertips in a white handkerchief, which he had carefully placed in his pocket.

Soon after being admitted to Casualty, he was interrogated by the duty doctor about his injuries. He said that he had suffered the accident while making a meat stew. He had chopped his own fingers off. The hospital appeared to accept the explanation.

The doctor told him that it was too late to attempt any remedial procedures. He would have to accept the fact that he had lost his fingers permanently.

He was admitted for minor surgery, and his wounds were then stitched and dressed, and he was given antibiotics. He was told he would be detained in the hospital for twenty-four hours. He was asked for details of next of kin. He declined. He was told that it was a policy that someone had to be contacted about his admission into hospital. It could be either a relative or a friend. Leo gave the hospital Rebecca Stein's name and telephone number, which had been disconnected when she had died.

As he settled into the hospital bed, he wept profusely.

Part 2

Chapter 72

WEDNESDAY

The weather in London had turned, and there was a chill in the early morning air as the United Airlines Airbus landed at Heathrow.

Arnold Fischer was relieved to have been told by the FBI that he was now free to travel to England. The condition was that he would only be permitted to stay for a week. But that would give him enough time, he thought.

His plan was to make contact with Alexandra Matviyko that morning, and then see Leo Connell. He would also meet with Maria Gubin as soon as he could.

He had told Marcia Segarra that he would check in with her from time to time, so that she and Martin Schaeffer would know where he was, and he had promised the FBI that he would do likewise.

Arnold was temporarily detained in the Terminal Three arrivals area while immigration officials checked his passport, into which the FBI had stapled an official note. It stated, "Arnold Fischer cleared to travel to UK July 1st, and to remain max. 7 days."

As he exited the airport building, and went to the taxi line, he felt that he was being followed.

*

Quentin and Alexandra had packed the night before.

They had an early breakfast, and ordered a taxi to pick them up in Oakley Street, in time to arrive at Heathrow, Terminal Three, by nine fifteen. As they got into the taxi outside the apartment, Quentin noticed the security officer standing just by the stoop. He called to him, "We're just getting a taxi, as you see. We're taking some of my things over to Wapping, to my flat. Miss Matviyko will be back shortly."

As the taxi driver turned into the Embankment at the end of Oakley Street, Alex said, "You're quite a good fibber, aren't you, Quentin. I shall have to watch you." She kissed him on the cheek.

*

Quentin and Alexandra were browsing in the Terminal Three duty free hall just as Arnold Fischer emerged from the baggage claim area in the arrivals hall one floor below, just a few hundred feet away.

Alex said, "I think it's time to call Roberts."

Quentin looked at his watch. "Let's leave it until we are at the gate, or even when we're on the plane. I don't want him trying to stop us for any reason."

They walked to the departure gate and sat in the lounge, waiting for first and business class passengers to be called for the flight. Quentin had bought a copy of The Times, and he started to read it. His eye went to a photo-fit picture on the front page. It was an artist's impression of a man wanted by Scotland Yard. He recognized the face as being that of the intruder Alex had described to the police.

The short caption mentioned that the man was wanted for questioning in connection with the death of Petya Gubin.

Quentin decided not to show the newspaper to Alex. He was determined that she would enjoy the trip to New York as much as possible, free from the stresses and pressures of the last few days.

The flight was called at ten forty-five, and they found their seats. Quentin then rang Roberts on his mobile phone.

"Good morning, Superintendent Roberts, Quentin Dart here."

"Good morning to you," said Roberts. "How are you and Alexandra today? I was wondering why I hadn't heard from you yesterday."

"We have been busy. As a matter of fact, we will be away for the next three weeks. We wanted to let you know that we are going to New York. I am covering the Lincoln Center Festival there, for The Times. Alex is traveling with me. In fact we're on our way right now."

Roberts expressed surprise. "Really? Why didn't you mention this to me before? I'm not sure that I am happy about this."

"I must apologize. Also, I'm afraid I lied to the security officer who was outside Alex's flat this morning. I told him we were going to my flat in Wapping."

"Why did you do that?"

"We didn't want you to know we were leaving the country, at least not until we got to the airport. It's very important to us that we get away for a while. Alexandra needs the break. Is that a problem?" asked Quentin.

Roberts hesitated, then said, "I might require you, or more likely Alexandra, for the purposes of identifying Bryce, if we bring him in. And I'm sure there will be other developments for which we will want Alexandra to be in London."

"I understand," said Quentin. "But we really have to do this. We'll call you regularly and let you know where we are, at all times. I am sure the police in New York can help if there is a requirement for Alex to look at any paperwork, or identify someone."

"That may be a little awkward to arrange, but so be it. Very well. Thank you for advising me. Please let me know where you will be staying."

"We will be at The Plaza hotel, by Central Park, Superintendent. Thank you for everything. By the way, I assume you will now ask the security officer at Alex's apartment to stand down."

"I'll think about that. Did the entrance door get repaired, Mr. Dart?"

"Yes, it's all secure. Locked up."

"Please give Alexandra my best wishes, and say I hope she has an enjoyable trip. Good bye."

Alex smiled and hugged Quentin. "You're getting to be quite the expert. You handled that beautifully. Thank you, darling."

Chapter 73

Leo Connell was feeling drowsy from the painkillers. He had been detained by the hospital an extra day, due to the possibility of an infection, but he had been allowed to go home that morning.

He had to speak to Alexandra. The wire transfers had to be stopped, or reversed, if it was too late to abort. She would understand, he thought. He would show her what they had done to him, and she would be too terrified to refuse.

He called her number. There was no answer and so he left a voicemail message for her to contact him, saying, "Leo here. Something terrible has happened to me. We need to talk. Please ring me as soon as you get this message."

He then left to go to his office.

*

Akbar Sattar sat in his room at The Embassy. He picked up the phone, and dialled.

"Do you have any new instructions for me?" he asked.

"Where is Connell?"

"Still in the hospital, I think. He was there last night."

"Are the police still guarding the girl?"

"Yes."

"When Connell is released by the hospital, go and see him again. You also have to find a way to get to the girl. That's critical. You have to scare the shit out of her. If you can't find her, get to her through her boyfriend. He works at The Times newspaper. His name is Quentin Dart. Don't delay. The funds are needed this week. We cannot wait."

"Anything else?"

"Yes. Don't make any mistakes. And move out of the hotel. I understand your face is all over the British papers this morning."

Chapter 74

Arnold got out of the taxi at The Park Lane hotel, where Marcie had suggested he should stay. He checked in at the desk.

As he was walking towards the lift, he noticed that the man who had been following him at the airport was again immediately behind him. The man spoke as they entered the lift.

"Mr. Fischer?"

"Yes."

"FBI," said the man, showing his ID. "Mr. Stone would like to see you this afternoon, at two o'clock. Here at the hotel. Please be in the lobby at that time."

Arnold was not surprised that the FBI was tracking him so closely. But he was a little taken aback that Stone was in London. He went to his room, and unpacked.

He then called Leo Connell's office number. Leo answered.

"Hello, Leo. Arnold Fischer here. How are you?"

"Not good. I am not good at all, in fact. Why are you calling me? What do you want? It's early for you, isn't it?"

"I'm in London. At The Park Lane hotel. Can we meet today? I also want to see Alexandra. Do you know how I can contact her?"

"I would like to know where she is myself. She's not answering her phone. When do you want to meet?"

"I'll come to your office, this afternoon, around three. Is that OK?"

"Yes. I'll keep trying Alex in the meantime."

Chapter 75

Alexandra had slept a little. They were now over Ireland and setting out over the Atlantic Ocean, as they started their lunch.

They talked about what they would do in New York. They would be staying at The Plaza, on the corner of Central Park South and Fifth Avenue. Quentin had made the reservation at The Plaza because he wanted Alex to be as comfortable as possible. She deserved a bit of luxury, he thought. And The Times would pick up the bill, he said to himself, smiling.

The Guggenheim Museum was a "must-do" as far as Alex was concerned. Quentin wanted to see some new movies, and spend some time in Central Park, just relaxing. They agreed to do everything together, and not to overtax themselves.

Quentin said he would call The Lincoln Center soon after they arrived to make certain that reservations had been made for him for the various festival performances. He said there were at least ten concerts, an opera and two ballets that he would have to cover, with some performances at The Metropolitan Opera House. "You'll be OK with that, won't you, darling?"

"Sure," she said. "I love The Met. I used to spend a lot of my time there, before I worked for Petya." She immediately regretted saying this, and anticipated that Quentin would query it. He did.

"But I thought you went to New York to work for him. That's why you left Kiev, isn't that right?"

"It wasn't quite like that. There was a period of a year or so while I had to wait for a visa. So I didn't work for him until afterwards."

"How did you manage, financially, during that year?"

"Well, I had some money."

"Did Petya support you?"

"Er …Yes, he did, to some extent."

"Let me get this straight, Alex. He was supporting you when you arrived. So you were already involved with him at that time, right?"

"Quentin, it really doesn't matter now, and I don't want to talk about it."

"OK, but tell me one thing. How did you meet him? You never told me that."

"It's not a very nice story."

"But Alex, we said we would not have any secrets from each other. Just tell me how you met. I want to know. I'm curious."

"You don't want to know."

"What do you mean, I don't want to know? I do."

"You don't Quentin. You really don't."

"Why, what have you got to hide? Do you have some other dark secret, something I still don't know about? Tell me, please."

Alex stared at the back of the seat in front of her. She thought about whether she should tell him. He would be horrified. On the other hand, he had been so wonderfully understanding about all the other revelations. Maybe she should tell him. Maybe it wasn't such a bad thing to do.

She said, "If I do tell you, I'll have to tell you the full story. I'll have to explain things from the beginning." He nodded in agreement.

Alex then recounted the events that led to her first meeting with Petya Gubin. She held on to Quentin's hand as she did so, never letting go.

Alexandra had been raised by her grandparents in Nezhin, near Kiev. Her father had deserted her mother when she was young, and her mother could not afford to keep her, so her mother's parents had come to her rescue. She lived with her grandparents until she left school, at the age of sixteen. She had lost contact with her mother during that time, because she had remarried and had gone to live in Moscow with her new husband. Alex said she did not attempt any reconciliation with her mother, at any time.

Alex had never been particularly happy at home with her grandparents. By the time she was fourteen, she looked for opportunities to go out at night, dancing, and spending time in bars with friends. There were a few young men in her life, and although she was liberal, and would experiment and sleep with them from time to time, she was not involved with any of them seriously. Her grandparents did not fully understand how to deal with this determined, sometimes petulant, young girl, and they tried to keep her at home as much as they could. But Alex defied them.

When Alex was due to leave high school, she persuaded her grandparents to pay for her to study in Kiev. She had learnt French and English at school in Nezhin, and she had a natural flair for languages.

She had been optimistic about getting into university in Kiev at first. She had dreams of becoming a linguist, perhaps an interpreter. She wanted to travel to other parts of the world, and she thought that knowing languages would be a passport to the fulfilment of her dreams.

But soon after arriving in Kiev, she became involved with an older man, whom she had met at a nightclub. He was a soldier who was stationed in barracks near Kiev. His name was Yevgeny. They became lovers, and she moved into an apartment with him, after just one month. He promised to support her financially.

Yevgeny turned out to be rotten to the core. He was dealing in drugs, and he had a number of friends and acquaintances who were involved in narcotics and prostitution. Yevgeny introduced Alex to drugs, and she quickly became addicted to heroin.

Alex said she had been totally seduced by Yevgeny, and that she only realized her terrible mistake when it was already too late. By then she had become dependent on Yevgeny in every way, and for the supply of drugs in particular.

Yevgeny often forced her to have sex with other men, and he paid her fifty percent of what he received from them. She then discovered that he had a group of five other girls who were working for him in the same way.

She had become a prostitute, and was a drug user. She was at an all-time low.

Alex said that at that moment in her life, she hated herself. She could not go back to her grandparents in Nezhin, and she considered suicide.
Then one night she was at a club, and she was approached by a tall, distinguished looking, older man, who invited her to join him for a drink. It was Petya Gubin. He was in Kiev to conduct a series of concerts.

Petya did not know about her drug dependency at first, although she did tell him later, she said. She slept with him that night, at his hotel, and he invited her to the concert hall the following morning, to see a full orchestra rehearsal.

They had lunch together, and she went back to his hotel with him that afternoon. She then told him about her situation, and how she wanted to get away from Yevgeny. She said she was afraid that he would harm her, particularly when he discovered that she was spending time with Petya.

Petya asked Alex to stay with him at his hotel while he was in Kiev, and he bought her some clothes and other essentials. She never returned to Yevgeny.

When it was time for Petya to leave Kiev, he asked Alex to go with him to the United States. The lure of his music world, the prominent position he had as a conductor, and the opportunity to leave her life in Kiev behind was too much to resist. She did not hesitate.

Maria and the children were in Paris when she and Petya arrived in New York, and for two weeks Alex stayed with him in the Gubin family apartment in Manhattan. Then he found her an apartment of her own. He helped her to get over her drug dependency.

She undertook some work for him occasionally, on an unofficial basis, and he gave her a monthly allowance.

When her work visa eventually came through, after a year, she was appointed as Petya Gubin's Personal Assistant, and she worked in his office, at The Met.

"So you see, I owe him a lot," Alex said.

Quentin was silent. He was shocked. Deeply shocked. But Alex had told the story from the heart. And he sympathized with her in her predicament as a young girl in Kiev. He thought it was not surprising at all that Petya had made such an impact on her, and that her loyalty to him had survived the subsequent years of suspicion she must have had about his undercover activities.

He leant over and kissed her on the side of her neck. "I'm so sorry you had to suffer so much."

Alex burst into tears.

Chapter 76

Franklin Stone arrived at The Park Lane hotel, and quickly found Arnold Fischer, in the lobby. He suggested that they adjourned to the bar nearby.

"So, what are your plans while you are here, Mr. Fischer?" asked Stone.

"I'm hoping to see Alexandra Matviyko, and Leo Connell. I must also meet with Maria Gubin."

"Alexandra and Quentin Dart left for New York this morning."

"What?"

"I'm afraid so. Also, we seem to have lost track of Mr. Connell. He hasn't been seen since Monday."

"I don't understand that. I spoke to him at his office, earlier," Arnold said. "In fact, I have arranged to go over there this afternoon, at three o'clock."

"Really? I wanted to meet with you again, Mr. Fischer, to tell you that Alexandra Matviyko and Leo Connell transferred funds back to the foundation, on Monday. Six million dollars, from a number of bank accounts. The funds should be in the foundation bank by the end of the week. I have this on good authority from Scotland Yard. The FBI and the CID here have been working together on this. We will meet with you again in New York to discuss the affairs of the foundation, after you return."

Arnold Fischer let out an audible sigh of relief. "Thank God," he said. "I think that is the best news I could possibly have expected. Who can give me written confirmation of this?"

"Scotland Yard. Also I agree you should go and meet with Connell, but not at three o'clock. Perhaps later. You should call him and postpone the meeting. The reason is that I want you to join me with Mrs. Gubin and her two children first, and I have already arranged to meet them, here, also at three."

"I see. Well, I guess that's OK."

"Mr. Fischer, call Connell back now, if you would. I will call the CID. I want to alert them that Mr. Connell has reappeared. Shall we meet here again, say in thirty minutes?"

*

Maria Gubin, Antonio and Chloe had spent the morning with Henry Walton, their new lawyer, and then they met with Detective Superintendent Roberts. With Walton representing them, they tried to get authorization from the police to take Petya Gubin's body back to New York, but it was proving to be difficult.

Henry Walton reviewed the will, and advised Maria that she would need to appoint someone in the United States with a Power of Attorney, to administer Petya Gubin's estate. She would also have to file in the States to contest the will, and an attorney in New York would have to handle that for her.

She was feeling that this would all be too difficult to handle, and she wondered whether Antonio would have sufficient time to help.

Maria waited in the hotel lobby as arranged, together with Antonio and Chloe.

Franklin Stone arrived, and Arnold Fischer joined them shortly afterwards.

The group sat in the small patio lounge, and ordered coffee.

Arnold mentioned the concern he had about the foundation funds being in limbo, in spite of Stone's earlier reassurances. He said he was praying that by the weekend the wire transfers would be completed and that the funds would be safely returned to the foundation's bank. Antonio asked him to explain what these funds were.

"They were grants from the foundation and other sources to various holding accounts in Alexandra Matviyko's name, as requested by your father," he said. "The funds were to have been forwarded to certain overseas accounts over the next twelve months, but your father requested that in the event of his death those funds should be wired immediately to those overseas accounts as a single lump sum. Nevertheless, Alexandra and Leo Connell apparently signed papers earlier this week to transfer the funds back to the foundation. In my view that was the correct thing to do."

"What were the grants supposed to be for?" asked Antonio.

"I cannot say," said Arnold. "It's probably best you don't ask."

"But I'm a trustee of the foundation, aren't I?" asked Antonio.

"Yes. You are. And so is your mother, as well as Fred Ballard, his brother and myself. There were six of us, including Petya, and now there are four."

"Then I am entitled to know what the grants were for," Antonio repeated.

"Well, that is not as easy as you might think. There isn't a full paper trail on that. But in a way it's now academic, Antonio, because the funds are being returned."

Antonio persisted. "I would still like to know what the funds were for, and whether they were linked to my father's death in any way. I have a right to know."

Stone interjected. "Yes you do," he said. "But until the investigation has progressed further I don't think we can provide you with that information."

Antonio thought for a moment. "I think I would like to meet with Alexandra, and ask her a few questions. She must know a lot."

Stone responded, "That's not a good idea, at least not for the time being. And in any case she left London for New York today. Antonio, all I can tell you is that the FBI, and the CIA, are working closely with the British CID to resolve this matter."

Antonio then asked, "Mr. Stone, what does Lord Jaeger have to do with all this?"

Stone thought for a moment, and then quietly said, "Among a number of other individuals Lord Jaeger is a person of interest in our inquiries."

"What does that mean?"

"We haven't ruled him out."

Antonio threw his hands up in the air. "I give up," he said.

Stone then turned to Arnold. "What did you and my agents find in your office over the weekend?"

"There was a lot missing."

"I'm not surprised. Let's hope that the reports back from our search of Petya Gubin's offices are more enlightening."

Antonio then asked Stone to explain what had happened in Arnold Fischer's office, and what had been going on in his father's office.

Stone gave Antonio, his mother and sister a generalized account of the FBI's work in reviewing critical documents and preparing files, as an aid to the investigation. "The IRS will also be provided with these files," he said.

Antonio, said, "We have to go back to New York, to sort this out. Mom. We're not going to get clearance on Dad's body for some time, that's obvious, and now you have to do all this legal stuff in the States. I think we're wasting our time here."

Maria said, "Let's make a decision tomorrow, after speaking with Roberts again. Then if there's no news on when Petya's body will be released, we'll go back. On Friday."

Chapter 77

Akbar Sattar had gathered from The Times office that Quentin Dart had left for New York.

He made a telephone call.

He said, "They've gone. Dart went to New York today, and he will be there three weeks. He's taken the girl with him."

"Are you sure?"

"Well, I assume she has gone with him."

"What else? Where's Connell?"

"Connell is in his office. There's someone with him. I'm waiting outside."

"We can't do anything without the girl. Leave that to me, and don't touch Connell again for now."

*

It was eleven-thirty in the morning in New York.

Mark Novelli received a call on his cell phone.

"Alexandra Matviyko is on the Virgin flight from London. It gets in to JFK at two thirty. You should find her as soon as you can. Quentin Dart is with her."

Chapter 78

The rest of the flight had been uneventful. Alexandra had slept some more, and Quentin had dosed intermittently, but he had been thinking about Alex's life in the Ukraine. As he looked at Alex's profile in the seat beside him, he wondered how she still managed to look so lovely.

They were through immigration and baggage claim in less than an hour, and they got a cab into Manhattan.

At four thirty they checked in to The Plaza and were soon unpacking their bags in their room overlooking Central Park.

Quentin said, "I think I'll call The Lincoln Festival office."

"OK," Alex said. "While you're doing that I'll go down to the lobby and get some things. I need some toiletries." She kissed him on the forehead, and closed the door behind her.

Quentin made a call to the Festival press office, and confirmed his seat requirements for the various performances. He asked them to be certain to reserve two seats for him for each event.

The Festival would open on Friday evening with an all Beethoven concert at Avery Fisher Hall, with The Metropolitan Opera Orchestra. Dominique Lieberman was the soloist. Then on Saturday there was "Mitridate, Re di Ponto" to be given at The Met, a rare early Mozart opera to be performed by a visiting company from Brussels. On Tuesday, there was to be the first performance of a new production of the ballet "Swan Lake", to be given by the Kirov Company, from St. Petersburg. Quentin asked the office to fax him full details of all the performances.

Quentin then thumbed through a few magazines. He looked at his watch. He had not adjusted it for the five hours time difference with London, but he quickly calculated that Alex had been gone thirty minutes already.

He wondered whether she had forgotten their room number, but if so, she would surely have asked at the reception desk. He assumed that she had got absorbed in her shopping.

A further fifteen minutes went by. He began to get concerned.

He decided to go down to the lobby to find her. He walked around the lobby and the ground floor boutiques for several minutes, but could not see her anywhere.

He phoned back to their room from the house phone in the lobby to see if she had returned. She had not.

It was now a full hour since they had checked in at the hotel.

He went round the hotel lobby once more.

He then decided to ask the reception clerks if they had seen her. He gave them a description, but they could not help. He then repeated the inquiry in each of three small boutique shops, and then finally in the pharmacy. No one had seen her. He then asked the doorman, who was standing outside the lobby.

The doorman thought he might have seen her leaving the hotel, he said.

"Was she with anyone?" asked Quentin.

"Yes, Sir, I think she was. She was escorted out of the front door by a gentleman. He had his arm round her, and then I believe they got into a cab. But I couldn't be sure that they got into it together."

Quentin's stomach turned over. "Could you describe that man to me, please? Did you get a good look at him?"

"Yes. He was of average build, well dressed, with black hair, going bald. He looked as if he might be from the Middle East."

Quentin stood rooted to the spot.

*

It was now six in the evening, equivalent to eleven at night back in London. Quentin was exhausted. He picked up the telephone in his room, and said

"911 please. Police." After a pause he said, "I wish to report a missing person."

Quentin then described the circumstances of Alex's disappearance to the NYPD officer on the line, and gave him a description. The officer said, "We will send someone over to get a statement and a full description. Do you have any photographs of the young lady?"

"Yes. When will someone be here?"

"In the morning."

"But it can't wait until then. She might be in danger."

"I am sure the young lady will turn up, my friend. They usually do. We'll be round in the morning, around nine o'clock."

Quentin could not believe what had occurred. He suddenly thought that her disappearance was probably connected to the funds that had been wired back to the foundation, and what had been happening back in London. "God, she's been kidnapped!" he said under his breath.

Chapter 79

THURSDAY

Franklin Stone met with the Deputy Commissioner and Detective Superintendent Roberts at Scotland Yard. It was ten in the morning.

Roberts gave him and Canning a detailed update on his investigation.

First, Roberts reported that Bryce had not yet been picked up. He said that Leo Connell had phoned Scotland Yard earlier that morning, to say that he had received a visit at his home on Monday from someone he thought was Bryce, based on the artist's impression published in the newspapers. Connell told him that Bryce had viciously attacked him using a meat cleaver, and that he had chopped four fingertips off his left hand.

Stone slammed his papers on the table in front of him, saying, "We're dealing with savages here. They will stop at nothing."

Roberts continued that he had told Connell that Alexandra Matviyko was now in New York, with Quentin Dart.

Roberts then mentioned the request the CID had received from Maria Gubin for the return of Gubin's body to the United States. He said a decision could not be made pending ongoing inquiries.

Roberts said that inquiries at Covent Garden had so far not yielded any further evidence or relevant information. A watch was being maintained on Lord Jaeger, and he said that his private phone was being tapped. Jaeger was probably now using a mobile phone that was not registered in his own name. Therefore it was impossible to monitor all the phone calls he was making, or receiving.

"Anything further suspicious there, Toby?" asked Lanning.

"No, Sir. Nothing at all since we observed him with Derek Grant on Monday."

The Deputy Commissioner said, "The possible Grant connection is a very sensitive matter, gentlemen. Unless and until we are sure that the envelope Lord Jaeger handed to Grant contained some relevant and incriminating material, I am not prepared to pursue that particular line of inquiry. However, there is another important issue here. Let us assume, for the sake of argument, that Lord Jaeger is implicated in this case in some way. If he is, he may try to leave the country. What are we going to do in such circumstances? Let us suppose for a moment that he decides to fly to the United States. Should we let him go, and then put a tail on him in the US, which no doubt the FBI could help us with, or should we detain him?"

"My advice is to let him move around feely," said Stone. "We're not getting anywhere, and if he decides to take off, he might become careless, in which case the surveillance will yield some useful information."

Roberts then asked the Deputy Commissioner, "Sir, did you mention Lord Jaeger to The Commissioner?"

"Yes, I did. They do know each other, but not that well."

Roberts then said, "There's only one other thing I should mention. Geoffrey Wright, the Opera Company General Director, has been away on vacation. He returns to his office tomorrow. I propose to interrogate him myself. He was, if you remember, the first person to see Gubin dead, after the initial report was made by the senior dressing room attendant, and we haven't yet taken a statement from him."

"Very good, Toby. Thank you very much," said Lanning.

Stone stood up and said, "Unless there are major new developments I plan to return to Washington this afternoon. Thank you for all your help, and I will stay in touch with you both, on a daily or as needed basis. Keep me in the loop on Jaeger's movements."

Chapter 80

Quentin slept only fitfully. When he did finally get some sleep, he dreamt that he and Alexandra were in heaven, and that Petya Gubin was there, handing out checks.

The dream woke him. He looked for his watch. It was five thirty. It was just getting light.

He called the hotel front desk to see if there had been any messages from Alex. There hadn't been.

He wondered how he could use his time before the police arrived, and he decided to call Detective Superintendent Roberts, in London.

Roberts answered the phone.

"Hello there, Superintendent Roberts. Quentin Dart here."

"Good day, Mr. Dart. How are you, and how is Alexandra?"

"Unfortunately, I have some very bad news. Alex has been abducted, I think. It happened shortly after we arrived at the hotel yesterday afternoon. She went down to the lobby to buy some toiletries, and she didn't return. The doorman thinks he saw her leave, escorted by some guy."

"My Goodness. How distressing. Do you have a description of the man? Do you really think she was taken against her will?"

"Yes, I do, Superintendent. I have a description, and I am sure she was abducted. Do you think this could be connected to what has been going on in London?"

"Quite possibly," said Roberts. "Have you seen the police there yet?"

"The NYPD are coming round to the hotel at nine."

"Well, that's good, but we might need to spread the effort to locate her, especially if it is connected with events here. I think we have to involve the FBI in this."

"What can you do to help?" Quentin asked.

Roberts said, "Let me contact Franklin Stone. He is still here but he plans to fly to Washington this afternoon. I will advise him of your phone call, and ask him what he suggests. I am sure he will contact you."

"Thank you, Mr. Roberts. Please do all you can. I am very worried about Alex's safety. Very worried indeed."

*

The NYPD officer arrived at eight forty-five. He took a statement, and Quentin gave him a description of Alexandra, and a photo of her that he had taken the previous summer, when they were on the Serpentine Lake one afternoon.

The Officer asked Quentin if Alexandra had any friends or contacts in the New York City area. He could only think of The Metropolitan Opera House, where she had worked, in Petya Gubin's office, and Dominique Lieberman. The Officer suggested he contacted them as soon as possible.

*

Quentin first called Martin Schaeffer's office at The Met. Marcia Segarra answered the phone.

He introduced himself, and then told Marcie about Alexandra being missing. He asked her if Alex had contacted her, or anyone else at The Met.

Marcie said Alex had not been in touch, but that she would mention Quentin's call to Martin Schaeffer as soon as he returned from a short business trip, the following day. In the meantime she would ask in the theater to see if anyone had seen Alex or heard from her.

"If she's been here, someone will know," said Marcie. "Everyone here remembers her well."

"Thank you," said Quentin. "I'll check back with you tomorrow. Please call me at The Plaza in the meantime if you hear anything."

*

Quentin then considered how he could contact Dominique. He suddenly remembered that he had her mobile telephone number in his own phone memory. It was a UK number. He dialled it and got an automated greeting from her that said, "I regret that I am unable to answer this call. I am in the United States. If it is urgent, please call me in New York, on 212 555 1617."

He didn't know why, but Quentin felt the first surge of optimism since Alex had disappeared. He didn't see how Dominique could possibly help, but at least hers would be a friendly voice. He called the Manhattan number. Dominique answered.

"Hi Dominique. I'm so pleased to hear your voice. It's Quentin here."

"Hello. What a nice surprise. Where are you?"

"At The Plaza. Here in New York."

"Fantastic. Are you here on your own? Or are you with Alexandra?"

"I came here with Alex yesterday. But she's missing. It's a long story. Dominique, can we meet somewhere?"

"Of course. Come over to my apartment." She gave him the address, on the corner of Third Avenue and East 72nd Street.

Quentin took the elevator downstairs to the lobby. He left a message for Alex at the front desk saying that he would be at Dominique's apartment, and he wrote down the address.

He took a cab over to the Upper East Side.

*

Stone went in to Roberts' office, to bid him farewell, and to see if there were any further developments.

Roberts told him of Quentin Dart's phone call. "We might have a ransom situation here", he said.

Stone nodded in agreement. "I'll fly in to JFK instead of Dulles. This afternoon. I'll see what I can do."

Roberts said, "I'll leave a message for Dart at The Plaza. Au revoir, Mr. Stone."

Chapter 81

Dominique changed into her favorite flowered dress. She sat at her dressing table, in her bedroom, and looked at herself in the mirror. She smiled. She put some make-up on her face, and combed her hair. She sprayed perfume on her neck.

Quentin was now downstairs, and pressing her apartment bell. "Come on up, Quentin. It's the tenth floor."

She was waiting for him by the elevator. As the doors opened she fell into his arms, and kissed him, on the mouth. A long, passionate kiss.

"Wow, that's quite a welcome," said Quentin, as he struggled for breath.

"Come in and have some coffee. You must tell me what you're doing."

While they stood in the kitchen, Quentin recounted the story of how Alexandra had disappeared. He said, "I am very worried about her. I think she may have been kidnapped."

"If she has, the kidnappers will make contact," Dominique suggested. "It is terrible, for sure. But it will be resolved. Tell me, mon cherie, how have things been between you and Alex?"

"Not good, last week especially. We were going to separate. Then on Sunday or Monday Alex decided that she would come to New York with me, and it's been fine since then."

"She has had a complicated life, Quentin. Do you know about her past?"

"Yes, I do."

Dominique then offered to make Quentin some lunch, and he readily accepted. "Can I use your phone, please? I want to find out if there are any mes-

Conducting Terror

sages at The Plaza, and see if there's any news of Alex."

"Of course."

Quentin called the hotel. There had been no sign of Alexandra. There was a message from Roberts, which he asked the hotel clerk to read to him. It said that Franklin Stone would be in New York that afternoon, and that he would contact him. He gave the clerk Dominique's address and telephone number.

"Franklin Stone is flying over from London today. He will help."

"Who is he?" asked Dominique.

"A very senior guy in the FBI."

They ate their lunch. Dominique talked about the Beethoven Violin Concerto she was playing at the opening Lincoln Center Festival concert the following night.

"I am reviewing it for The Times," Quentin said.

"You will have to give me a good write-up. What can I do to persuade you? No, I'm just kidding! But I have a serious suggestion to make. You should bring your things over, and stay here, with me. You should not be alone."

"That's very kind. Thank you. But I'm not sure I should."

"You will not regret it. I will look after you. Take care of you. Will you, please?"

Quentin was concerned about what Alex's reaction would be. He said, "Let me think about it."

"OK. Now, let's relax a little. Take off your shoes, and sit with me on the sofa."

He did, and Dominique sat next to him. She placed her hand on his knee, and she nestled her head into his chest. He relaxed, as he caught the sweet aroma of her perfume, and he felt her breasts pressing against his own body. He sensed that she desired him, but he felt that he was allowing her to get too close to him.

He said, "Dominique, I like you, and I'm very happy to be in your company, I really am, but you must back off a little, please. You're being too forward. I hope you don't mind me mentioning it."

Dominique moved away from him. "Of course. I'm sorry. I like you too, very much."

Quentin felt overwhelmingly tired, and he yawned.

"Mon cherie, you poor thing. You must be exhausted. Why don't you slip into bed and have a nap. It will do you good."

"I think I will," he said.

Dominique put her arm round his waist and guided him into the spare bedroom. He sat on the bed and started to undress. She helped him remove all his clothes, except for his boxer shorts. He got under the covers, and shut his eyes. She closed the drapes, took off her dress, and slipped into the bed beside him. He was already asleep.

Chapter 82

Arnold Fischer was in his room at The Park Lane hotel, watching television. It was ten o'clock and he was thinking of going to sleep.

He was satisfied with the way events were developing.

He had called Marcia Segarra and advised her that he was doing well, and he mentioned that he had met with Franklin Stone, together with Maria Gubin and her children.

He also said that he had met with Leo Connell that afternoon, and had been relieved to see the bank transfer documents. Marcie said she would advise Martin.

He decided to check with the foundation bank in New York the next day, to make certain that the funds had arrived.

He thought he might take a couple of days to do some sight seeing in London, before returning home.

His phone rang. "This is hotel reception. We have an urgent message for you, Mr. Fischer. We will deliver it to your room."

"Thank you." Arnold thought it might be from Maria Gubin, or maybe the FBI.

After a delay of a few minutes, a white envelope was pushed under his door.

He opened the envelope. There was a single sheet of white paper inside, folded in half. On the paper there was a note, hand-written, in capital letters.

ALEXANDRA MATVIYKO IS BEING DETAINED. SHE WILL BE RELEASED IF AND WHEN $6 MILLION IS PAID, EITHER BY THE FOUNDATION OR ANY OTHER MEANS AT YOUR DISPOSAL. FUR-

THER INSTRUCTIONS WILL BE GIVEN TO YOU TOMORROW. YOU HAVE UNTIL 5 PM MONDAY, US EST, TO PAY. MATVIYKO WILL BE SAFE, UNTIL THEN. BUT IF YOU FAIL, SHE WILL DIE. YOU HAVE ONLY 4 DAYS. THERE WILL BE NO NEGOTIATION. COOPERATE OR YOU WILL ALSO DIE

Arnold's hands shook as he read the note. He at once knew that he was in great danger. He decided that he would advise Franklin Stone, and he wondered how he should contact him. He telephoned Scotland Yard, and asked to speak to the officer dealing with the Gubin case. DI Bartholomew answered.

"This is Arnold Fischer. I am the President of the Anisimov Foundation, and I am here in London, at The Park Lane hotel. I have an emergency, and I would be grateful if you would tell me how I can contact Franklin Stone, of the FBI."

"What is the nature of the emergency, Sir?" asked Bartholomew.

"I have a received a ransom note for the return of Alexandra Matviyko."

"Stay there, Sir, and we will be round."

*

An hour later, Roberts and Bartholomew arrived at the hotel. Arnold invited them to his room, where he showed them the hand-written note he had received.

Roberts said, "We will need to take this away with us. Mr. Stone returned to the United States today. He should be in New York shortly. I will make certain that he is informed."

"Thank you," said Arnold. "What should I do?"

"Go back to New York, as soon as you can. Tomorrow. Mr. Stone or we will be in touch with you directly."

Roberts and Bartholomew left, taking the ransom note with them.

Arnold thought he should advise Maria Gubin that he would be leaving the next day. He telephoned her room, and told her. He did not mention the ransom note.

She said, "We are also returning to New York tomorrow. Why don't we all travel together? Do you have your flight confirmed?"

"No, not yet."

"Neither do we. Let's try to get on the same flight, if we can. Shall we meet at breakfast?"

Chapter 83

Quentin woke. Dominique was sitting on the bed, beside him, reading a book.

He rubbed his eyes, and said, "What time is it?"

"You have had a long sleep, mon cherie. It is just after midnight."

"My God! I must have slept for over eight hours."

"Yes, you have. How do you feel?"

Quentin sat up. "Have there been any phone calls?"

"Yes, one. From Franklin Stone. He said you should call him, and he left a number."

Quentin got out of bed and called the number Dominique gave him. Stone answered.

"You woke me, Quentin. It's late."

"Yes, I know. I'm sorry. Is there any news of Alex, please?"

"Yes. Arnold Fischer was the recipient of a ransom note in London earlier this evening. It is quite clear that we have a kidnap situation, and that it is linked to the funds Alexandra and Leo Connell remitted back to the foundation. Fischer has been given until Monday afternoon to pay six million dollars."

"Oh God, that's terrible. Is there any information on Alex? Is she safe?"

"We can only hope that she will be safe until the deadline for the payment of the ransom. We have to try to find out where she is."

"Do we know who her captors are? What can I do, Mr. Stone?"

"Nothing at all. Just wait. It's out of your hands. You have presumably reported it to the NYPD."

"Yes, I met with them this morning. They have a description, and I gave them a photograph of Alex."

"I will liaise with the police here in New York, Quentin. I will contact you again in the morning. Try to sleep. Good night."

Dominique asked, "What is happening?"

"That was the guy from the FBI. Alex has definitely been kidnapped. They want six million dollars."

"That's a lot of money," said Dominique, stating the obvious

"Yes it is, but the funds are available, or they should be, at least. They will be in the Anisimov Foundation bank tomorrow. Hopefully."

"I warned you that Alex is a person with a complicated life, mon cherie."

"Yes. I just hope she's safe." He went to the window, overlooking Third Avenue. He said, "I wonder where she is?"

Chapter 84

FRIDAY

Akbar Sattar received a phone call.

The caller asked, "Did you deliver the note to the hotel?"

"Yes, I put it under his door last night."

"You have one final assignment. Connell knows too much. Eliminate him."

"He still has police surveillance."

"Get to him, somehow. Then you will be paid, and you can leave, tomorrow."

Chapter 85

Detective Inspector Roberts arrived at the stage door of the Royal Opera House, ten minutes early for his nine thirty appointment with Geoffrey Wright.

Wright joined him, and they adjourned to his office up two flights of stairs.

"Thank you for this meeting, Mr. Wright. Is Lord Jaeger here, by the way?"

"No. Do you need to see him, Superintendent?"

"Not right now. Where is he, do you know?"

"I'm not certain. He is not expected back in the theater until next week."

"I see. Mr. Wright, I want to ask you about the night Petya Gubin died." He pulled the artist's drawing of Bryce from his briefcase. "Have you seen this newspaper article?"

"No, I haven't."

Roberts said, "This is the man we believe was in the theater last Thursday night. He met Petya Gubin just before the curtain went up. Please look carefully, Mr. Wright. Did you see this man in the opera house at any time that evening, either back stage or in the front of the house?"

Wright studied the drawing. He nodded. "Yes, I believe I did. During the first interval."

"The first interval?"

"Lord Jaeger came backstage during the first interval, to have a word with me about the reception that we were mounting for UNHCR after the performance. He wanted to finalize the order of speakers, acknowledgements, that kind of thing. We met in his office, and then he said he had to speak to Petya Gubin. Lord Jaeger and I then walked from his office down to the conductor's dressing room. He went in to see Gubin, and I walked round to brief the Assistant Stage Manager about the arrangements for the reception. It was supposed to have taken place on the "Onegin" Act III set, immediately following final curtain. As I was going round to the back of the stage, and they were setting Act II, I saw that man. At least I think I did. He was wearing a dress suit. He was standing by a table that had flowers on it. I am pretty certain it was him, anyway."

"Mr. Wright, this could be very important."

"Yes, I am sorry I haven't mentioned it before. But I haven't seen the newspapers. I was down in Cornwall for a few days, from Saturday morning onwards."

"Another question, Mr. Wright. Could anyone leave the backstage area of the theater during a performance, or an interval, through an exit other than the stage door?"

"Yes, very easily. There are several fire exits that cannot be accessed from the street, but they can be opened from the inside."

"I see. Do you know what Lord Jaeger and Petya Gubin were discussing during that first interval?"

"No, I don't. I have no idea."

"Mr. Wright, do you know of any reason why anyone would want to kill Mr. Gubin?"

"No. I cannot think of any reason."

"Thank you. DI Bartholomew will be round later on today, to take a full statement from you."

"Yes, of course."

Roberts then left the theater, and he called Bartholomew on his mobile phone. "Terry, I have just left Geoffrey Wright. Bryce was in the theater in the first interval. He is our man, I am sure of it. Step up the search for him. Put out another national alert. Airports, railway stations, everywhere. Don't leave a stone unturned."

"Right, Sir."

"And Terry, make sure you have a tail on Lord Jaeger. Where is he now, by the way?"

"In his limo, Sir. On the A4, heading out of London."

Chapter 86

Arnold Fischer, Maria Gubin, Antonio and Chloe had arrived at Heathrow, Terminal Four. They had shared a taxi from Central London. Their British Airways flight was due to leave for JFK at three thirty.

It was now two fifteen. They were waiting by the gate, having checked in and gone through security together. Arnold decided he would call the foundation bank in New York. He went to a telephone kiosk nearby, and used his long distance calling card. He spoke to the bank's Assistant Manager, and asked whether six million dollars had been credited to the account. "Yes, Mr. Fischer. The funds arrived this morning. What are your instructions?"

"Place the funds on twenty-four hour renewable deposit. I will contact you on Monday morning with further instructions. Thank you."

He then called Detective Inspector Roberts and told him the news.

He made his way back to Maria Gubin. He could not resist the temptation to tell her that the funds were safely back in New York. He did not mention the fact that there was a ransom demand out on Alexandra's life for the same amount.

Chapter 87

Dominique was at Avery Fisher Hall, at The Lincoln Center, for the final rehearsal for the concert scheduled for eight o'clock that evening. She had promised to return mid-afternoon, and she left Quentin a front door key to her apartment.

She asked him to answer the telephone if anyone called.

Just before noon, Franklin Stone telephoned. He asked Quentin if he had heard from Alexandra. He said he had not.

Quentin then asked, "Will Arnold Fischer pay the ransom money? Does he have a choice?"

"That remains to be seen. In the meantime, we are doing our very best to locate Alexandra. I will let you know as soon as we have any new information."

*

Quentin wrote a note for Dominique, saying that he would meet her backstage during the interval, immediately after her performance. The Beethoven Violin Concerto concluded the first half of the concert, he remembered.

He then let himself out of her apartment and returned to The Plaza. He wanted to change into more formal clothes later that afternoon, and to be ready for the evening concert at Avery Fisher Hall. He thought that if he could maintain a normal schedule as far as possible, he would manage to keep his anxiety about Alex under control.

Chapter 88

Alexandra did not know where she was. The room was dark. She only knew that she was near other people. She could hear their voices, but was confused because some of them seemed to be Russian. Her hands were bound behind her back, and her legs were tied together at the ankles. She was lying on a mattress on a concrete floor. There were blindfolds over her eyes. She thought she could hear children playing in the sea. She cried out for Quentin.

Chapter 89

Franklin Stone had requested Scotland Yard to give him copies of all the documents retrieved from Alexandra Matviyko's apartment, and he had them with him in New York. He had also collected reports and copies of relevant documents from the FBI agents who had searched Arnold Fischer's office, and Petya Gubin's office and home. He set aside the rest of the day to make a detailed study of all the material.

Another major issue for him was that he wanted the search for Alexandra to move forward as quickly as possible. He was concerned that the ransom deadline would arrive and that her captors would still have the upper hand. He was also worried that even if they found Alexandra in time, the identity of those who were behind the ransom demand might elude him.

One of the FBI agents in London had advised him earlier that Lord Jaeger had boarded a Lufthansa flight at Heathrow, London, headed for New York. He consequently increased the number of agents positioned at JFK.

At four twenty, Stone's cell phone rang. The caller was an FBI agent, at JFK. "We have Jaeger under surveillance. He is alone, and is waiting for a cab outside the airport terminal building."

Stone said, "Good. Go wherever he goes."

Chapter 90

Leo arrived home late, after a long day at the office. He was suffering severe pain from the injuries to his hand, and was tired.

He placed an oven ready meal in the microwave. He heard the French doors in the bedroom burst open. Akbar Sattar was standing in front of him, in the kitchen.

Leo looked at him pleadingly. "Why are you here again? Leave me alone!"

"You were warned. Make peace with your God," he said, as he plunged a nine-inch knife into Leo's heart.

Leo fell to the floor, lifeless. The microwave alarm bell rang intermittently, as Akbar Sattar made his exit through the French doors.

Chapter 91

The opening Lincoln Festival concert was full to capacity.

Quentin arrived at his seat with plenty of time to spare, and he read through the evening's program notes. He glanced at the empty seat beside him, thinking about where Alex might be. How she was coping with her ordeal?

He read the biography of Dominique Lieberman in the program, and was wondering about her parents. He would ask her how a young French woman had an apparently German last name.

The concert started. He did not concentrate on the playing of the Leonora Overture. His mind focused on Alex.

Then suddenly, there was Dominique walking onto the stage. She was wearing a floor length, tight fitting, strapless dress, in shimmering gold lame. She looked beautiful, he thought. She stood bolt upright, like a ramrod, with her violin poised, her right profile to the audience, as the orchestral introduction started. From this vantage point, she appeared much taller than her actual height, thought Quentin.

Her playing of the Concerto seemed inspired. She achieved a wonderful combination of technical accuracy and emotional, lyrical playing, supported by the orchestra at the top of its form. Dominique conducted the work herself, an unusual and sometimes risky thing to do, especially with such a demanding work as the Beethoven Concerto, but it worked well, Quentin thought. At the end of the finale, the audience gave her a prolonged standing ovation, and she returned to the stage time and time again, for several calls.

Quentin made his way backstage, and he was not surprised to see that Dominique's dressing room was full of admiring visitors. He patiently waited for most of them to leave, and there now remained only a handful. Dominique spotted Quentin, and she shouted out, "Hi. Come and meet my father. Quentin, this is Hermann Lieberman. Papa, this is the man I was telling you about."

"Delighted to meet you at last," said Lieberman in a loud voice, with a German accent. "Wasn't Dominique sensational? I am so proud of her."

"And so you should be," answered Quentin. He then turned to Dominique, "You were wonderful."

She then kissed Quentin on his cheek, and said, "I was playing for you, mon cherie, did you know that?"

Quentin blushed. Lieberman put his arm around Dominique, and said, "Don't embarrass the young man. Now, let me take the two of you out for dinner. Where would you like to go?"

"That's very kind, Mr. Lieberman, but I have to go back for the second half of the concert. I'm supposed to be working, you know."

"Papa, why don't we wait until the end of the concert, and then have dinner," Dominique suggested. "Let's meet here after the concert."

*

Quentin did not focus on the "Eroica" Symphony at all. He wondered how he might make his excuses and avoid dinner with Dominique and her father.

As the concert ended, and he rose to his feet, he found that he was standing face to face with Hermann Lieberman. "I will take you to dinner with my daughter now. Please, let us go."

They joined Dominique at the artists' stage door entrance, and then took a cab to "The Four Seasons." Dominique had changed into a short cocktail dress. At every opportunity she took Quentin's arm and caressed him.

During dinner, Hermann Lieberman asked if Dominique and Quentin would object if he left the table and returned to his apartment. He was suffering from a headache, he said.

During the reminder of dinner, Quentin asked Dominique about her father, and her life with her parents.

Dominique said that her father, who had been born and raised in Hamburg, had been working in Paris temporarily, and met her mother there. They married about a year later, and decided to live in Paris permanently. Dominique's sister, Juliette, was born a year later, and Dominique two years after that. At a very young age Dominique was encouraged to play the violin and piano, and she showed great potential with the violin. She was entered for the Juillard School, in New York, and was accepted. She moved to New York to complete her studies.

"Where did you meet Petya Gubin?" Quentin asked.

"Here in New York," Dominique said. "I had just finished at The Juillard, and I was at a party. My father was there, and Petya was with him. Papa and Petya were old friends, you know. Then shortly after that, Petya asked me to audition for him, and he liked my playing. When they wanted a stand-in at the last minute for a concert Petya was conducting at Carnegie Hall, I covered it. My career took off from there."

"How do you feel about having his baby, now that he's dead?"

"He was not a trustworthy man, Quentin, and I do not grieve for him, but I want a father for my baby."

After coffee, Quentin said, "Dominique, do you mind if we leave now? I am very tired."

"Of course."

They made their way out of the dining room, and through the lobby. Quentin noticed that in one corner of the lobby, Dominique's father was talking with two other men. One looked familiar, Quentin thought, but he could not place him. It bothered him, but he said nothing.

They got into a cab, and Dominique gave the driver instructions to go to her apartment on Third Avenue. "Back to my apartment, right?" she said, smiling at Quentin.

Quentin felt he should resist. But replied, "Yes, but I will sleep in the spare bedroom."

"You are a very old-fashioned man, but sweet. I like that. Whatever you say."

Chapter 92

Quentin slept soundly at first, but he had a dream that woke him.

He sat up in bed, retracing the dream.

He had been at a restaurant with Alex, and they were told by the waiter that they would have to leave. They were escorted to an open field. In the middle of the field, Roberts was sitting at a desk. Roberts started slapping Alex on her face, and Alex said she would report him to her father. Then they were transported to a lake on a monorail train, high in the sky. There was a stage by the lake, and there was an audience waiting. Quentin was asked to sing. He did not have the sheet music and was sweating profusely, not able to remember the words or notes. At that point he woke up.

As Quentin thought about his strange dream, he wondered if Dominique was asleep in her bedroom. He suddenly remembered seeing Hermann Lieberman at The Four Seasons as they had left through the lobby the night before. He knew the identity of one of the men Lieberman was talking to. It was Lord Jaeger.

Chapter 93

SATURDAY

It was very early, before sunrise. Stone slept in his bed in his hotel suite. He was disturbed by a call from Detective Superintendent Roberts.

"Apologies for calling you so early, Mr. Stone, but I wanted you to know that Lord Jaeger is in New York."

"Yes, I know he is."

"He's staying at The Four Seasons," said Roberts.

"Yes, I know," replied Stone.

"I can see you're on top of things. Did you know he had a visitor at the hotel last night?"

"Surprise me, Toby," said Stone, becoming exasperated.

"The Assistant Under-Secretary of State. That's who. Forbes Taylor."

"Really! That does surprise me."

"I took the precaution of getting NYPD to tail him from the airport, and then keep watch at the hotel."

"Toby, you should have told me you were doing this. We have to work together."

"Yes, I agree. That's why I'm telling you now."

"Toby, this is serious. But my concern is why Jaeger should be meeting with Forbes Taylor? He's very senior in the government in Washington. I wonder what is going on?"

"Well, I rang to make sure you knew, and I'll leave it to you to follow up. Also may I ask if you would make contact with Arnold Fischer today? He returned from London yesterday, and will need some briefing on the ransom situation as it develops."

"Yes, Toby. Thanks for calling."

Chapter 94

Arnold Fischer was pleased to be back in his own apartment. He hoped that the weekend would bring some clarification on how he should deal with the ransom situation.

Stone called him at that moment. "Oh good. I was wondering when I would hear from you," Arnold said.

"Arnold, I am staying at a hotel, near The Lincoln Center. I would like to meet you later this morning. Can we have coffee together, say at eleven?"

"Yes, I could manage that. Where?"

"How about Avery Fisher Hall, in the ground floor lobby cafeteria. I left a message for Martin Schaeffer to join us. I'll let you know if there's a change of plan."

"OK. Thanks."

Arnold then had a shower, and made himself a light breakfast.

His telephone rang again. The male voice on the line was difficult to understand. Arnold thought he might be Russian.

The man said, "We have Alexandra. She will be OK if you pay us the money, on Monday. She wants you to know that she is comfortable."

Another voice then came on the line. It was Alexandra. "I am well. Please tell Quentin I am OK. You must pay them. No mistakes. By Monday afternoon."

The line went dead.

Arnold immediately called Stone back, and recounted the call.

Stone asked him if there was any background noise during the call. Arnold thought hard, and then said, "They were very faint, but yes, I did hear voices, I think, and the sound of water and children playing."

Stone asked Arnold to think about it some more, and said they would discuss it further over coffee.

*

A few minutes later, Dominique answered her telephone. She was still in bed.

She called Quentin into her bedroom. "It's for you. You can take it in here," she said.

He took the receiver from her. As he did so, she kissed him lightly on the cheek. "It's Franklin Stone."

"Hello, Mr. Stone."

"Good morning. I have some good news. I have just heard from Arnold Fischer. He had a call from Alexandra's captors this morning, and they put her on the line. She spoke to him. She said she wanted you to know she is well."

"Thank God. Any idea where she is?"

"No. We're working on it. I'll let you know more as soon as I can."

"Mr. Stone, please do. Anything, whatever it is. By the way, Lord Jaeger is here, in New York. I was dining at The Four Seasons last night, with Dominique Lieberman and her father. Her father departed from the table early, before we finished dinner, and later when Dominique and I were leaving, I saw him talking with Lord Jaeger and one other man."

"What time was that?"

"I would say around eleven."

"OK. Thank you. I'll contact you as soon as we have more news on Alexandra."

*

Quentin told Dominique the news about Alexandra.

"That's good," she said. "Let's hope they find out where she is. Quentin, what shall we do today?"

"I have to go to The Met tonight, for "Mitridate," but other than that I have no plans. I ought to stay by a phone in the meantime, in case there is any more news."

"Then let's stay in, and we will have a nice quiet day together. I will make you lunch. You can write your review from last night. I will dictate it to you!" she said coyly.

Chapter 95

The cafeteria at Avery Fisher Hall was half empty when Arnold Fischer arrived. Franklin Stone and Martin Schaeffer joined him shortly afterwards, and they ordered their coffees and sat at a table.

Stone said he wanted to go over a short summary of the Gubin affair.

"We are conducting matters in a coordinated way, and I am moderately confident that we have a satisfactory resolution in sight. We have some way to go, however. Since you and I met here at the opera house last week, Martin, we have had a number of developments. Some of them are disturbing. On the other hand we know a lot more than we did, even a week ago. Petya Gubin's murderer was probably the man we know as Bryce. Bryce threatened Alexandra Matviyko and we believe he was also responsible for torturing and injuring Leo Connell. So far we have been unable to link Bryce with any organization or network in London, or establish exactly who or where his control is. But I hope that will become clear very soon. We are obviously pleased that the transfer of funds to terrorist cells overseas was stopped, just in time, thanks to Alexandra Matviyko and Leo Connell, but that has now developed into the Alexandra kidnap situation. Her captors want six million dollars for her release, this coming Monday. The involvement of Lord Jaeger is under scrutiny. We are not clear exactly what his role is. We are regarding him as a person of interest, even with suspicion. We are watching him closely. We want to know the reason he met with Forbes Taylor last night, at The Four Seasons, together with Hermann Lieberman. He also had a meeting with the Shadow Foreign Secretary in London, last week and we do not yet know why."

Martin Schaeffer said. "Lieberman was a close friend of Petya Gubin's. I expect you know that. Have you determined how Fred Ballard's murder and Arnie's break-in are linked to all this?"

"Only that from a logical point of view there has to be a connection. The general picture seems to be that whoever was responsible for last week's events in New York was trying to obtain documents, or alternatively to eliminate the paper trail of the flow of money. We have an APB out on Novelli, but since the break-in at your office, Arnold, there have been no sightings."

"Is there anything I can do?" asked Martin.

"Yes, there is, and that is why I suggested we should all meet. The ransom deadline is Monday afternoon. There is no doubt in my mind that until then, Arnold, you are likely to experience serious intimidation and threats, and we have to give you protection. They will not harm you enough to jeopardize the handover of the ransom money, but you are vulnerable. I have a suggestion to make."

"Do you want me to go into hiding, Mr. Stone?" asked Arnold.

"In a way, yes. But I want you to be free to talk to Alexandra Matviyko's captors whenever they make contact. I need your cooperation on this, Martin."

"Tell me what you have in mind, Mr. Stone," said Martin.

"Is there anywhere within the opera house complex, where Arnold can stay, where there are telephones, where he can sleep, at least for tonight and tomorrow night? Somewhere totally secure."

"Yes, there is the private boardroom suite, near my office," said Martin. "But won't they find it?"

"I doubt that they will work it out, especially if we put an undetectable forwarding mechanism on your home telephone, Arnold, to the phone in the opera house suite."

"I would feel much safer there," said Arnold. "Thank you. And thank you, Martin."

Stone stood up to leave. "Good. We will have the telephone in the boardroom suite monitored, so that we can trace any incoming calls from the kidnappers. If it's all right with you, Martin, we'll set that up at once."

Chapter 96

DI Bartholomew called Detective Superintendent Roberts' home telephone number.

"Sorry to disturb you, Sir. Connell has been murdered. A neighbor noticed that the doors at the back of the flat were open, and he went in. He discovered Connell on the floor. He had been stabbed. He then called the local police, and they contacted the Yard."

"I'm very sorry to hear that. It's Bryce, we assume?"

"I don't know, Sir."

"Meet me at the flat in an hour, Terry. Get forensics there too."

Chapter 97

It had been a quiet afternoon. Quentin and Dominique listened to a taped relay from the Chicago Lyric Opera of "Tosca", on WQXR, and Quentin then got ready to leave for The Met.

Dominique escorted Quentin to the door. She said, "Quentin, may I come with you? Perhaps we can get a ticket for me. I doubt they are sold out, not for "Mitridate.""

"In fact, I have a spare ticket," he said. "It was supposed to have been Alex's".

"Oh, do take me. Please. Pretty please?"

Quentin thought for a moment. He could see no harm. "OK. But we have to go now."

Dominique then quickly changed, and they hailed a cab to The Lincoln Center.

They arrived thirty minutes before curtain up and decided to have drinks in the orchestra stalls bar, before taking their seats.

Quentin bought the drinks and handed one of the glasses to Dominique. Out of the corner of his eye, he saw Lord Jaeger. He then noticed the man that Jaeger had been meeting with the night before. They were standing together at the other end of the bar.

The five-minute warning bell then sounded, and Quentin suggested they should go into the auditorium.

They settled into their seats, which were in the fifth row, center orchestra stalls. Quentin looked around. He had been to The Met before, but as ever he was astounded by the size of the theater. His eye scanned the seats in the Grand Tier, and he saw Lord Jaeger once again. He was sitting next to

Hermann Lieberman, and on his right side was the man he had been with at the bar.

"Your father is here, Dominique. Did you know he was coming?"

"No. Where is he?"

Quentin pointed out where Lieberman, Lord Jaeger and the other man were sitting.

"Oh good," she said. "We should meet up with him in the interval."

*

Arnold Fischer felt more secure. Franklin Stone had arranged for him to have an FBI agent with him in the boardroom suite where he was now staying, and the telephone equipment had been set up. He sat in his temporary living room, on the sofa, getting ready to listen to the relay of the evening's performance.

*

Quentin could not concentrate on the music. He thought it interesting that the plot was about a woman loved by both the king's two sons, and that it was set against a background of political threats and plotting. He would have been very intrigued by it musically, but he could not stop thinking about Alex. Her face haunted him. He felt she was crying out for him.

The first Act was over quickly, and Dominique suggested that they should go up to the Grand Tier bar, to look for her father.

They left the orchestra stalls, and climbed the two sets of stairs to the Grand Tier level. They walked around the balcony overlooking the entrance lobby, into the bar.

The three men were standing by the bar, with drinks in their hands.

Lieberman noticed his daughter, and waived. Dominique and Quentin moved through the crowd to where they were standing.

"Hello Papa. I didn't know you were coming to the opera tonight."

"No, I didn't know you were coming either," he said. "Hello Quentin, how are you?"

"Very well, thank you."

Lieberman took his hand, and said, "I'm so pleased Dominique has found such a splendid young man. May I introduce you to my friends?"

"This is Lord Jaeger, Chairman of the Royal Opera House, Covent Garden. And this is Forbes Taylor, a friend of mine. Gentlemen, this is my daughter, Dominique. She is a violinist. This is her friend Quentin Dart, who is here from London, covering the Lincoln Festival. He is from the London Times newspaper."

"Nice to meet you again," said Lord Jaeger, holding out his hand to Quentin. Turning to Lieberman, he said, "Hermann, Quentin was at The Garden last week, the night Petya died. We met then, briefly."

Lieberman spoke again. "Really?" Indicating to Forbes Taylor, he added, "Forbes is a wonderfully generous patron of the arts, you know."

"Delighted to meet you," said Quentin to Forbes Taylor. "I'm sorry to appear to be rude to you gentlemen, but Dominique and I had better return to our seats now, or we will be late for the next act. We'll see you later, perhaps," he said, addressing all three men, but looking at Lieberman.

As they descended the stairs to the orchestra stalls, Quentin was thinking. He knew from Stone and Roberts that they were concerned about Jaeger, but he did not understand the connection with Dominique's father. He supposed it could all be quite innocent. After all, the international opera world was very small, and it should not be surprising that the Chairman of Covent Garden was at The Met, in New York.

*

There was a call coming in to the telephone in the boardroom suite. As Arnold picked up the phone, the FBI agent leant over and showed him a note he had just scribbled. It said, "Keep them talking as long as you can."

The male voice said, "We will harm you, unless you cooperate. Do you understand?"

"Yes. What do you want me to do?"

"The six million must be in cash. You will be contacted again on Monday, and given instructions on where to take the money. You must be on your own. You must not have anyone with you. No one."

"Wait a minute," Arnold said. "It might be difficult to get the money to you in cash. Perhaps it would be easier if I wire the money to you. It might be safer."

There was a delay, and then the voice said, "The money must be in cash. US dollar bills. You will be told what to do."

The line went dead.

Arnold said to the agent, "Do you have any idea where the call was made from?"

"Yes," he said. "Coney Island."

The agent then made a call on his cell phone to Stone. He gave Stone the information. Stone said, "I will arrange to get some agents over to the area."

*

The opera finished at ten fifteen. Stone had already deployed agents to Coney Island. Arnold waited in case there was another call.

Chapter 98

Quentin continued to agonize over the possibilities as they traveled back to Dominique's apartment.

He was torn between thinking there was no particular significance in seeing Lord Jaeger in New York, and speculating on a massive conspiracy of which Alex's kidnapping was a part. He contemplated calling Franklin Stone. But he did not want to trigger any events that would place Alex in further jeopardy.

He decided to do nothing until the following day. There were still two days to the ransom deadline.

They let themselves into the apartment. Dominique went into her bedroom, and changed into a nightgown. She then suggested they had a light supper, and Quentin agreed.

Dominique was proving to be a good companion, he thought. Even though she tended to be too cloying for his liking, Quentin felt he could trust her. He asked her if she knew how long her father had been friendly with Lord Jaeger. She didn't know. He then asked her about Forbes Taylor, and she said her father had mentioned his name before, but she had never met him.

As they ate their sandwiches, the street door entry phone buzzer sounded. Quentin asked who was there. A voice said, "Pizza delivery."

Quentin said that there must have been an error. "This is 1020. Are you sure you have the right apartment?"

"I must have pressed the wrong apartment buzzer. Sorry, pal. I wanted 1011. Can you bell me in?"

Quentin pressed the entry button on the phone.

"Wrong apartment. Pizza delivery," he said to Dominique, as he returned to the table.

They then settled down to their supper once again.

Now the apartment front door bell sounded. "They've got the wrong one again," Dominique said.

Quentin got up from his chair, and went through the living room, to the front door. He slid the safety chain into its slot, and opened the door a little. Immediately the door was forced open, against his body, and the chain snapped, as a man charged in.

Dominique ran from the kitchen into the living room. She screamed, and went to Quentin.

The intruder shut the apartment door behind him.

"It's you I want. You are becoming a problem," the intruder shouted, pointing a pistol at Quentin. He then glanced at Dominique. "Not you," he said.

Quentin held on to Dominique and managed to stutter, "What do you want?"

"Keep your mouth shut. Do not contact the police again, or the FBI, or anyone. Do not talk any more. If you do, Alexandra Matviyko will be killed."

"But that's ridiculous," said Quentin, gathering some courage. "She's been kidnapped and there's already a ransom for her release."

"Shut the fuck up," the intruder yelled at Quentin. "Don't get smart with me. She will be killed after the ransom is paid, unless you cooperate and cause no trouble." Dominique let out another scream.

The intruder grabbed Dominique's arm, and pulled her away from Quentin. He tore at her nightgown, and ripped it off her shoulder. He tightened his grip on her arm. She screamed again, and started to sob.

"You shut up too," the intruder said, holding the pistol to Dominique's head. He then said, to Quentin, "Cooperate or I shoot her. Get it?"

Quentin instantly leapt forward and tackled the intruder around his waist, pushing him backwards. The pistol went spinning into the air. In the same moment, the man roughly pushed Dominique aside, and she was thrown against a table by the sofa, which sent everything on the table flying onto the floor. Dominique was now slumped on the carpet, her body twisted and motionless, her torn gown around her hips. The man quickly recovered, picked up the pistol, and held it to Quentin's head. In a sotto voce whisper, through clenched teeth, he said, "You've been warned."

The intruder then moved to the door, and said, "This never happened. Understand?" He left the apartment, and Quentin heard him running down the steps to the floors below.

Quentin went to where Dominique had fallen. She was unconscious, but breathing. He propped her head up onto a cushion, and straightened her body. He placed a cover from the spare bedroom over her body.

He picked up the telephone to call Stone, and the NYPD, but he hesitated. He thought again, and replaced the receiver. He then picked it up once again, and dialled 911. "Ambulance, please. There's been an accident." He gave the emergency services the address.

*

Dominique recovered consciousness, and it was another five minutes before the ambulance arrived. Quentin heard the siren as it drew up outside the apartment building.

Dominique had injures to her head, and she was bleeding. "It's OK," she said to Quentin, "but make sure you tell them I'm pregnant."

The EMTs checked Dominique over, and then placed her on a stretcher. She was carried out to the elevator, from the elevator out to the street, and into the waiting ambulance. Quentin gathered up her clothes that were on her bed, and went with her to Mount Sinai Medical Center, just a few blocks from the apartment.

*

Quentin had been waiting in the Medical Center Reception area for two hours. He felt guilty that he had provoked the intruder's retaliation against Dominique unnecessarily, and that otherwise she would not have suffered any injury. He wanted to report the event to Stone, but clearly the intention had been to intimidate him. He was concerned that if he said anything, there might be a further attack.

His thoughts turned to Alex. He wondered whether she was being fed, and how comfortable she was. He hoped they were not harming her.

The duty doctor approached Quentin, and after verifying who he was, sat down beside him.

"Miss Lieberman has suffered a concussion. She has lost the baby I am afraid. I'm very sorry. But she will recover, and we will see how she is tomorrow. Maybe she can go home tomorrow afternoon. Will you be able to collect her?"

"Yes, of course."

"Do you want to see her before you go?"

"Yes, please," said Quentin.

Quentin was escorted into a small ward, where Dominique was lying on a bed. Her left arm was bandaged and in a sling. She had a dressing on her forehead. Quentin knelt by the bed, and cupped her head in his hand, stroking her cheek. He noticed that she had been crying.

"I am so sorry," he said. "I should never have charged that guy down. If I hadn't, this would never have happened."

"Nonsense," she said, stroking his brow with her right hand. "You were so brave. I am lucky to be alive." The tears rolled down her cheeks.

Quentin shook his head. "If it hadn't been for me, and Alex, you would not be involved in this. It's my fault."

"No, it's OK, really it is," she said, soothingly. "They told me I have lost the baby, but I think I'll get over it, and maybe later on I might think that it is for the best."

A nurse interrupted. "You will have to leave her now."

Quentin stood up. "I'm so sorry to have to leave you like this, Dominique. I'll see you tomorrow. They say you might be able to go home tomorrow afternoon."

Dominique half smiled, and weakly blew him the gentlest of kisses. "Good night, mon cherie."

Quentin left the hospital, and hailed a cab to The Plaza hotel.

*

It was two thirty in the morning as he let himself into his room at The Plaza.

The light was flashing on the telephone. He dialled to retrieve his messages. There was just one, from Franklin Stone.

"Quentin, it's Saturday, around midnight. I cannot get an answer from Dominique Lieberman's apartment. I just get her voicemail. When you receive this message call me back immediately. Thanks."

Quentin sat on the bed. This was a real dilemma, he thought. The intruder's threat was uppermost in his mind. Then he considered how anyone would know if he made a call to Stone. They couldn't possibly be tapping the phone in his hotel room, surely?

He dialed Stone's number. There was no response, just a voicemail greeting. He decided to leave a message. He said, "Mr. Stone. It's after half past two, early Sunday morning. I just got your message. I'm at The Plaza. Please phone me whenever it's convenient. Don't call Dominique Lieberman's number, please. You'll be able to reach me here until late morning. Thank you."

Quentin slipped into bed, wishing he was back in Oakley Street with Alex.

Chapter 99

SUNDAY

Quentin was awakened by Stone's call. It was nearly ten.

"We have taken a small task force out to Coney Island, and the Brighton and Manhattan Beach areas, where we believe they may be holding Alexandra. A thorough search is under way. I want you to stand by in case there are any developments."

"Mr. Stone, that's good news, isn't it?"

"I hope so, but we are up against some desperate people here. And the stakes are high, as you know."

"I understand. I have to tell you something. But it is highly confidential," Quentin said.

"You can rely on me. What is it?"

Quentin then explained what had happened at Dominique's apartment. "I am taking a big risk by saying anything, to anyone. I think Dominique is now at risk as well."

"Describe the intruder, if you would, Quentin."

Quentin said that he was of slight build. He was dressed casually, and had dark hair, balding. He said he was probably Eastern European or Asian.

"That sounds like it might be Novelli," said Stone. "He gave us the slip. I would put money on it being Novelli."

"Who is he?"

"He's a paid hatchet man, like Bryce, in London. He may be Fred Ballard's killer, and he was responsible for breaking into Arnold Fischer's office."

"Who does he work for?"

"That's what we're trying to establish, Quentin. How is Dominique, by the way?"

"She was very shaken by the whole experience, Mr. Stone. Please do not use this information in any way that rebounds on me, Alex or Dominique. Please be careful."

"You have my word."

Chapter 100

Another call was coming into the boardroom telephone. Arnold Fischer answered it.

"Yes, Fischer here."

"You are to drive to the British Airways Cargo building at JFK tomorrow, by cab. Be there at two pm. No later. Bring six million dollars in suitcases. Large bills. You must be on your own. You will then be taken to another location, where an exchange will take place. If it is satisfactory, you and the girl will be allowed to leave. If there is anyone with you, the girl will be harmed, and you will be in danger. Serious danger."

"Where is the Cargo building? I am not sure I know how to find it."

"You will receive final instructions tomorrow morning."

"I thought the deadline was five, tomorrow afternoon."

"Two."

Arnold replaced the receiver. "Did you trace the call? He asked the FBI agent.

"Yes. It was a phone box on the lower east side, in Manhattan."

*

Stone and his FBI agents continued with their search of Coney Island but found nothing. He had just been advised by the agent in The Met boardroom that the most recent call from Alexandra's captors had apparently originated in Manhattan. He reluctantly concluded that they were on a wild goose chase in the Coney Island area, and that they should assume Alexandra was now somewhere else.

He set about planning the detailed modus operandi for Monday.

Chapter 101

The telephone rang again, and at first Quentin thought it was Franklin Stone back on the line.

"Good morning Quentin. Hermann Lieberman here. How are you today?"

"Very well, thank you."

"I tried to call Dominique but there's no answer at her apartment, so I called your hotel. I just wanted you to know how much I enjoyed your company last night. I'm so pleased that you and Dominique are ….. an item, shall we say?"

"I think that's a bit of an exaggeration," Quentin said, "but we're good friends, certainly."

"Oh, you can be straight with me, young man. I've been round the block a few times."

Quentin was trying to think, fast. He did not want to give Lieberman the impression that he had placed Dominique in any jeopardy, even unintentionally. He certainly did not want to mention that Dominique was in Mount Sinai.

He said, "Dominique thought we should have some brunch out today, so we came over to The Plaza."

"Good. Excellent idea. Well, I hope we'll meet again soon, maybe at the ballet, on Tuesday night. Are you going?"

"Yes, that's the plan," said Quentin.

"Wonderful. Take Dominique with you, and I'll see you both there."

Chapter 102

Detective Inspector Roberts had been working all day. It was now nearly five in the evening.

He decided it was time to speak to Franklin Stone again.

"Mr. Stone, I have some bad news. Leo Connell was found murdered in his flat yesterday. The forensic team picked up fingerprints identical to those they found in Alexandra's flat."

"I'm sorry to hear about that. It might be worth going back to the dressing room at Covent Garden to try for a prints match there too, if you haven't already done that."

"Unfortunately, the whole of the conductor's dressing room was thoroughly cleaned when the contents were removed. Someone has done an effective job in eliminating all prints."

"Pity. Any luck with tracking down Bryce?"

"No, not yet."

"We've had some developments here. Novelli, at least we think it was him, broke into Dominique Lieberman's apartment last night, and threatened her and Quentin Dart at gunpoint. We haven't located Alexandra and her captors, but I'm setting up an operation for tomorrow."

"I wish you luck with that, Mr. Stone. There's one other matter I wanted to share with you. It may be related, but I'm not yet certain."

"What's that?"

"Derek Grant has a question down for Prime Minister's Question Time in the House of Commons, this coming Tuesday. It's concerning terrorist cells in Chechnya, among other things. Seems he's trying to embarrass the government. I'm not sure, but I have a hunch it could be linked to our inquiries, if only indirectly."

"Could be. Let's not jump to conclusions."

*

Stone called Arnold Fischer in the boardroom suite at The Met, and advised him that he would meet him there at eight the next morning, to go over the planned strategy for the day.

Chapter 103

Mount Sinai advised Quentin that Dominique was cleared to go home, but only if she rested.

The injury to her left arm was such that she would be unable to play the violin for several weeks. She was advised to cancel all her engagements for a month.

Quentin suggested to her that they should go back to The Plaza from Mount Sinai, and stay in his room there, rather than returning to her apartment. He said it would be safer, and she could use room service. It would be a more convenient place to recuperate. She readily agreed, saying that she didn't mind where she was, providing she was with him. He said that he would collect some clothes for her from her apartment later.

He arranged for a cab to take them to The Plaza. They settled into the hotel room, and Quentin helped Dominique get into bed.

She asked him to lie on the bed beside her. They were quiet for a while, and then Dominique said she wanted to know more about him, about his past. "Tell me, Quentin, about what your life was like before you met Alexandra."

"There's not much to know, really."

"Did you have any serious girl friends, before her?"

"I was engaged once before, to someone called Wendy. We met at college. We were at Cambridge together. She became a journalist, and we both worked at The Independent newspaper."

"What happened?"

"We got engaged, and her parents planned a big wedding. We were going to be married in Worcester, where her parents lived. But then she asked if we could delay the wedding, because she was having doubts. But in fact, unknown to me, she had met this other guy, and eventually she dumped me."

"How long did you go out with her?"

"About seven years."

"Were you very hurt?"

"Yes, I was in a way. Surprised."

"Meeting Alexandra must have made a very big change in your life."

"It completely changed it. I was working at The Times by then and I was enjoying my job, but suddenly my life became a lot more interesting. She was so vibrant."

"But it was on the rebound from Wendy, wasn't it?" Dominique suggested.

"I never thought about it before, but yes, I suppose it was."

"Are you worrying about Alexandra now, mon cherie?"

"Yes. I hope she's all right. She must be terrified."

"Alexandra is very tough. She will always survive, I think."

Dominique then took Quentin's hand in hers, and settled her head back into her pillow. She said, "I think I'm a little tired." She then went to sleep, holding his hand. Quentin did not move for a while.

Then, when he was certain he would not awaken her, he got up from the bed, and let himself out of the room. He took a cab to her apartment, and randomly gathered some of her clothes from her closet and various drawers, and put them in a case. He returned with the case to The Plaza, again by cab, and was back in his room, in less than an hour. Dominique was still asleep.

Chapter 104

Alexandra was feeling wretched. Other than the brief phone call to Arnold she had not had a conversation with anyone since she had been captured. And even that had been under duress. She was dirty, suffering from stress, and was beginning to hallucinate.

She was not certain, but she thought three or more days must have passed since she was with Quentin.

Every four or six hours, during the days she assumed, and she wasn't certain how frequently it really was, her hands and legs were untied, and the blindfold removed from her eyes. Each time the routine was the same. She was given a bowl of water in which she could wash, and a bucket to use, as an alternative to a toilet. She was then given food, usually rice.

Her captors rarely spoke, but when they did it was monosyllabic. They gestured to her when she was required to move, eat or wash.

On a few occasions she asked questions, but she was always ignored.

She did not think she could endure this deprivation much longer.

She passed the time by re-enacting her life with Quentin, and with Petya. Sometimes she developed different versions of events, speculating on what might have happened in varying circumstances. She often thought about her grandparents, and her mother. She wondered if her mother had raised any children with her new husband. She thought about the brothers and sisters she might have in Moscow. Maybe she would see them one day.

She reasoned that if the ransom was paid she might be freed. If she was to die, she hoped it would happen suddenly, without warning.

Her fitful sleep was broken by voices. The door to her room was unlocked. A man was now looking down at her. In broken English, he said, "Tomorrow you will be taken to another place. You will not speak or try to escape. If you do you will be shot."

In spite of the threat, Alex felt a sense of hope. She prayed that she would be freed and that she would be with Quentin and maybe even see her mother again.

Chapter 105

MONDAY

He was in an opera house, standing on a bare stage, looking out into the auditorium, which was full of people. Alex was in the audience, watching him, as he watched her. A man sat down beside her, kissing her. They were making love. Quentin wanted to go to her, but his feet were rooted to the stage. Alex then got up and walked to the back of the theater, and looking over her shoulder, waved to him. Quentin then flew, as a bird takes flight, and was hovering over a grassy path, by a cliff top. He ran, his feet not quite touching the ground, in big airborne strides, chasing Alex. He could not see her, and then suddenly he was over the cliff, falling, falling, falling.

Quentin stirred. Dominique was asleep. She slept on, as he arose from the bed and went to the window. He looked out to Central Park.

He thought about Alexandra. He wondered where she was. He thought about his dream. It had been so vivid.

*

The telephone rang. It was Franklin Stone. "I would like you to come to a briefing I'm having with Arnold Fischer this morning, in the boardroom suite in the opera house, by Martin Schaeffer's office. I want you to be with us when Alexandra is released, hopefully this afternoon. She will need you to comfort her and help her recover from her ordeal. Be there at eight for my meeting, please."

Quentin looked at the clock on the wall. It was only five-thirty.

Chapter 106

In London it was a warm, sunny day. Detective Superintendent Roberts was browsing through the newspapers, reading the results of the Wimbledon finals that had taken place over the weekend.

Detective Inspector Bartholomew telephoned. "I have some good news, Sir."

"What is it, Terry?"

"We have apprehended Bryce. He was at Gatwick airport this morning, trying to board a plane to Hamburg. An officer in the security screening area identified him. He was arrested without incident, and he is now in police custody, at Gatwick. The name in his passport is Akbar Sattar. He is an Iranian. We have no previous record of him here at the Yard, but the FBI or CIA might have some information on their files."

"This is very satisfactory, Terry. Arrange to bring him up here, to London, and get a match on the prints."

"I hope we can make the case stick, Sir, providing the prints match. We still have no murder weapons. Not for Gubin or Connell."

"I know. Get him up here straight away. I want to interrogate him today."

"Yes, Sir. But because he's an Iranian citizen, we'll have to inform the Iranian Embassy, and eventually hand him over to them."

"Let's see what happens."

Roberts sat for a moment, thinking that it would be difficult unless more evidence came to light to pin the Gubin murder on Sattar. It might be easier to make the case for his killing of Connell. But he could foresee diplomatic difficulties, in any event.

He went to his computer files, and looked up the name Sattar. Nothing. Then he did a search on Iranian names. He was surprised to read that the name Akbar meant Bad in English, and that Sattar translated as Concealer. The Bad Concealer, he said to himself. How ironic.

He picked up the telephone, and asked his secretary to get Franklin Stone and the Deputy Commissioner on the line, in that order, he said.

Chapter 107

Arnold Fischer was feeling ill, and he was apprehensive about what he had to do.

Franklin Stone arrived. As he was taking some documents out of his briefcase, the telephone rang. Arnold answered, his voice quivering with nerves. "Yes, Fischer here."

"Your final instructions are these. Listen. Take the suitcases with the money to the British Airways cargo building at JFK, building 66, on Cargo Service Road. The cases should not be locked. Be there at two pm, in a yellow cab. No later than two. Apart from the cab driver you must be alone. Tell the driver to stop in the parking area at the front of the cargo building, and then you will get out of the cab, with the cases, and tell the driver to leave. You will then wait in the parking area. If you do not follow these instructions you will be harmed, and the Matviyko girl will be killed. That is all. This is final."

Arnold replaced the receiver. "They were calling from a Queens number," said the FBI agent.

There was a knock at the door. Marcia Segarra entered, greeting Stone and Arnold Fischer. "Martin will be here in ten minutes. I have Quentin Dart outside. Should he come in?"

"Yes, thank you," said Stone.

Quentin entered, and was surprised to see all the monitoring equipment. Stone welcomed him. "Good morning again, Quentin, please take a seat. You know Arnold Fischer, I assume?"

Quentin shook Arnold's hand, saying, "No, I don't think I've had the pleasure."

Martin Schaeffer arrived, breathing heavily. "Sorry I'm late, gentlemen. Good to see you again, Mr. Stone. Hello Arnie, how are you bearing up?"

"I'm feeling a bit queasy, to be honest," he said.

Stone then introduced Quentin to Martin Schaeffer. Quentin said, "I suppose you must know Alexandra quite well."

"Yes. She worked here, for quite some time. Let's hope we can get her released safely, today."

Stone then invited them all to sit at the conference table. He had several documents in front of him.

"Arnold, in about thirty minutes, I want you to call the Manager of the foundation bank, on the speakerphone. I will introduce myself to the Manager and I will say a few words. You will then ask him to prepare the six million dollars cash for collection at noon. I assume you can do this on your own authority."

"I am authorized under the mandate to make payments on my own, yes."

"Where exactly is the bank?"

"On Broadway, just across the street from here."

"Good. This is what will happen. Arnold, you will wear a bulletproof vest under your everyday clothes, and you will also wear a concealed homing device. I will explain how this will work in a moment. You will take two large empty suitcases that we have procured to the bank, leaving here at eleven fifty. When you get to the bank, you will ask the Manager to escort you to a secure room at the back of the bank, away from the public area. Together with two FBI agents, I will follow, and join you there, just after twelve. You will be given the money, and you will place it in the cases. You will then complete the paperwork necessary for the bank. A yellow cab will arrive at twelve forty-five, to take you and the cases to JFK. The cab driver will in fact be an FBI agent. A dozen FBI agents, in six cars, all unmarked, will follow the cab, at a distance. There will be radio contact between all cars. I will be in one of those cars. Quentin, you will be in the car with me. When we get to the airport vicinity, the six cars will disperse, and then stop, each in a different location within one mile of the BA cargo building. The cab driver will drop you and the cases at the cargo building, Arnold, as requested by the captors just now, and he will leave you there in the parking lot, on your own."

Stone then paused, and asked, "Is everyone clear, so far?" There was no comment from anyone.

"I'll move on. We do not know for certain that Alexandra is still alive. The demands that have been made for the cash may be based on a false premise. If that is the case, it is likely the captors will make off with the cash from the cargo building, leaving you stranded there, Arnold. On the other hand, it is equally possible that what is being offered is a genuine exchange. If so, we assume that the exchange will not take place at the cargo building. This will be the stage of the operation where it is essential for you to hold your nerve, Arnold. We anticipate that what will happen will be that someone will emerge from the cargo building, or that a car will draw up, soon after you are dropped. Either the money will be snatched from you, which I think is unlikely, or you will be taken by Alexandra's captors to another location. They may well look in the cases first, to see that you have all the cash. Do not resist if they do this. You must not panic, or try to deviate from the strategy, at any time. Do you understand?"

Arnold nodded.

Stone continued, "Each of the six cars will be equipped with electronic monitoring units, and will be able to track where you are at any given time, and where you are being taken. You can assume that the agents in one or more of the cars will always have you in their sight. But you must never look round or behind you, or give the captors the impression that you are not alone or are being protected. We don't know where you will be taken, of course. We have no idea. It might be Coney Island. We don't know. Wherever it is, once you have arrived at what you believe is the destination, you must insist on being able to see Alexandra, that she is safe. If at any time they try to escape with the ransom money, before Alexandra is handed over to you, we will immediately move in, disarm the captors and retrieve the money."

After a pause, Arnold said, "It seems very well thought out, Mr. Stone, I have to admit, but I will be too vulnerable outside the cargo building, while I wait for them. Especially if they plan to take the money and run."

Stone shook his head. "They will have calculated that somehow we will have them under surveillance there, based on the ransom directions they gave you, so that is improbable."

Arnold persisted. "They may shoot me. Or they may shoot both of us, Alexandra and me, later, after they have the money."

"There is that risk. You're right. But we will have two snipers on the roof of the cargo building. They are checking out the vicinity already, in fact. Also, each of the groups of agents in the cars that will be in pursuit will have a marksman with them. If events develop in the way you fear, the captors will be shot."

Arnold still wasn't convinced. "But what if they shoot me first?"

"I don't think they will. They will want to verify that the cases contain the money. There will be a small window, so to speak, that will give our snipers the chance to shoot the captors, if they have to. But our strategy is to allow them to take you to Alexandra."

"What if I refuse to do this?" asked Arnold.

Stone leaned forward, his eyes looking directly into Arnold's. "Mr. Fischer, the FBI, and especially the IRS, have certain serious charges that can be made against you and the Trustees of the Anisimov Foundation, regarding your handling of grants, and in dispersing, or attempting to disperse, not-for-profit funds for the purposes of aiding terrorist activity. Do I make myself clear? You can be charged with treasonable activity, as an enemy of the state."

Arnold blinked, and shrunk from Stone's gaze. "My God!"

"Yes, Mr. Fischer. If, however, you fully cooperate today, those charges could be reduced considerably, and your actions taken in mitigation. And if Alexandra is rescued, and we retrieve the ransom monies, as we hope will be the case, you will be asked to provide further cooperation by endorsing those funds over to the State. In such circumstances, I believe you may be able to look forward to a future free of incarceration, and free of any financial penalties."

Arnold looked at Martin Schaeffer, who had been listening closely, and said, "What do you advise, Martin?"

"You have a choice, Arnie, but I think you should do the right thing, and cooperate with the FBI. You are at some risk, I agree, but I am sure Mr. Stone and the FBI will do all they can to protect you. You are in expert hands."

Quentin asked Stone if he could say a word. Stone nodded his consent.

"Arnold, Alexandra's life is at stake here. If you do not do this, she will be killed. And her kidnappers will then be after you. They will not stop until they have the money. Please do this today, for Alexandra's sake, and for your own sake." He broke down, sobbing. "I'm sorry," he said, "I am feeling very emotional about this."

Arnold then sighed heavily. "I will do it, Mr. Stone. I hope I am doing the right thing."

Stone said, "Good. Now, we should discuss briefly what will happen if and when we have sight of Alexandra. You will say to her captors that you want to make the exchange in an open area, where you can see her, walk towards her, and continue to keep her in your sight. You should agree that once you have started to walk towards her, they can drive away with the money."

"Surely, we're not letting them get away with this?" said Martin.

"No", said Stone. "We will make our move as soon as we see Alexandra is safe. We will then deploy the cars to run them down. Remember, we will be close."

Quentin was recovering his thoughts. He was impressed by Stone's plan, but he could see the risks, as Arnold could. His abiding wish was that they would rescue Alex, whatever happened.

Stone then said, "Arnold, it is time to call the bank."

Chapter 108

The door to Alexandra's locked room was opened, and she was lifted up from the mattress where she was lying. She was already tied by her arms and feet, and blindfolded. She was now gagged. She was then carried out of the room and dropped into the trunk of a car. She heard the trunk being slammed shut, and she could smell oil.

She heard voices. They were Russian and Arabic. She then heard some other voices that she hadn't heard before. She couldn't make out what was being said.

The car started to move forward. They were in traffic, at first, with some slowing down and stopping. But then they seemed to be accelerating again, and driving fast, on an open road. Then there was traffic again, and the noise of other vehicles.

The car stopped, and Alexandra was lifted out of the trunk. She was carried a distance, and then put down onto a hard, wooden surface. She felt the warm sun on her face. She thought she heard the sound of water. Then the noise of a motor, and she was moving again, on a boat. Definitely a boat. The boat slowed down, and then stopped. She was lifted, and then put down again, this time on a softer surface. She could feel that she was still on water. She could smell the sea air.

Chapter 109

Maria Gubin was sitting with Antonio and Chloe in Petya's Manhattan apartment. She had decided she would make a decision about a memorial service for Petya today, regardless of whether there was any news about his body being returned from London.

She made a telephone call to Detective Superintendent Roberts, and asked if there was any change in the status of the release of her husband's body. He told her that they had apprehended a man they believed was his killer, but that there could be international implications and difficulties. It would take a few days of diplomacy and further investigations before any charges could be made in connection with her husband's murder, he said.

Roberts then recounted the circumstances of Leo Connell's death to Maria. He said he was hopeful that there would be a good chance of making a murder charge stick in connection with Connell. He believed the man who had killed her husband had also killed Connell. In the Connell case, there was a better trail of evidence. But he cautioned Maria that there were still the diplomatic issues to be overcome.

Maria expressed surprise and horror at the news of Leo Connell's death, and said she would leave the matter in Roberts' hands until she heard anything further. She thanked him.

After explaining the situation to Antonio and Chloe, she said, "I don't think we should wait for Scotland Yard any longer. We should arrange a memorial service for your father, perhaps this Friday."

"I agree," said Antonio.

Maria added, "I would like to hold it at St. Nicholas Russian Orthodox Church. It's on East 97th Street, between Fifth and Madison. I think it will be a most suitable venue, and it will give us some closure, at least."

"That sounds good," said Chloe. "Who should we invite?"

"Tonio, please check with the church, and then have a notice put in The New York Times tomorrow. Ask Martin Schaeffer to send a notice out to everyone he has on The Met's VIP and Board mailing lists. We'll need to think about eulogies, tributes and speakers, though."

Antonio said, "Maybe Martin will have some ideas."

"The only thoughts I have at present are Arnold Fischer maybe, or perhaps better, Martin himself. Let's ask Martin, as you suggest Tonio."

"OK, Mom. By the way, the petition to contest the will is being handled by a well known New York firm that is affiliated to Henry Walton's, in London. Robert Gerard is dealing with it."

"Good. He's quite high-powered, isn't he?" said Maria.

Chloe asked, "Did you find out about the insurance policies, Tonio?"

"I'm having Fred Ballard's papers, or what is left of them, sent over to Robert Gerard's office, and Mr. Stone and Superintendent Roberts are assisting us, by arranging for copies of everything they have to be sent to Gerard as well.

Chapter 110

It was nearly one o'clock. It was now over ninety degrees, and humid. Storms were forecast for later that afternoon.

The arrangements made at the bank had gone well. Arnold Fischer had watched carefully as the bank clerk, supervised by the Manager, had placed three hundred sealed, transparent packets, each consisting of one hundred $100 bills, into each of the two cases. As FBI agents kept guard, Arnold heaved one of the filled suitcases out to the cab that was waiting curbside, shortly followed by a bank clerk carrying the other filled suitcase. The cases were heavy, and Arnold had some difficulty with his. Both the cases were placed in the trunk of the cab. Arnold was already sweating.

The cab moved away, turned east toward Central Park, through the park, and then south down Second Avenue to the Midtown tunnel. Quentin was in one of the cars following, code-named Alpha One, together with Franklin Stone, and an agent armed with a rifle with a telescopic sight. Quentin watched, as the beeping unit on the dashboard in front of the driver monitored the exact location of Arnold in the cab ahead.

From time to time, the driver checked communications with the cab, and with the five other cars in the convoy.

Quentin thought of Dominique as they sped through the park. He imagined her looking out of the window of his room, across the park, and ordering her lunch from room service.

The convoy continued out towards JFK, making its way through heavy traffic, and approached the airport at one forty-five.

Instructions were given to the driver of the cab to proceed to the BA Cargo building, in Cargo Service Road. Alpha One stopped on the shoulder near the Van Wyck Expressway, and the driver cut the engine. Quentin gathered that the other cars were moving to various locations nearby. He sat still, nervously awaiting news on the radio of what was happening at the Cargo building.

The cab driver stopped in the parking lot in the forecourt of the Cargo building. Snipers on the roof of the building that overlooked the forecourt reported no other activity, and Arnold got out of the cab, and asked the driver to open the trunk. Arnold and the driver then removed the two suitcases and put them next to each other on the tarmac. The cab driver was then cleared by radio to drive away. Arnold waited, standing next to the suitcases.

Shortly after that, two identical black Lincoln Town Cars sped into the forecourt. Both had black tinted windows. The snipers reported what was happening on their radios. Stone asked whether the snipers could see how many individuals there were in the cars. They said they couldn't see clearly. Then suddenly a man emerged from the front passenger door of the second car, and approached Arnold. He was wearing a black ski mask. He motioned Arnold into the back of the car, and the rear door opened from the inside. Arnold hesitated, knowing that he was supposed to wait until they had verified the contents of the suitcases, and said, "Do you want to check the cases first?"

"Into the car," was the response.

Arnold then got into the car, and the door closed. Arnold heard the trunk slam shut.

The two cars then sped away, up ramps and onto the Van Wyck Expressway. They passed Alpha One that was parked to one side of the Van Wyck, and turned west into the Belt Parkway. Alpha One's driver then pursued the Town Cars, keeping a distance of half a mile, and the other five cars followed behind, at regular close intervals. Alpha One was now moving fast down the Belt Parkway, and had the two Lincoln Town Cars in its sights, about one hundred yards ahead. The two Town Cars sped in tandem formation, side by side, so close to each other that they were almost touching. Suddenly, one of them veered down the ramp to the left, heading north into Flatbush Avenue, and the other continued west towards Manhattan Beach and Coney Island, still on the Belt Parkway.

Stone shouted, "Driver, follow the Town Car still on the Belt Parkway, and Alpha Three and Alpha Four, do likewise. The other cars, Alphas Two, Five and Six, follow the Town Car going up Flatbush. Keep it in your sights."

The monitoring unit in Alpha One indicated that Arnold was in the Town Car they were following. Stone breathed a sigh of relief, and said, "I took a

Conducting Terror

gamble. It was difficult to distinguish between the two at the moment they parted. I hope the money is in the car with Arnold. Driver, radio back to the snipers and get that verified if you can."

The Town Car with Arnold now slowed and turned off the Parkway, and headed towards the west side of Manhattan Beach, close to Brighton Beach. "Do you think this is where they are holding Alexandra?" asked Quentin.

"Probably," said Stone. "Driver, keep your distance. Stay back, but keep them in your sight."

The driver was on the radio. He then reported that the snipers saw the cases being loaded into the trunk of the car that Arnold was in.

"Good," said Stone. "Keep it in view."

The Town Car slowed, almost to a walking pace. It turned left into a narrow lane, and then right, towards the boat moorings. "Stay back," barked Stone, watching the beeper on the car dashboard.

"Where could they be hiding her?" asked Quentin, rhetorically. "There are no buildings around here, except those small boat sheds."

The Town Car stopped. Three men got out of the car, two from one rear door and one from the front, passenger side. They were all wearing masks. They opened the other rear door, and manhandled Arnold from the car towards the pier. The trunk opened, and the men carried the two cases also towards the pier.

Stone now had a radio in his hand. "No one make a move," he shouted, as he watched events unfolding.

The three men then threw Arnold and the suitcases into a small motorboat. Two of the men got into the boat. One started the engine, and the man remaining on the jetty untied the moorings. The motorboat then sped off away from the beach, heading south.

Stone took out a pair of binoculars. He said, "For Christ's sake, they're taking him out to sea! Where are they going?"

The third man then got back into the Town Car, and it quickly turned round, and passed Alpha One, going in the opposite direction.

"What's happening?" asked Quentin. "What can we do?"

"They've thrown us completely. They're clever, very clever," said Stone. "I didn't anticipate a transfer to water. That was my error." He continued to watch the motorboat through the binoculars. He seemed momentarily confused, unsure what to do next.

"But wait, I think I know where they might be going," Stone suddenly shouted. "They're probably heading out to Rockaway Point, or Breezy Point, to the peninsular."

"Where's that?" asked Quentin.

"Not far. Driver, turn round. Go back to Flatbush Avenue, via the Belt Parkway. If I remember correctly, you can drive out to the peninsula by going south over the causeway. It's at the bottom end of Flatbush Avenue, heading out in the direction of the ocean. We should go down Flatbush, over the bridge, then turn west at Roxbury, on the peninsular. It will take us to Rockaway Point and Breezy Point. Go! Go! Quick!"

At that moment, Alpha Two reported on the radio. "The Town Car we were pursuing going north has done an about turn, and is now heading south on Flatbush, very fast. We might have lost them. Shall we turn round as well, and try to maintain pursuit?"

"Yes," said Stone into his radio. "Good. That tells me we're going the right way, but they've got at least three or four minutes on us."

Quentin was now frantic, although he was encouraged that Stone didn't seem to think they had been thrown off the scent altogether. "How did you know about Breezy Point and Rockaway Point, and how to get there from here by road, Mr. Stone?"

"I sometimes used to bring my kids here when they were young, that's how. Just a lucky break."

Alpha One, followed by Alphas Three and Four, was now speeding south on Flatbush Avenue, with the three other FBI cars that had turned round in pursuit. The convoy was more or less together again. They reached Roxbury, and then turned west on a narrow road, heading out to Breezy Point. The beeper was showing that Arnold was ahead, quite near.

"Slow down, Driver. Look out for the motorboat." Stone was peering through his binoculars. "Hold it, I have Arnold Fischer in my sights. They're pulling him out of the motorboat. Driver, get much nearer." He then called on the radio, "All other cars, come up close behind us." He then leant forward and put his hand on the driver's shoulder. "Driver, nearer, much nearer! I want to be within thirty yards." And then he was on the radio again, "All cars, all operatives, be ready for an attack! Be ready to shoot!"

Stone could now see clearly that both the Town Cars had already arrived, well ahead of the FBI convoy. They had parked at the very end of the peninsula. There was a large yacht anchored about fifty feet off the shore, and the motorboat was already moored alongside the yacht. Four men and Arnold Fischer were now getting out of the motorboat, and were boarding the yacht, carrying the two cases.

"Can anyone see Alexandra?" asked Stone.

The yacht was now suddenly free of its anchor, as well as the motorboat, and was speeding away from them, out to sea. The motorboat, empty, was left drifting just off the shore.

"My God, we've lost them. My God!" Stone slumped back into his seat.

Quentin had been watching carefully. He was now subdued and deep in thought. He quietly said, "Mr. Stone, I'm certain Alexandra is on that yacht. I didn't see her, but I'm sure of it. Apart from Arnold, two of the men who got out of the motorboat and are on that yacht, were familiar. I think I recognized them, even though they were wearing masks."

"Who are they?"

"Lord Jaeger and Hermann Lieberman."

Storm clouds had gathered overhead, as the beeper on the dashboard of Alpha One faded, fast.

Chapter 111

The weather had now deteriorated. There were gale force gusts, and torrential rain. Visibility was poor.

Stone strained to follow the yacht through his binoculars, as it disappeared out to sea. He was now on the radio. "I want helicopters to comb the area south of Breezy Point. That yacht could be going further out to sea, but more likely because of the weather, is heading for the New Jersey coast. Or maybe, east, towards Long Beach and up the Long Island south shore."

The reply came back that helicopters were not able to fly until the storm abated.

Quentin was now totally despondent. He was watching Alexandra disappear from his life forever, he felt, and powerless to do anything about it.

"Don't worry," said Stone, gripping his arm, "We'll find them. It won't be long before we can get the helicopters out."

*

The yacht turned west when two miles out to sea. Unknown to Stone, it was now heading north, into the calmer waters of the Upper New York Bay.

Chapter 112

Dominique had spent the day awaiting news from Quentin. She was feeling better physically, but she was still recovering from her ordeal. She slept occasionally, half listening for the telephone.

She was beginning to get apprehensive. It was now after six, and she still hadn't heard anything.

Then the phone rang. "Quentin?"

"No, my dear, it's Papa. How are you? I hear you have been in the wars, a little."

"It was nothing. I'm fine."

"Are you sure? I heard that you were in hospital."

"Yes, Papa. But don't worry. I am very well."

"OK, if you say so. Is Quentin there?"

"No, he has been out all day."

"Really? What he been getting up to?"

"Oh, the Alexandra Matviyko situation, you know."

"OK, sweetheart. Well, when am I going to see you next? Will you be at the ballet tomorrow night?"

"Yes, perhaps, if we go. I'll see you then. Bye bye, Papa."

Dominique wondered how her father had learned about her stay in hospital. She would talk to Quentin about it.

*

The telephone rang again, and woke her. "Quentin?"

"Hello, Dominique. How are you?"

"Oh Quentin, I've been so worried. Are you all right?"

"Yes. I am not in the city, though. I'll be back at the hotel later, in a couple of hours. See you then, OK?"

"Did you get Alexandra back?"

"No, she has been taken on a yacht, together with Arnold Fischer."

"Is she all right?"

"I don't know, Dominique. I have no idea. I must go. I'll call you later."

Dominique lay on the bed, happy that Quentin was safe, and that he would soon be with her.

Chapter 113

The winds had dropped. The helicopters were now out, combing the New Jersey and Long Island coastlines.

Stone decided that it was time to move. "We're not going to learn anything more staying here," he said. He ordered two of his agents to drive back to Manhattan, and to go back to base, and stand by.

Quentin telephoned Dominique, to tell her he was on his way back.

As they approached the city, and the Manhattan skyline came into view, Quentin asked Stone, "What do you think Alexandra's captors will do now? You must have dealt with situations like this before. What is your best guess?"

Stone was staring into the distance. Almost absentmindedly, he said, "It doesn't look good. They have the money, and they have Alexandra and Arnold. Both of them are now dispensable."

"Where do you think they went?"

"If you're right about Jaeger and Lieberman being on the yacht, maybe overseas. They might have a private plane. After all, their business is now concluded here. They have the cash in their hands. They can get it to wherever they want. They have no obstacles in their way."

"Be straight with me, Mr. Stone. Do you think they will kill Alexandra?"

"We must still have hope that she will be released, Quentin. But I have to say I think the chances are slim, very slim indeed."

"Can't we do anything at all?"

"We will make the very best effort we can to pick them up. I'll have an alert put out to all airports, and if and when we find the yacht, we may learn more."

*

The car was now in the city, on Madison Avenue. "Shall I drop you at The Plaza, Quentin?"

"Yes. I should check that Dominique is OK."

Stone said, "Ask her about her father, Quentin. See what you can find out."

"I don't think he tells her much," replied Quentin. "They are friendly, but not terribly close."

Chapter 114

Quentin let himself into his room at The Plaza. Dominique was waiting for him, dressed.

She welcomed him with a kiss, and invited him to sit down, and tell her about the events of the day.

"It's very bad," he said. He then recounted everything as it had taken place, in detail, except that he did not mention that he thought he had seen Hermann Lieberman get onto the yacht.

"So what will happen now?" she asked.

"I don't know, I really don't," replied Quentin.

Dominique suggested they order room service. "You should eat, mon cherie. You must be starving."

Their dinner arrived, and they sat on the sofa, with their trays on their knees. As they started to eat, Quentin asked her, "Do you think your father could be implicated in this?"

Dominique shrugged. "I would be very surprised," she said.

"I saw him, your father, with Lord Jaeger, after we had dinner with him, at The Four Seasons. Then you'll remember we saw them together again, at the opera house, Saturday night. And Franklin Stone suspects Jaeger is involved in this. So what do you think?"

"I don't know. Papa called earlier. He knows I was in hospital. Who would have told him?" Dominique stopped eating, and put her tray down. She knelt in front of Quentin, facing him. Looking him in the eyes, she said, "Believe me, Quentin, I know nothing of any of this. It is very scary. So I prefer not to think about it."

They finished their dinner, in silence. Quentin was re-living the drama of the day in his mind, over and over again. He then turned on the television. He wanted to take his mind off things, he said.

But his mind kept going back to the image of the yacht, going out to sea, and to Jaeger and Lieberman. "Did your father say where he was calling from?" he asked.

"No, he didn't. He said very little. He just asked me about my hospital stay, and we talked about the ballet tomorrow night. I think he'll be there."

The telephone rang. It was Franklin Stone.

"Hi there, Quentin. I have some news."

Quentin braced himself for the worst.

"We have just found the yacht. It is moored at one of the piers, by the West Side Highway, opposite 55th Street, in Manhattan. We are there now. There's no one on board. No sign of anyone."

"Why would they come back to Manhattan?" asked Quentin.

"I assume they sheltered in the Bay because of the weather conditions. If Lieberman contacts his daughter, please let me know, immediately."

"He called her earlier, before I got back. Dominique doesn't know where he was. It was only a very brief conversation, I think. I will make sure you know if he calls again," said Quentin. "Thank you."

Quentin then said to Dominique, "There's no news, except that they found the yacht. It's moored on the west side."

Chapter 115

TUESDAY

Quentin woke first. He turned on the television, to check the early morning news on CNN. After an item about the Chechnyan situation, and growing insurgencies there, there was a local item that immediately caught his eye.

The report was live, from the ferry terminal at Staten Island. The bodies of two men had been found washed up on the shore. Both had their throats cut. NYPD was investigating, together with the FBI, the report said. More would follow later.

Quentin went to the phone, and dialled Stone. He answered. "I've just seen a news item about bodies found at Staten Island. Did you know about this?"

"Yes, we're investigating. They were found at dawn this morning. We have provisional identification."

"The report said there were two men," said Quentin. "Is that right?"

"Yes. We think it's Novelli and Fischer."

"My God!" Quentin then said, "Please let me know if your hear anything about Alexandra. I'll be here at the hotel."

Dominique was now awake.

Quentin had replaced the receiver. He said, "Arnold Fischer has been killed. And the man they think attacked us in your apartment has been killed too. They were both found washed up on the shore near Staten Island. There's no sign of Alexandra though." Quentin's whole body was shaking with fear and apprehension.

Chapter 116

The House of Commons Chamber was full to capacity, as was the custom for Prime Minister's Question Time.

The Prime Minister slipped into his seat on the front bench, and rose to make a short statement on Her Majesty's Government's plans for reducing peacekeeping forces in Afghanistan and Iraq.

After several routine questions from the Leader of the Opposition, which The Prime Minister answered adeptly, the Shadow Foreign Secretary, Derek Grant, rose to his feet.

"Would the Prime Minister tell us what the Government is doing to halt the growing build up of terrorist cells in Chechnya, Iraq, Afghanistan and Iran? Some of these groups are known to have plans to launch attacks on specific United Kingdom and United States targets. The situation is becoming increasingly dangerous, with a growing threat of weapons of mass destruction being deployed against innocent citizens. What can the Prime Minister tell us, to reassure this House and the country?"

"My Right Honourable Friend opposite will be aware that we are constantly improving our security, and that whenever we have intelligence that there is a specific threat, we respond with increased security, to safeguard the people of the United Kingdom. We are constantly diligent. If My Right Honourable Friend has any particular information that is relevant, no doubt he will hand it over in the appropriate way, at the earliest opportunity."

The Shadow Foreign Secretary was on his feet again, waving a file of documents in his left hand. "The Prime Minister might be surprised to know, shocked even, that I have in my possession here certain documents that show beyond any doubt whatsoever that plans have been laid to fund terrorist cells from subversive sources in the United States, through channels in Saudi Arabia, Switzerland, France and Great Britain. They provide details of biological and chemical weapons that are being manufactured at secret sites in

Chechnya, Iraq, Afghanistan and Iran, to be used by terrorist insurgents in those countries, and against Great Britain and the United States. These documents, which I will hand to the Prime Minister, demonstrate that the Government has been painfully negligent in monitoring security matters, and that it is seriously out of step with public opinion, and with our friends and allies, especially those in the United States. The Government has failed to keep our country safe, and it should resign, forthwith. I shall be asking The Speaker to table a 'No Confidence' Motion, this week, and we expect to win it, and to win the next general election. It is time for change!"

There was now uproar in the House. Ballot papers were being waved, and Members of Parliament were shouting, and calling for the Prime Minister to resign.

Derek Grant turned to his Leader, sitting next to him on the Front Bench, and smiled. "I think we have them on the run now," he said.

Chapter 117

There was still no news about Alexandra.

The killing of Arnold Fischer appalled Quentin. But he reasoned that if Alexandra had been killed at the same time, her body would have been found by now.

He was intrigued by the fact that Novelli's body had been washed up with Arnold Fischer's. Logic suggested that Novelli must therefore have been on the yacht with Arnold Fischer. But why had he been killed?

Quentin felt he had to do something to take his mind off this and other related questions, and he decided to draft his review of the "Mitridate" performance. He would write more about the opera than the performance itself, since he was so distracted during the performance.

He thought that it would be good for Dominique to get out of the hotel, now that her condition had improved so much, so he invited her to join him for the performance of "Swan Lake" taking place at The Met that evening. Perhaps they could have something to eat beforehand, in the dining room on the Grand Tier level. She was enthralled, and started to get ready early mid-afternoon. They decided they would plan to get to The Met at six. The performance did not start until eight.

*

Quentin wrote the "Mitridate" piece, and then he showered and dressed. Dominique was ready to leave by the time he had finished.

Dominique's arm was still in a sling, but she no longer wore a dressing on the wound on her head. She had washed her hair, and had put on a little make-up. She was wearing one of the two black evening dresses Quentin had collected from her apartment. It was knee length, with lace trimmings.

"You are looking so much better," Quentin told her.

Dominique smiled, and touched his hand.

"Let's go," he said. "We'll get a cab, even though it's not far. I have to look after you."

*

They enjoyed their dinner. They talked about Dominique's schedule of engagements over the next twelve months. She would cancel the concerts she had previously committed to in July and August, and she would concentrate on being prepared for the concerts for which she was booked at The Royal Festival Hall in London, in November. She would also go ahead with her other engagements after that, in Paris, Vienna and Rome, and in the United States. She had secured some recording contracts, and would work in the studios in London in December and January.

They discussed the Beethoven Concerto that she had played the previous Friday. Quentin complimented her on the performance once again, this time going into much more detail than he had covered in his review.

Dominique followed his every word.

Quentin then told her about some of the features that The Times had asked him to write, and he mentioned other commissions that he would be working on when he was back in London. He was developing an idea for a book. It would be about the effect of the collapse of communism on music making in former Soviet Union countries, and the consequential effects in the western world. Dominique offered to help him research the book. Quentin said he would welcome her assistance.

Quentin then told Dominique that he had seen Petya Gubin's will, and he told her that when all the legal formalities were overcome, she should expect to receive a large inheritance. Dominique surprised him by saying that she did not need the money, and that she would donate it to charity.

They finished their dinner, and slowly walked to the orchestra stalls lobby, where the audience was already gathering, in the bar and at the entrance doors to the auditorium.

Quentin collected two programs from an usher, handing one to Dominique. As they were reading their programs, Hermann Lieberman approached from behind Dominique. He tapped her on the shoulder, taking her by surprise. "There's my favorite daughter," he said.

"Papa, you're here. How nice."

Quentin was shocked to see him standing there. He wondered if he knew he had been out at Breezy Point with the FBI the previous day. Lieberman held out his hand to him, saying "Nice to see you again, Quentin. Thank you for taking such good care of my daughter."

He then took Quentin by the arm, and said, "Dominique tells me you were out of the city yesterday, doing something on the Alexandra Matviyko kidnapping case. What were you doing exactly, if I may ask?"

"I was with the police. How did you know she had been kidnapped, Mr. Lieberman?"

"I saw something on television about it, I think. Do you know if she's been found?"

"No, she has not. But she will turn up soon, I hope."

"Yes, indeed. Well, I must leave you young things now. I have to entertain my guests upstairs. Enjoy the ballet." He disappeared into the crowd

Quentin whispered in Dominique's ear, "There has been nothing on television about Alexandra and the ransom. The police and the FBI have deliberately been keeping it quiet, away from the media. I wonder how he knew?"

Dominique shrugged. "I have no idea."

Chapter 118

The ballet was a good diversion for both Quentin and Dominique. The production was new, and unusually modern and provocative. Quentin was intrigued that the Kirov Company should break away from tradition so radically, given its history with Tchaikovsky's ballets. The dancing was of the highest possible quality, and the orchestra played the score with a freshness that was captivating.

At the start of the first interval, Quentin asked Dominique if she would like to go to the bar for a drink. She said she was a little tired, and she would prefer to stay in her seat. She told him he should go on his own.

Quentin made his way to the bar at the back of the orchestra stalls. He was about to order a drink, when he thought he would go up to the Grand Tier, to see if Hermann Lieberman was in the bar at that level. It was where he and Dominique had talked briefly with Lord Jaeger and Lieberman before.

Lieberman was there, with Forbes Taylor, and one other man. He approached them, not ready with anything in particular to say.

Lieberman acknowledged him, saying "Hello there, Quentin. Where's Dominique?"

"She's downstairs. I would like a word with you."

"What about? As you can see I am with my friends here, and it is not the best time."

Quentin heard himself saying, " I'm wondering if you know where Lord Jaeger is? I would like to speak to him."

"Why is that, young man?"

"Do you know where he is, Mr. Lieberman?"

"Not at this moment, no. Why do you want to speak to him?"

"It's about Alexandra Matviyko."

Lieberman took Quentin by the arm, and steered him away from Forbes Taylor and the other man. He whispered in Quentin's ear, "I suggest you forget about Alexandra. Take care of my daughter. Do that and you will be left unharmed. Continue to dabble in affairs that are none of your business, and you will regret it. Take that as a friendly warning."

Quentin nodded. "I see. Thanks for the advice. I must get back to Dominique now. I expect I will see you later."

"Good bye, Quentin."

Quentin returned to the orchestra stalls. He was trying to think of the reason Lieberman might be involved in the Jaeger affair, and in Alex's kidnapping. He worried that Alex might now be in even more jeopardy, due to Lieberman's declared interest in having him permanently attached to his daughter. He did not intend to say anything to Dominique about his brush with her father.

He would talk to Franklin Stone again. He would call him in the morning.

*

After the performance Quentin took Dominique straight back to The Plaza. She was now exhausted.

She turned to him in the cab as they arrived at the hotel, and kissed him on the cheek. "Thank you so much for this evening, Quentin. I had a lovely time. You make me very happy."

"My pleasure, Dominique. I enjoyed it too."

They took the elevator to the room, and started to undress. Quentin noticed that the message light on the telephone was flashing. He picked up the receiver and dialled to retrieve his messages. He was stunned to hear Alex's voice.

"Quentin, where are you? I have managed to get to a phone, and this must be very short. I am buying time for myself, but they have killed Arnie. They have the money. Lord Jaeger is involved in this, but it's complicated. Be very careful. They know you have been talking with the FBI. Do be careful. I miss you. I will call again when I can. It's very difficult. I am a long way ....I must go."

The message ended, suddenly, as if she had been interrupted.

"What was that?" asked Dominique. "You look like you've seen a ghost."

"Oh it's nothing really. Just Stone. I'll call him back in the morning."

They got into bed. Quentin wished he had been there when Alex had phoned.

Chapter 119

WEDNESDAY

Quentin got up early, and he telephoned Franklin Stone while Dominique was still sleeping. He used the telephone in the bathroom, to avoid being overheard.

He told Stone of the meetings with Hermann Lieberman at the opera house the previous evening, and about the voicemail message he had received from Alexandra.

Stone said, "It's clear that they're still holding her as some sort of collateral. It's a good development, Quentin. From your account, I would say she's some way from here, but safe. I've received no information on the whereabouts of Lord Jaeger since you saw him on the yacht on Monday. I'll get on to Roberts at Scotland Yard, and see if he can do some work over there, through Covent Garden, to try to ascertain where Jaeger might be."

"Anything I can do in the meantime, Mr. Stone?"

"No, and I don't think you should talk to Lieberman any more, unless he calls you, of course. You must be cautious, Quentin."

*

Detective Superintendent Roberts was pleased to receive the telephone call from Stone, but distressed to hear of the failed attempt to thwart Alexandra Matviyko's captors, and to learn of Arnold Fischer's murder.

He said he would immediately make more inquiries about Jaeger through Covent Garden.

Roberts told Stone that they had been unable to get any information out of Akbar Sattar. He was assumed to be protecting his control and the wider network.

Roberts then rang Geoffrey Wright, at Covent Garden. He asked him if he knew where Lord Jaeger was. Wright replied, "We were expecting him back yesterday, but he has been delayed. He is in the United States, I understand, and he is planning to attend the memorial service for Petya Gubin, this Friday."

"Could you tell me how I might contact him?" asked Roberts.

"I'm afraid he has left no number on which we can phone him. He told his secretary that he would check in from time to time, and that he would return to London next week."

*

Quentin and Dominique showered and dressed, and were having breakfast, in the hotel room. Stone called Quentin back with the news from London. "I find it hard to believe that Jaeger will risk being seen in public, but I will be at the memorial service on Friday, just in case he shows up."

"That's good," said Quentin. "I'll also attend myself. I don't know where it's being held, but I'm sure it will be in New York."

"It's being held at St. Nicholas, the Russian Orthodox Church, at eleven. It was announced in the New York Times."

Chapter 120

Dominique asked Quentin if they could spend the day in Tarrytown, up river from Manhattan. The boat trip on the Hudson would be enjoyable, she said, and they could take the tour round Washington Irving's house.

Quentin was a little reluctant to be away from the telephone at the hotel, and perhaps miss another call from Alex. But, he reasoned that Alex was severely restricted in what she was able to do, and that it was therefore unlikely that she would have any time to talk on the phone. He would check for messages as soon as he and Dominique returned to the city.

So he agreed, and they set out for the ferry terminal on the West Side, by 43rd Street, and boarded the boat for Tarrytown.

The river breezes were refreshing after the heat and humidity in the city, and Quentin quickly put his worries about Alex to the back of his mind. Dominique was being a wonderful companion, and he was enjoying her company increasingly every day. She had stopped being so demanding physically, and was allowing him more space. As a result Quentin did not feel pressured, so their relationship was developing naturally.

They enjoyed their relaxed tour of the Irving home, and had lunch in a small bistro in Tarrytown. They spent the afternoon walking near the river, and in the early evening made the return trip to Manhattan.

When they finally settled back into the hotel room, Quentin was relieved to find that there were no messages. He questioned his own reaction in preferring not to have to deal with any messages from Alex, and he decided it was because he needed some relief from the strong feelings of obligation that he had been experiencing. If he didn't hear from her, he didn't have to do anything. Not for the time being, at least. He felt a twinge of guilt, nevertheless.

He turned to Dominique, who was now in bed. She had undressed, washed and changed into her pyjamas. He had not yet changed. He lay down beside her on the bed, and stroked her hair. "You have done so well, my sweet. You got over that nasty attack so bravely. I'm so proud of you."

"Thanks to you, mon cherie," she said smiling. She kissed him on the lips. Quentin did not turn away or shrink from her, but kissed her, several times, on her cheeks, lips and on her neck.

Dominique held his face in her hands. She said, "I have fallen in love with you, Quentin, I really have. You are the nicest man I have ever known, and I adore you." After a pause, in which Quentin thought about how he wanted to respond, she added, "I'm going to sleep now. Night night."

Quentin was deeply touched by Dominique's constant devotion to him, and now by her declaration of love. He asked himself what he should do, and what he would do if Alexandra never re-appeared.

He speculated on how he would feel if Alexandra managed to escape the kidnappers, and wanted to be re-united with him. The prospect made him feel slightly uncomfortable, and he quizzed himself on the reasons for this. He felt that the more he had discovered about Alexandra's past the more he admired her courage, but the less his heart yearned for her. The various events of the past few days had not lessened his commitment to help her in any way he could, but it was almost as if every additional piece of information about her history incrementally damaged the prospects of keeping his love for her fully alive.

This made him feel guilty, and yet strangely liberated at the same time. He mused that perhaps it would enable his growing feelings for Dominique to develop in an uninhibited way, in spite of the fact that he had no idea what fate would befall Alexandra in the hands of her captors.

He vowed to do everything in his power to continue to bring about Alexandra's rescue. But as he slipped into semi-consciousness he thought how happy he was to be with Dominique, as she quietly slept by his side.

Chapter 121

FRIDAY

Quentin and Dominique had spent Thursday together, strolling in Central Park, and then at the Guggenheim Museum. He had invited her to accompany him to the chamber concert at Alice Tully Hall in the evening.

The concert had been worth attending, and Quentin was pleased that in spite of everything he was able to get his reviews written and sent back to London on time.

He awoke first, and ordered coffee for them both.

He had not heard from Alexandra since Tuesday. He assumed she was still in the hands of her captors.

Quentin and Dominique dressed to go to Petya Gubin's memorial service. Quentin wore a dark suit with a sober tie, and Dominique a turquoise blouse and black skirt. Dominique decided not to wear her arm sling. As they got ready, Quentin said he hoped the service would bring some closure for Maria and the Gubin family. Dominique surprised him by saying, "It will help me too. Now that I have lost the baby, I can put that whole chapter behind me."

It was a clear, sunny day. The storms earlier in the week had moved on, and humidity levels were now quite low. They took a cab to the Russian Orthodox Church, going through the park, to Madison Avenue at East 72nd Street, then north, and along 97th Street, which was one way only, going west. They were dropped outside the church, twenty minutes early, but crowds were already gathering outside, and there were journalists and television cameras lying in wait for those who might be prepared to say a few words about Petya Gubin.

Dominique spotted Maria, Antonio and Chloe in the crowd, but she held Quentin back, tightly holding on to his arm. Maria was wearing a veil.

Dominique said, "I'm sorry for Maria. She must be going through such a mix of emotions. I'm so pleased she has the support of her children."

Quentin saw Martin Schaeffer as they were entering the church. He was with a large group. Probably members of The Met Board and staff, he thought. He shook Martin's hand, and said, "Good to see you again, Mr. Schaeffer." He then presented Dominique to him, saying, "I don't know whether you know Dominique Lieberman?"

Martin nodded. "Hello, Dominique. How nice to see you. How is your father? Quentin, Hermann and I are old friends, you know."

Quentin then saw Forbes Taylor entering the church, with a small contingent he assumed was from the US State Department.

As they started to move into the church, down the aisle, each member of the congregation was handed a memorial service program. Quentin, not taking a glance at the sheet, looked up at the richly painted ceiling, and to the many banners with painted icons hanging from the roof. Other than the sound of hushed voices, gently echoing, the church was silent.

He then noticed Franklin Stone, with two agents, sitting in the back of the church, near the door, to one side. He saw that Maria and the children had taken their seats at the very front, just before the altar, on the left side of the aisle. Others were filing in behind them. On the right side of the aisle, in front of the altar, already seated, was a small chamber orchestra, the men dressed in morning tail coats, and the women players in long black dresses. Mourners were filing into the rows of seats behind the orchestra, and Quentin guided Dominique to two seats about half way back, on the same side of the aisle as the orchestra.

The church gradually filled as it approached eleven o'clock. Quentin thought the congregation must be in excess of three hundred by now. About twenty seats, two rows in front of Quentin and Dominique, were still unoccupied.

The orchestra started to play. Quentin recognized the slow movement from "Serenade for Strings," by Tchaikovsky.

There was a hush, and a procession slowly started to move up the aisle from the back of the church, towards the altar.

An elderly Russian Orthodox bishop followed two priests, who were both wearing richly adorned liturgical vestments. The bishop was wearing a mandyas, the mantle for processional dress for bishops. It was deep purple, embroidered with medallions of evangelists. He wore a kemelavkion, the clerical hat, and had a full, long grey beard. Around his neck he wore a pectoral cross and encolpa. He carried a paterista, a pastoral staff, adorned with serpents looking at an orb, surmounted by a cross.

Another bishop followed, a younger man, with a black beard, dressed as the first. He wore a saccos, an outer cloak, over a sticharion, and he too was carrying a cross. On his head he wore the bishop's crown, the mitra, embroidered with icons, surmounted by a cross.

Two priests followed, completing the procession. Each carried double candles.

As the procession reached the altar, the orchestra stopped playing, and the priests took their positions, facing the congregation.

Quentin heard muffled voices behind him, at the entrance door to the church. He turned around, and saw several men, and a woman, walking quickly, quietly down the aisle. They sat, silently, in the row two in front of where he and Dominique were seated. Lord Jaeger and Hermann Lieberman were accompanied by six men, all dark suited, and with them, now seated between two men Quentin did not recognize, was Alexandra.

Dominique gripped Quentin's arm tightly, and whispered in his ear, "Alexandra! And with my father!"

Quentin's heart was now pounding. He felt faint, and leant forward, trying to get some blood into his head. Dominique held his hand and stroked the back of his neck.

He recovered a little, and sat up. The priests were now chanting liturgical verses, in deep bass voices.

Quentin could see the back of Alexandra's head. She was staring straight ahead, not looking left or right. He assumed she had not seen him as she came into the church.

Jaeger and Lieberman were reading their program sheets.

The service proceeded. Chants and hymns were followed by the eulogy, read by Martin Schaeffer. He recounted Petya Gubin's achievements, especially at The Met, and paid tribute to his philanthropic work. He asked the congregation to pray for Maria, Antonio and Chloe, and all the friends that Petya had left behind. He finished by reading a verse by Goethe.

The orchestra then played Samuel Barber's "Adagio for Strings."

More chanting followed, and then after prayers, an arrangement of a movement from Mozart's Requiem Mass was played on the organ.

The bishops and priests then completed a final chant.

Quentin wanted to try to talk to Alexandra when she left the church. He had prepared a plan during the service, and he stood just as it finished, before the rest of the congregation did so. He took Dominique's arm, gently guiding her to the exit door, and out into the street. There he waited for Alexandra.

He noticed a Suburban SUV, together with a number of other vehicles, including several limos. The Suburban was parked immediately outside the church, one set of its wheels on the sidewalk. The windows were tinted black. He assumed it was waiting for members of the congregation.

He then saw Alexandra walking down the aisle towards him, arm in arm with Lord Jaeger. They were within a tight cordon, guarded by six men in very close proximity, two immediately in front, two behind, and one on either side. It was an eerie sight. Hermann Lieberman was following immediately behind.

As they moved nearer, Alexandra noticed Quentin and they exchanged glances. He saw in her face a pain and anxiety that touched him deeply.

The cordon had almost emerged from the church. At that moment, the Suburban doors burst open, and several men jumped out, brandishing rifles and handguns, pointed in the direction of the cordon approaching them. They were wearing black bullet-proof vests. There were shouts, and screams from several women leaving the church. The men in the cordon surrounding Alexandra and Lord Jaeger scattered, some of them diving to the ground.

Two of them were now kneeling, pointing handguns that they had removed from under their jackets. They started to fire on the men wearing bullet-proof vests. In an instant, the men from the Suburban returned their fire. Quentin had already jumped into the melee, and had grabbed Alexandra by the arm, pulling her to one side and to the ground, all in one movement. He covered her with his body, waiting for the firing to stop. He thought he heard Stone's voice, barking out orders. He then looked up to take in the scene. Two men were lying on the sidewalk by the Suburban, and three from the cordon surrounding Lord Jaeger and Alexandra were now also on the ground, lying still. Lord Jaeger was prone, face up on the sidewalk, blood streaming from his chest and neck. Stone was standing over him.

Quentin then looked for Dominique. He saw her crouched down behind the Suburban, in the street, on the opposite side of the vehicle. There was no sign of Lieberman anywhere.

Quentin shouted for Dominique to run, pointing in the direction of Madison Avenue. He pulled Alexandra up from the sidewalk, and ran with her, chasing after Dominique. As they threaded their way through the crowds, Quentin saw a delicatessen on the corner of Madison and East 97th Street. He shouted out, "Go in there." The three of them, now out of breath, fell into a booth at the back of the deli. Quentin heard the police and ambulance sirens, and saw two ambulances flash past from Madison Avenue.

Quentin was seated opposite the two women. "Are you all right?" he asked them. They both nodded, still out of breath.

Dominique was sobbing, and Alexandra was staring at Dominique. "Oh my God!" cried Dominique, "that was terrible." She was now shaking, and Quentin leant across the table, took off his jacket, and draped it across her shoulders.

Alexandra turned to Quentin, placed her hand on his, and said, "You saved my life."

"What happened out there?" Quentin asked, and then as if to answer his own question, said, "I suppose the men who came out of that Suburban were FBI. That was quite an operation."

Alexandra was now holding her head in her hands. She said, "I happen to know Jaeger was going to go to the police, and to the FBI I think, after the service."

"I don't imagine he's going anywhere, not now," said Quentin. "I think he's dead."

"He was working both sides, you know," she said, looking out of the window.

"What do you mean?"

"He was a kind of double agent. Very complicated."

"Alex, you're going to have to explain this, to the FBI, and to the police. You must."

"Yes. But first I want to tell you what happened. You have a right to know, Quentin."

They ordered coffees, and Dominique had now recovered a little.

Alexandra, sipping her coffee, said. "I never thought I would survive this. I am so lucky to be here, and I have you to thank you for that, Quentin. After I was taken away from The Plaza in the cab, I was put into another vehicle on the east side, near the Midtown Tunnel, and then blindfolded. I finished up somewhere near Coney Island, although I didn't know it at the time. They locked me in a room. It was horrific. I was given some food, but I was tied up and told I had to wash in this dirty water they brought to me in a bowl. There was no toilet. They just gave me a bucket to use. It went on for days. I thought I was going to go mad."

"Do you remember speaking to Arnold Fischer?" Quentin asked.

"Yes, I do. But they held a knife to my throat while I spoke. I was told what to say. Then a long time later they took me somewhere else. I had lost track of time by then. I had given up, really. They put me on this boat. I was still tied up, and I couldn't see anything, but the relief was amazing, to be out in the fresh air after being cooped up for so long. Then there was a lot of commotion on this boat, and suddenly it was moving. Jaeger was there. I could hear his voice."

Quentin interrupted. "That's when you were on the yacht. I suspected you were on it. I was there, watching helplessly as they motored off with you, with Arnold Fischer, and the money. It was out at Breezy Point."

"You were there?"

"Yes, with Franklin Stone, and the FBI, on the shore. The FBI nearly rescued you then, right there, but they were taken by surprise. They weren't expecting the getaway by boat."

"Well, the boat, or the yacht, went into the New York Bay. I knew they were heading for Manhattan, because I could hear Jaeger giving instructions to other men, in English. That's when there was a terrible scene, arguments, and they killed Arnie and this other man. They threw their bodies overboard. I thought they were going to kill me too. But Jaeger told them I wasn't to be touched. Then we got to the pier and they put me in the trunk of this car. We drove for a long time, for several hours."

"Do you know where they took you?" asked Quentin.

"Somewhere upstate. By the Canadian border, I think. It was a log cabin, near a lake. When we arrived there I was ill. I was vomiting, and I passed out, soon after we got into the cabin."

"Who was there with you?"

"Just Jaeger, me, and this other man, a guard. They took the ropes off me, and I was allowed to walk around the house, and bathe, and to recover a bit. They wouldn't let me out of the house, though. Jaeger told me that he would spare me if I slept with him, and if I promised to go with him back to England."

"You what?" exclaimed Quentin.

"I slept with him. I had to. I didn't have a choice. You've got to understand, Quentin, I was convinced I was going to die. And then suddenly I was given a chance. So I did as he asked."

Quentin stared at her, almost in disbelief that she had undergone such an ordeal. "Were you with him all the time, until the memorial service, today?"

"Yes. In fact I got to know him quite well. I think he trusted me, after a while. He began to talk, more and more. He was a bad man, Quentin, but there was another side to him, you know."

"What do you mean?"

"He was working at two levels at once. He was feeding the information he got from Petya to the British opposition party, but he wanted to provide hard evidence. That was the reason he had to have the CD. It contained all the documents that provided the proof the opposition needed. The CD had the payment information on it, as well as the details of terrorist targets, procurement of materials for making biological weapons, the cells in Germany and Italy, and in Chechnya. Everything. Petya didn't know Jaeger was double-crossing them. And Leo thought he was supposed to pass the CD on to the insurgency leaders, through Akbar Sattar. But Jaeger acquired it, from Sattar, who got it from Leo's safe. Jaeger then gave all the information on the CD to the Shadow Foreign Secretary. He did it deliberately, knowing that it was likely to result in chaos in parliament, and bring down the Government. The opposition party would then win a General Election, and form a new Government. That new Government would be much more sympathetic to the American position for dealing with the terrorists. That was Jaeger's plan, his motive from the very beginning to the end. But it got too complex, and it spun out of control."

"What about the money?"

"Jaeger let certain people think he was going to help to get the ransom money to the terrorists, but in fact his plan was to stop it, and safeguard me."

Quentin looked perplexed. "What would have happened if you and Leo Connell had not changed your minds, and you had wired the funds to those accounts in the Middle East, as Petya Gubin originally wanted?"

"Jaeger always intended to get the terrorist cells exposed. Also I think he knew that Petya was having second thoughts. Petya must have mentioned it to Jaeger."

"Do you know who shot Petya? Or why he was killed?"

"Akbar Sattar. Sattar was getting his instructions from someone here in the United States. Jaeger did not know Sattar was going to kill Petya, until afterwards. But by then Jaeger was double-crossing them. So he had no choice but to conspire to conceal the evidence regarding Petya's murder. He didn't want anyone to suspect he was playing both sides. Jaeger's main purpose was to get hold of the information that was on the CD. He was totally focused on that, and ruthless. As far as he was concerned, it had to come out in parliament, with all the legal protection that provided, as an expose from the Shadow Foreign Secretary, and as a total surprise. Actually, he had no regrets about Sattar killing Leo, which happened later, but it was not his decision. But he never intended that the money should get to the terrorists, or be used by them, at least."

"Why was he meeting with Forbes Taylor, here in New York?"

"For some time he had been working under cover with the US State Department, privately sharing the strategy to get a change of Government in the UK. It was in America's interests to cooperate with him, but covertly."

"Well, if all that is true, said Quentin, "why on earth didn't you tell me what was going on earlier, before we left London for New York?"

"Because I didn't have the whole picture. You have to believe that, Quentin."

"And where was Jaeger going to put the money, until this all died down?"

"He already has it deposited in a safe, here in Manhattan."

"But I still don't understand why he was so damned secretive about everything, even if he was double-crossing the terrorist network organizers."

"Just think, Quentin. He is the man responsible for probably bringing down the British Government. That's a treasonable offence. He could not afford to be open about it."

"OK", said Quentin, "but how did Jaeger know the money was in your bank account? When things got out of hand with Akbar Sattar, why didn't Jaeger do something?"

Alex said, "He knew from Petya about the money I was holding. But Jaeger didn't do anything about Akbar Sattar because he couldn't. Sattar's control was here, in the US. Apart from that, to some extent it suited Jaeger to have Sattar around, as a diversion, and to get the CD, of course."

"Yes, I understand that," said Quentin. "But bottom line, why did he do it?"

"He thought the British Government was leading the country into the greatest risk from the terrorists. He was convinced that Britain had become a soft target. He believed a new Government would put things right, more on the lines of the tougher, American approach. He strongly felt that we can only combat terrorism effectively if Europe and America stand together more effectively."

Quentin thought for a moment. "There's still something missing. There has to be someone else. Someone other than Jaeger, who didn't have his particular agenda. A real extremist, with sympathies to hard line Muslim fundamentalists."

"Yes. Petya."

"I understand that. And I know that Petya's loyalties to Chechnyan insurgents must have been part of the reason for that, but he had a partial change of heart, didn't he? You said as much yourself, Alex."

Alex lowered her voice to a whisper. "There was someone, yes. Someone who organized everything with Petya from the outset. And that person remains a hard line extremist, to this very day. He is very good indeed at covering his tracks."

"Who is that?"

"If you must know, it's your father, Dominique. Hermann Lieberman."

Dominique let out a gasp. "How do you know?"

"He was on the yacht. He killed Arnie, and the other man as well."

"Who was the other man?"

"He went by the name of Novelli, I think."

"Why would he want to kill Novelli?" asked Quentin.

"Because Novelli harmed you, Dominique, and he found out."

Alex sensed that Dominique was deeply shocked. "I know it's incredible, Dominique, but I saw what happened. Also Jaeger was constantly talking to your father on the telephone, from the log cabin. Lieberman was determined that the money would get to the terrorist cells, but he didn't know that Jaeger had other plans."

Dominique blushed. "So my father is a traitor and a murderer, then. Is that what you're saying?"

"Yes."

Quentin nodded in comprehension. "So Jaeger got his information from Hermann Lieberman as well as Petya"

"Yes, absolutely," said Alex.

"Well, where did Lieberman get his information from?" asked Quentin.

"From Petya originally, and then from all the stolen papers from the break-ins at Fred Ballard's and Arnie Fischer's offices," Alex explained.

Quentin said, "I see. You never know about people, do you? Where is Lieberman, by the way? I didn't see him after the shootings outside the church."

Dominique shrugged. "He must have run off," she said. "What are you going to do, Alexandra, now that Jaeger is probably dead?"

"I will help the police, and the FBI, and I will get the money back to the foundation. I'll go to see Franklin Stone first. Then I'll return to England and talk to Roberts. But Quentin, things depend on you, really."

"What do you mean?"

"You must decide what you want to do," said Alexandra, glancing back and forth between Quentin and Dominique.

Quentin knew what she meant. Here he was, sitting with both Alex and Dominique. He was engaged to be married to Alex, but because of everything that had happened in the last ten days, his perceptions had changed. She must already have guessed that he and Dominique had become close.

He thought to himself, looking across the table, first to Alex, then to Dominique, that he should decide irrevocably what he wanted to do, there and then. It was only fair.

He held out his hand to Alexandra. He said, "Alex, you know that I have loved you. You are an amazing person. So tough. So strong."

"And?" asked Alexandra.

He hesitated. Then, after smiling at Dominique, he said, "I have decided that I want to spend the rest of my life with Dominique. I'm so sorry, Alex."

Alexandra turned away from Dominique. "Whatever you decide, Quentin, it's your decision. I shall be very sad, hurt. But I know your belief in me has changed. There is so much about me you didn't know before. I still loved Petya after I moved to London, and even when you and I were dating and we got engaged. I understand."

Quentin turned to Dominique. " I love you, Dominique. I want to be with you."

Dominique smiled. "Mon cherie. Moi aussi."

Epilogue

Three months later

THURSDAY

Quentin was at his desk. Because it was the day of the General Election, he thought all the restaurants in London would be busier than usual that night. He telephoned The Savoy, to reserve a table for two, for dinner. He gave the receptionist the names, "Mr. and Mrs. Quentin Dart."

Dominique was at The Royal Festival Hall, rehearsing for that night's concert.

He looked up from his desk. Suddenly, on the other side of the glass screen, there was Alexandra.

"Hello, Quentin," she said, as she walked into his office. "How are you?"

"Very well, thanks. You look great, Alex."

"Thank you. I have decided to stay in London permanently. I am going to set up an artists' agency of my own. Maybe I'll be able to capture some of Leo Connell's clients."

"That's a terrific idea," said Quentin.

"How is Dominique, by the way? And how is married life for you both?"

"She's fine. Absolutely great, thanks. We're very happy. Alex, what happened about your inheritance under Petya's will?"

"Maria contested the will, and she lost, as you probably know. But I gave my legacy to her anyway. The funds that we returned to the foundation were then handed over to the IRS. I have the insurance monies though. Quite a nice little sum. It will enable me to make a good start with the agency."

Quentin said, "They never found Hermann Lieberman, did they? Dominique says she has disowned him anyway."

"She has done the right thing. I am pleased for you and Dominique, Quentin. I think you're very well suited."

"You're very kind. She's playing at The Festival Hall this evening. Do you want to come? You could join us for dinner afterwards."

"My names translated into English mean Defender of Man, and God's Gift, so perhaps there's another gorgeous man somewhere I can defend and be God's gift to, but unfortunately it seems it isn't going to be you. I don't think you and I were made for each other, Quentin."

Quentin laughed. "What's the harm in having dinner with us?"

"No, thank you. I had better not."

*